"And what would Liz Elliott say if I ask her to dinner on Saturday night?" Sheridan asked, still staring at the ground.

"Liz would say yes, she'd love to go to dinner with Coach Ross."

"It isn't Coach Ross who is asking," Sheridan added[.] [...] Sheridan who is asking."

"She'd say yes to Sheridan, too." Liz looked over [...] eyes meeting.

Sheridan stopped walking and reached out, takin[g] [...] She gently pulled Liz to her and kissed her. It was a b[...] one that sent Liz's heart to her throat and started it po[...] ously. Sheridan looked down at her and seemed as sur[...] at her action.

"I'm sorry," Sheridan said and started up the stre[...] strides.

"Hey!" Liz called. She perched her hands on h[...] stared, still standing on the spot where they kissed. "[...] sorry?" she asked.

"That was a mistake. A big mistake. Please, just forg[...] that." She kept walking.

"That's like telling someone not to think about el[...] too late. I'm already thinking about them."

"Rule number one. Coaches don't kiss players[.] [...] scowled.

"But the coach didn't kiss me. Sheridan did." There was tenderness in Liz's reply that floated up and gripped Sheridan, making her stop in her tracks.

Visit

Bella Books

at

BellaBooks.com

or call our toll-free number

1-800-729-4992

ROMANCING THE ZONE

KENNA WHITE

Bella
BOOKS

2006

Bella Books, Inc.
P.O. Box 10543
Tallahassee, FL 32302

Printed in the United States of America on acid-free paper
First Edition

Editor: Anna Chinappi
Cover designer: Stephanie Solomon-Lopez

ISBN 1-59493-060-0

This book is dedicated to *all* the players, both bench players and starters, who have unselfishly given themselves to their team. Whether on the court or off, with fanfare or in silence, they are the backbone and courage that drives a team to compete and to win. Also, to all of us who wish we had the ability and opportunity to play a sport but are relegated to the bleachers to watch, cheer and wonder what might have been.

Acknowledgements

A big thank you to all the coaches—Mari-Beth, Maryann and Joan—who allowed me to invade their practices and glean their training secrets. Their patience and dedication to their players is often overlooked. Kudos to you and your efforts.

A special thanks to my Ann for her help, understanding and unwavering love.

About the Author

Kenna White lives in a small town nestled in southern Missouri where she enjoys her writing, traveling, making dollhouse miniatures and life's simpler pleasures. After living from the Rocky Mountains to New England, she is once again back where bare feet, faded jeans and lazy streams fill her life.

Prologue

With less than a minute left in the game, the women's basketball coach, Ralph Hanley, grumbled to his feet and signaled for a time-out. His Chilton College Lady Stingers were suffering another in a long agonizing season of defeats. Thankfully, this was the last game for both the team and for Coach Hanley. His retirement was long overdue and came as a relief for the players who would be returning next year. The athletic department and the alumni, who stayed away from the women's basketball games in droves, were also looking forward to his replacement.

The Albany State Cardinals crowded around their coach, sharing high fives and wide grins over their imminent victory. The Lady Stingers stood in a circle, silently catching their breath and staring at the floor as Coach Hanley launched into his tirade.

He leered at Deb, a willowy blonde freshman center.

"I told you—shoot the goddamned ball when you're open." He poked Becca in the arm and frowned at her as well. "Why didn't you foul Robertson when I signaled you? She had an open layup and you just watched her take the shot. If they are going to run the score up on my last game you make them pay for it, you hear me?" He poked her arm again. "And what's this crap about shooting left-handed? You're a righty."

Becca leaned over and grabbed her shorts, watching the drops of sweat puddle between her shoes. There was little glory in this the last game. The crowd was small, quiet and only marginally attentive to the team's efforts. During the time-out, most of the remaining spectators used the opportunity to disperse and move toward the exits.

"You're doing okay," Sheridan Ross said to Deb quietly as she patted her back. Sheridan was the assistant coach. It was her first year at Chilton but her credentials were so impressive she was offered the head coaching spot as soon as Hanley announced his retirement. Her dream job was in reach or at least the next dream job on her ladder to success. Coach Ross was forty-two years old and had already led two teams to high school state championships and a junior college women's championship trophy in Wisconsin. Her ascension through the ranks was the result of hard work and not without cost. She had so immersed herself in the pursuit of her goal to be a Division I college coach that she left little time for out-side interests including personal relationships. She was, to say the least, all business when it came to being a women's basketball coach. Now Chilton College, a Division II school, was ripe and hers for the taking. She roamed the outside of the huddle offering encouragement to the frustrated players.

"Watch inside," she said in Becca's direction. "They are dou-bling up on you so there should be someone open under the bucket."

Becca Elliott was one of the bright stars on the Chilton team. She was a tall, dark-haired nineteen-year-old with simple but strik-ing features. Her hair was pulled back in a tight ponytail knotted into a small bun at the back of her head. She wiped the sweat from her upper lip with the neck of her jersey as she glanced up into the bleachers behind the bench. Her eyes met those of a woman in the second row. The woman offered an encouraging clap and gave a signal Becca knew meant to pass the ball. She then winked at Becca and smiled down at her with the eyes of an adoring mother, one who sympathized with her daughter's frustration.

"Okay, ladies. Let's wrap this up," called one of the referees as she stuck her head into the huddle. "Send them out, Coach."

"Becca," Sheridan called. "Look inside to Deb on a crossing pattern deep," she ordered quietly then patted Becca's rear and sent her into battle. Coach Ross made eye contact with her tall center and pointed to her.

Sheridan stood at the edge of the floor and signaled to her players, setting the play. Coach Hanley had returned to his seat and was visiting with the man at the end of the scorer's table, oblivious to the action on the court.

"Watch for a steal," Sheridan yelled to the girl who was about to inbound the ball. As soon as she said it, an Albany player broke in front of her and intercepted the pass. No one on the Chilton team made a move to challenge the play. It was a clean steal resulting in an easy layup and two more points for the Cardinals. Their entire team jumped to their feet and cheered the player. Becca ran the ball down and in-bounded from under the basket, scowling at the player who made the errant pass.

Sheridan crossed her arms and glared at the players. She continued to stare as the team brought the ball up the floor. With only seconds to play, Becca took the pass and moved to the side of the three-point circle. Just as Coach Ross had predicted, two Cardinal players swarmed to her position, leaving Deb open under the basket. Becca faked a pass to her then drew the ball back and offered a long arching three-point shot. The buzzer sounded just as the ball twanged on the rim and bounced away. Becca smirked and shrugged her shoulders at the missed attempt. Deb frowned at her but didn't say anything. The players looked at each other knowing it had been a fruitless year, one they were glad was over.

There were only a handful of spectators to applaud the end of the game and the season. Coach Hanley was receiving congratulations from the few remaining fans for his years of service to Chilton, paying little attention to his team. Sheridan shook hands with each of the players as they came off the floor, trying to instill some measure of self-respect on their glum faces as they headed for the locker room. Becca retrieved her warm-up shirt from a chair and searched the rack of water bottles for a last drink.

"Becca Elliott," her mother called as she rose to her feet. Her voice was scornful at best.

"Don't start with me, Mom," Becca replied, holding up a hand to roadblock the discussion.

"Becca," Sheridan said, striding over and offering her a handshake. Becca accepted it but offered only a pitiful smile. "Sixteen points tonight. Good job," Sheridan added proudly.

"Yeah, right."

"Next year, Becca," she said, trying to sound positive.

Liz Elliott stood at the railing and watched the assistant coach offer first aid to her daughter's wounded pride. She couldn't help notice the tall woman's smooth confidence and benevolent eyes as she commanded Becca's complete attention. From Coach Ross's self-assured composure no one could guess the team had just finished the season with a six and nineteen record. Liz couldn't hear everything she was telling Becca but whatever it was, her daughter listened intently and seemed to agree. Becca was a freshman with three more years on an athletic scholarship and a promising career at Chilton College. The thought that a fresh, caring and compassionate coach would be there to guide her brought a smile to Liz's face. And an attractive coach as well, Liz found herself thinking. Liz remembered her own coach at Chilton as a matronly looking woman with thick glasses, a deep voice and an abrasive disposition. Everyone on the team joked behind her back that she got her coaching skills as a drill instructor for the Marines. They had winning seasons all three years Liz played. It was as much out of self-preservation as anything else. Liz was glad for Becca. This coach was definitely better.

Chapter 1

With consistent and measured strides, Liz Elliott jogged through the summer's early morning mist. She moved almost unnoticed along the narrow streets and back roads of Ashton, Vermont as her running shoes tapped out an even meter. Liz dripped sweat, her hair, running shorts and T-shirt drenched and plastered to her body as she rounded the small brick church at the edge of town and started up Bell River Avenue. Bell River was also Vermont State Highway 50 that snaked through Ashton on its way south to Rutland. Ashton was a small New England town of 4,200 residents that swelled to over 6,000 during Chilton College's autumn and spring semesters.

Liz had just turned thirty-nine. She had been running since she was a teenager, first as a member of the Ashton High School cross country, track and basketball teams. She continued to run to stay in shape for the three years she played for the Chilton College basketball team. Five years ago she had entered and completed the grueling twenty-six-mile Boston Marathon, partially at Becca's urging. She didn't need the competition to feel complete as an athlete. Now she ran for the peace and solitude it provided. Her world was hectic and rewarding enough as a single parent of a college-age daughter and as a business owner.

Liz was a trim five-foot-eight. When it wasn't matted to her head with sweat, her short blonde hair was soft and bouncy with an impish pixie look about it. She was average height but there was nothing average about her body. It was lean and sculpted with well defined leg muscles and a tight butt that turned heads. There was a purity about her body that was the result of twenty-five years of running ten miles a week through summer heat, fall rain and winter cold.

She crossed Bell River where it made a wide bend at the Congregationalist Church. The towering white steeple and clapboard siding of the historic church could be seen from any spot in the valley and was the object of many a tourist's camera, especially during the spectacular fall foliage season. The leaf-peepers, as the locals called the flood of visitors during October and November, and the winter skiers were a vital part of Ashton's economy. During late summer Vermont was quieter, left to the local residents who lived, shopped and raised their families in the rich natural splendor of Vermont's simplicity.

Liz moved down the shopping district, her reflection accompanying her in the store windows. The sleepy town seemed almost abandoned as she made her way along the sidewalk. She passed the city park with its white-columned gazebo and marble statue of John Howard Ashton, the town's founding father. The plaque at the base of the bronze statue also mentioned Abigail Grisham Ashton as a steadfast wife and mother of six children who helped carve their homestead in the Vermont valley but there has never been any talk of a statue in her honor.

She kept her pace constant as her shoes patted over the wooden footbridge that crossed Spencer Creek at the edge of the park. The same narrow bridge, made from native cedar trees, had been part of Ashton's sidewalk system for over a hundred years. The city council had threatened to replace it with a cement culvert and steel walkway but the tourist bureau squawked their disapproval arguing that this historic site brought many a tourist to snap a picture and spend a dollar in the Ashton business district. Many of the buildings throughout Ashton dated back to the mid-1800s, a few even earlier. Liz was thankful for the little pieces of history and splendor that brought visitors to the sleepy New England town for they were the customers that kept her restaurant, The Sugar Bush, the success it was.

She slowed her pace as she rounded the corner at Bell River and Ivanhoe, passing under the sign that swung from the mast over the double doors to her restaurant. The Sugar Bush, named for the grove of trees where maple sap was collected to make Vermont's famous maple syrup, was closed. It wouldn't be open for breakfast for another forty-five minutes. The lights in the kitchen could be seen through the port holes in the swinging doors at the back of the dining room. Liz opened the back door off the alley and stepped inside, her breathing heavy and labored as she gulped for air. She ducked in the employee's bathroom and emerged a minute later, her face and arms washed and her hair toweled dry. Her breathing was already slowed and controlled.

"Good morning, Liz," a woman called. She was loading trays of pastries into the large stainless steel refrigerator. "How was your run?"

"Morning, Pauline." Liz replied, checking the clipboard hanging by her office door. "Fine. Millie Timm's roses are in full bloom. Have you seen them?" Liz continued to read through the invoices.

"Yes, dammit. I am *so* jealous." Pauline smirked and shook her head. "She just plants them to torment us."

Liz laughed.

"I think she plants them to treat us to some color."

"Not Millie," Pauline scoffed. "If she knew we admired them she would pull them up and burn them."

7

"Has Ernie brought the strawberries yet?" Liz looked in the refrigerator intently.

"Not yet, but I called them again. He said they would be here by seven thirty, no later."

Liz rolled her eyes and smirked.

"Do you think it is safe to put them on the menu for today?" Pauline asked cautiously. "You had a fruit plate planned for one of the lunch specials."

"Yes. Put it on the menu. If they don't arrive in time I'll get some strawberries from the IGA. And then I will tie Ernie's ears together for promising something he couldn't deliver." Liz closed the refrigerator and headed for the back door. "I'll be back in a half-hour. You need anything?"

"Nope, we have everything under control. Georgia is setting up. Rosita is already here. Tina and Ellen will be in any minute. Take your time."

"Call me if you need me," Liz said then disappeared out the back door. She started at a slow trot then moved up to her normal pace as she headed down Ivanhoe. It was an easy fourteen blocks to her house and a hot shower before returning to her restaurant and a full day's work.

Liz felt comfortable leaving the pre-opening chores in Pauline and Georgia's capable hands. At least she was learning to be comfortable with it. She had hired the sisters eight years ago, soon after she took over complete ownership of the café. They had never worked in a restaurant before but were efficient, dependable and considered by many to be the best cooks in the county. Liz found them trustworthy and consistent. Pauline was best at organizing the kitchen and making sure it was stocked correctly for Liz's menu. She was a bustling energetic woman who understood Liz's demands for punctuality and order. Georgia, Pauline's older sister by three years, was the hands-on cook and baker. She could turn a refrigerator full of odds and ends into a feast fit for a king. Her cakes were rich, her quiches were works of art, her homemade soups were hearty and filling and her omelets were fluffier than a summer cloud. She couldn't make a decent pot of coffee in the large commercial machine to save her life but she could make a piecrust flaky enough to bring customers back time after time. Liz was a strict and deliberate businesswoman. She also knew the importance of reliable employees, something Pauline and Georgia understood as well. The prep cooks, dishwashers, busers and waitresses all knew Liz was a strict but kind taskmaster. She didn't expect her employees to do anything she wouldn't do herself.

Liz turned down Danforth, a dead-end street. Her house was the last one on the right and backed up to a thick grove of pine trees. It was a small two-story brick home dating from the 1920s. It had a living room, dining room and kitchen on the first floor with a laundry room and half bath out the back. There were two good size bedrooms upstairs with a remodeled bathroom and a tiny room under the dormer for an office. The front porch was centered between two bay windows and there were red petunias in the flower boxes suspended under the windows. The yard was full of trees. Scrubs dotted the corners of the property. When Liz was house hunting, the two most attractive features for her had been the cozy fireplace in the living room and the unattached garage with a two-room apartment above it. The previous owner had installed a small elevator in the corner of the garage to assist his mother with her independent living. When Becca earned her scholarship to Chilton College, Liz agreed to allow her to move into the apartment. It meant Liz wouldn't be getting the income from a renter, but Becca agreed to trade the living arrangement for her assistance at The Sugar Bush, with a little extra for Becca's spending money. As a former college student herself, Liz understood the need for privacy and independence. The garage apartment also afforded Liz's mothering instincts to keep Becca close to home.

Liz pulled the key from her sock and unlocked the front door. Once inside she placed the key in the ceramic shoe on the table by the couch. It would be there on Sunday evening when she planned on running out Blue Water Road and over Greeley Ridge to watch the sunset then back again. It was a shorter run, but one she enjoyed for the unobstructed and picturesque view of the valley. She went into the kitchen and poured herself a glass of juice. She checked out the window but the light in the garage apartment was still dark. Since Mark's car was in the driveway, she assumed Becca had company and she decided not to key the intercom just yet. She went upstairs to shower. When she returned fifteen minutes later, fresh and dressed for a busy day at The Sugar Bush, she again peered out the kitchen window. The light was on in the apartment.

"Mom!" Becca called over the speaker.

"Good morning, honey," Liz replied, keying the switch.

"Mom, will you see if my black nylon sweatpants are in the dryer? The ones with the white stripe."

"Good morning, Becca," Liz repeated persistently.

"Good morning, mother," Becca quipped finally. "Will you look?"

"Just a second." Liz went into the laundry room and returned with the pants, shaking them vigorously. "Yes, they are here but you can't wear these. They are all wrinkled."

"Could you put them back in the dryer with a fabric softener sheet? Please." Becca was good at whining. "Mark will be over to get them in a minute." The intercom squealed which meant she had turned it off.

"I'd love to, daughter. You're welcome," Liz muttered sarcastically as she returned them to the dryer. She added a moist towel to help discourage the wrinkles.

Before she could open a granola bar a tap at the back door meant Mark Bateman, Becca's on-again-off-again boyfriend since junior high school, had been sent to retrieve the sweatpants.

"Come in, Mark," Liz called.

"Hi, Ms. Elliott," he said quietly. Mark was a shy young man who was growing faster than his body could recognize. He was tall and gangly with a round baby face and soft eyes. He had buzzed cut his hair to a few millimeters in length. He was dressed in a New England Patriots T-shirt and green plaid pajama pants. He was barefoot and looked like he had been awake less than a minute. He was clean and polite—something Liz hadn't been able to say about all of Becca's boyfriends. His smile was small but genuine. As a concerned mother for the men Becca chose to share her bed and her life, Liz was thankful Mark seemed to be kind. That was the quality she had used to judge him by.

Mark retrieved the pants from the dryer and checked for wrinkles, something Liz suspected Becca had instructed him to do. He then threw them over his shoulder like a gym towel.

"Becca said to tell you thanks," he said sheepishly.

Liz nodded as she swallowed a bite of bar. Mark stood at the back door and watched as she sipped her juice.

"Would you like some juice, Mark?" she asked, noticing his stare. She handed him the container of orange juice.

"Thanks," he replied brightly and headed out the door with the pants and the quart of juice.

Liz smiled to herself and shook her head. Mark stuck his head back in the door.

"Becca said to tell you not to wait for her. I'll bring her to the restaurant in a few minutes, okay?"

"Thirty minutes, Mark. You tell her I said thirty minutes." She narrowed her eyes at him and pointed menacingly.

"Okay, I'll tell her," he replied then closed the door.

Liz knew she wouldn't see either of them for at least an hour. He had been out of town for three weeks and as Deb, Becca's best friend, had said they had the hots for each other. Liz finished her granola bar as she backed out of the drive and headed for town. She eased into the narrow space between the dumpster and the back door to Lidderman's Insurance Agency. Her shiny new lemon yellow Volkswagen Beetle fit perfectly in the space. She had needed a new car for several years but waited until she could pay half of it in cash. She handed down her old tank of a car to Becca. It was heavy, cumbersome and ugly but Liz decided it offered extra protection because of its size. She was sure Becca would complain about driving the twenty-year-old Oldsmobile with the mismatched doors but to the contrary, she was thrilled to have it, saying she couldn't hurt it and it was a conversation piece among her friends. It was christened Becca's moldy oldie.

The Sugar Bush was open and filling with customers as she re-entered the bustling kitchen. Two cooks, three food preparers and a dishwasher were all on task at their work stations as three waitresses bustled through the tight spaces, balancing trays and plates. Pauline was standing at the grill, turning the bacon and rolling the sausage links so they would brown evenly. Georgia was adding spices to the huge pots of soup that would simmer for hours before being served to the lunch crowd.

"Number two, over easy. Grilled onions on the home fries. Rye," one of the waitresses read from her order pad then attached the paper to the cord with one of the spring clips. "Where are my biscuits and gravy?" she called.

Pauline ladled a generous scoop of white sausage gravy over two large opened biscuits. She added a sprig of mint to the edge and sprinkled paprika on the top.

"Pick up, Ellen," she said, sliding it down the counter. "Ernie just dropped off the strawberries," she called as Liz donned an apron. "Six flats."

"How do they look?"

"Nice ones. Good color and heavenly smell."

Liz opened the refrigerator and checked the boxes.

"There are seven flats, Pauline. I only ordered six." Liz frowned at the extra box.

"Ernie said that one is on the house for being late. I told him what you said about tying his ears together. I guess he figured he owed you one."

"I hope he doesn't think he can offer a freebie and continue being late. I need my deliveries on time, not bonuses for his mistakes."

Pauline laughed.

"I told him you'd say that. He promised you'd be at the top of his list from now on."

"Uh-huh," she muttered and closed the door. She headed

through the swinging doors for the dining room. The pastry case was full of Georgia's creations, everything from muffins and home-made donuts to turnovers and powdered sugar funnel cakes. Ellen, Tina and Rosita, three of Liz's long-time waitresses, were busy with customers. Liz made a circle of the room, greeting her clientele and filling coffee cups. She corrected a gentleman's order, insisting his eggs would be cooked just the way he wanted them in no time. She seated guests and mopped a toddler's spilled cup of milk. She even handled the cash register, something Becca was supposed to be doing.

The door opened and a tall woman strode in, her steps determined and purposeful. She scanned the room with narrowed eyes as if she was searching for someone. After a complete perusal of the restaurant she gave a heavy sigh as the muscles in her cheek rippled. She seemed disappointed over not finding whoever she was looking for.

Liz took a menu from the podium and smiled her welcoming smile at the woman. It suddenly occurred to her who the woman was.

"Coach Ross," she said, offering a handshake.

"Hello," she replied, shaking her hand. "I'm sorry, should I know you? I'm terrible with names." She continued searching the room for something or someone.

"I'm Liz Elliott. Becca's mother."

"Oh, yes," Sheridan Ross declared, acknowledging her. "Hello."

"Would you like a booth or a table?"

"Actually, I am here to see Becca. I was told she worked here."

"See does but she isn't here right now. She should be along shortly. Can I help you with anything?" Liz didn't mean to intrude with her daughter's affairs.

"No, that's all right. I need to talk with her as soon as she gets in."

"Why don't you have a seat? Would you like a cup of coffee while you wait? Or maybe some breakfast?"

"Just a glass of water with lemon, no ice. Thank you."

"How's this, Coach?" Liz said, pointing to a booth by the windows.

"Please, call me Sheridan. I'm only *coach* to my players." She slid in, her long frame easing into place.

Liz poured her water and brought a small dish with lemon wedges and a sprig of mint tucked in the side. This was one of the little extras she had incorporated into her service, the little touches that meant the customers were special and their satisfaction was paramount. Sheridan sat sipping her water and checking her watch for fifteen minutes. Liz assumed she would give up on her daughter and walk out, leaving a message that Becca should contact her at her earliest convenience. Instead she stayed, staring at the door and drumming her fingers on the table. Finally Liz could hear Becca's voice from the kitchen. So could Sheridan. As soon as Becca entered the dining room, Sheridan was on her feet.

Becca stood in the doorway, leaning on a pair of metal crutches, her left leg covered with a plaster cast from her thigh to her ankle, the nylon sweatpants stretched tightly over it. She had a fuzzy yellow sock covering her bare foot. Mark stood behind her, carrying her backpack and looking like an elderly husband standing outside a dressing room with his wife's purse while she tried on dresses. Becca's hair was long and flowed over her shoulders in rich brown strands. She was an attractive woman, nearly six feet tall with muscular arms and shoulders and a small waist. She looked like an athlete, a beached athlete. She stumped her way into the dining room, still growing accustomed to the awkward crutches. It had been six weeks since her accident and two weeks since the surgery needed to correct the bone that wasn't healing properly. Becca was taller than Liz and didn't have her fair complexion or blonde hair but Becca had her mother's eyes and smile, one that produced dimples in both cheeks. She had come into the dining room with a broad smile but it quickly melted when she saw Sheridan staring at her.

"Becca," Liz said, going to her. "Coach Ross is here to see you. She's been waiting for almost a thirty minutes. Where have you been?"

"Trying to get my pants on over this freaking thing," Becca replied with a snippy attitude.

"How are you feeling, Becca?" Sheridan asked, going to help her. "I hear the surgery went well."

"I have no idea. I was napping at the time," Becca replied, shaking out the tingling in her hands from supporting her weight on the crutches.

"Dr. Corbin said she will have the cast on another six weeks then a brace for a month or so while she starts physical therapy. The doctor thought she should be good as new in four or five months. It'll just take some time to regain the muscle tone." Liz tried to help Becca navigate a chair so she could sit down.

"I can do it," Becca advised, lowering herself gingerly. Mark waited for her to get settled then hung her backpack over her chair.

"You're doing pretty well. I'm impressed. I never did get the hang of using crutches," Sheridan said.

"You broke your leg too?" Becca replied.

"Knee," she said as she pulled out a chair and sat across from her.

"Freaking pain in the ass, huh Coach?"

Sheridan laughed and nodded. Liz was tempted to stay and visit with them but she knew whatever Sheridan had to say to Becca was none of her business and she had customers to tend. She went back to work and left them to their conversation. Mark excused himself and went across the street to the bookstore.

"Becca, I got an e-mail from the registrar's office that you haven't sent in your class schedule yet. In fact, you haven't done anything yet. Classes start in ten days. You need to get that stuff taken care of ASAP. It just takes an e-mail to get it done. If you are having trouble getting around campus I can help. Tell me what I can do to get this completed." Sheridan seemed deeply concerned.

"Coach, I don't know yet if I'm going back," Becca said dispassionately.

"I thought the surgery took care of your leg. Your mother said after rehab you'll be good as new."

"Yeah," she replied, rolling and unrolling the corner of her napkin.

"You can use the whirlpool tank in the locker room and the trainer will work with your physical therapist to bring your leg along slowly so you'll be ready to play next year. This is what they do and our trainers are very good. I know it hurts now but give yourself some time to heal."

"It's just I haven't decided if I really want to play." Becca looked up at Sheridan plaintively. "God, Coach. We only won five freaking games all year. We were the butt-ass joke of the conference. The games we did win weren't even from rated schools." She lowered her eyes. "Why bother?" she muttered.

Sheridan covered Becca's hands with her own and squeezed firmly.

"Why bother? Becca, we have to bother. It's what people do. They keep trying to improve. You can't just give up and roll over. We learn from our mistakes. We don't let them defeat us. Is that what you do when things get tough? Quit? I didn't think that was in your personality. I thought you were a fighter."

Becca kept her eyes diverted as she discreetly wiped a tear from her eye.

"It's been a tough year for you," Sheridan offered soothingly. "A losing season, the accident and the surgery then finding out you can't play this year. It's all very depressing, I'm sure. Hey, I'm depressed over last year's record and I didn't even have a motorcycle accident," she joked, trying to bring a smile to Becca's face.

"You never get depressed, Coach," Becca replied. "You can adjust to changes. Old people adjust to changes better than we do." She smiled at her, knowing she sounded impudent.

"Old people?" Sheridan laughed. "I'll have you know this old person understands where you are coming from. And I'll have you know I'm only forty-two," she added leaning in and whispering.

"Wow, forty-two," Becca sassed then grinned.

"Yes, and I'm plenty old enough to take you over my knee if you don't get your class schedule turned in this week," Sheridan declared, wagging a parental finger at her. "You're too good not to play, Becca." She looked at her with sympathetic eyes. "I'm here if you need help. A year from now we'll be talking about new plays and practice and how many points you'll score per game."

"I'll think about it, Coach," Becca said quietly.

"Okay," Sheridan said, patting her hand. "Come talk with me if you have any questions. My office is always open to my players."

"That's new. Coach Hanley was never in his office."

"Well, Sheridan Ross is the head coach now. You're a Chilton Stinger, Becca. Don't you forget it. We are a tight-knit family and we help each other."

Sheridan stood up and pushed her chair in.

"There is one rule you need to remember as a Chilton Stinger," Sheridan said with a scowl. "Stay off motorcycles. At least while you're on my team."

"I wasn't driving. I was just riding on the back," Becca offered.

"Even worse. You have to always be in control of your world, Becca. Your future is in your hands, no one else's. Don't let someone else put you in jeopardy."

"It wasn't as much fun as I thought it would be," Becca declared then tapped on her cast.

Chapter 2

Becca stumped along the hall outside the locker room with her rubber crutch tips squeaking each stride she took. The hallway had a gentle bend to it as it circled the back of the gymnasium. As she rounded the corner to the lobby she noticed Coach Ross kneeling in front of one of the trophy cases. She was removing the contents of the bottom row and dusting the shelves, something that looked like it hadn't been done in years.

"Hello, Becca," she said, looking up from her work. "How's the leg?"

"I'd tell you but it wouldn't be pretty."

"That bad, huh?"

"I hit it on my locker door." She grimaced and leaned heavily on her crutches. "I wish I could scratch it. It itches *so* bad."

"I'm sure it does. But that means it is healing."

"That's what mom said."

"Have you done anything about registering?" Sheridan gave her a serious stare.

"Not yet," Becca replied hesitantly. "What are you doing with that stuff?" she asked, trying to change the subject.

"Cleaning out this case. No one has gone through it in years. I had to have new keys made for it. No one knew where the old ones were."

Becca looked down into a box of pictures and statistic sheets that had been folded and taped to the bottom of some of the trophy bases. One of the photographs caught her eye. She balanced on one foot and leaned down to retrieve it.

"This is my mother," she declared with a chuckle. "I didn't know her team won anything."

Sheridan looked for the trophy that went with the photograph.

"Connecticut Valley Conference Championship," Sheridan read, handing it up to Becca. "Wow, they had a twenty-four-and-two record. Now that is how you play to win," she muttered.

"I don't think she ever mentioned that. I knew she played but I didn't know they were that good." Becca offered the photograph for the coach to see.

"I think there is a stat sheet in here somewhere." She dug in the box and finally pulled out a typed list of the players' season and career scoring records. "Liz Elliott, point guard, number twenty-three. Ninety-four percent free throw shooter. Wow! Hey, look at this, Becca." She stood up and held it out for her to see. "She was only two hundred and twelve points short of the Chilton all-time career scoring record. At the rate she was going, she could have done that in a walk. Now there is something for you to work for," she suggested. "She is just a junior in this picture. I wonder how they did her senior year. They only graduated one player. They should have been a threat to repeat as conference champs the next year as well."

"Mom didn't play her senior year." Becca seemed almost ashamed to have to admit that.

"Why not? What happened?"

Becca gave a broad and artificial smile.

"Me," she offered.

"Oh," Sheridan replied and chuckled.

"So your mom got married and gave up college, huh?" she asked, replacing the articles in the box.

"My mom married?" she chuckled. "Not exactly." Becca wiped the dust from the trophy before putting it in the box. "I don't have a father. At least not one you could identify."

"That's okay," Sheridan replied reassuringly. She didn't want to pry into what sounded like a personal family matter. "I'm sure your mother would tell you how important it is to finish college."

"She tells me that all the time. She thinks I should do what you said, take classes this year and be redshirted while I rehab my leg."

"Smart woman," she replied quickly. "Are you taking her advice? I'd hate to see you waste your talents, Becca. You have the chance to be a really good player. Chilton can use someone with your shooting talents. I don't want to judge your mother but I bet she would tell you if she had to do it again, she would love to have a chance to play that last year of college ball. Looks like she was an excellent player herself. I hope you don't give up your chance to play."

Becca frowned at her then looked away pensively.

"Coach, isn't it true that in Division II colleges the players have ten semesters to participate in sports, not just five years like it is in Division I universities?"

"Yes, I told you all you have to do is let me redshirt your sophomore year and you can still play. Even if you need an extra semester to finish your classroom work for your degree, you can play."

Becca stood thinking for a long moment.

"I have to go to the registrar's office. See you later, Coach," she said as if she just remembered something important she needed to do. She turned on her crutches and stumped her way out the door. "Thanks."

"Good for you," Sheridan said, obviously pleased with Becca's change of heart over returning for her sophomore year.

Becca crossed the campus, taking long awkward strides on the crutches as she rushed into the administration building.

"Meredith?" Becca whispered in the direction of the lady busily digging in the filing cabinet. Meredith Rubinward had worked at Chilton College for over thirty years. She was assistant director of student services and well-liked by her fellow employees and the countless students who passed through her office over the years. On the surface, Meredith was the slick professional type, wearing tailored suits and stylish hairdos. Underneath she was kind and caring yet efficient, the perfect personality for her complex job. She also had a memory like an elephant.

"Hi, Becca," she said, grinning up at her. "I hear you had to have surgery. How's the leg?" She rubbed Becca's arm soothingly.

"It's okay. Mom about passed out though." Becca laughed. "The bone was sticking out and way gross."

"Yuk," Meredith smirked. "I would have passed out too. I'm so sorry to hear about the accident. I hope you are going to give up riding on motorcycles. Will you be able to play this season?" she asked cautiously.

"Nope," Becca replied and heaved a deep sigh. "I'd have to be redshirted this year."

"That's okay," she quickly inserted. "You can play next season then. Your scholarship will still cover you while you recuperate."

"I know. Coach Ross told me all about it."

"Is that why you are here? To check on your scholarship?" Meredith asked.

"Well, sort of," Becca replied, looking around to see if anyone was listening. "I need your help checking on something, Meredith."

"Sure, honey. What do you need?" She helped Becca into a chair next to her desk.

Becca looked around again then leaned in.

"Can you look up my mom's records, her transcript and scholarship?" Becca whispered hopefully.

"Why do you want to know Liz's records, honey?"

"I just want to know how close she was to finishing her degree when she quit. But please," Becca said, placing her hand on Meredith's arm. "Don't tell anyone I asked, okay?"

Meredith sat back in her chair.

"What are you up to Miss Becca?" she asked, narrowing her eyes.

Becca pursed her lips as if she was trying not to let anything slip out.

"Student records are private and privileged information. I could get fired for doing that, honey."

"I know." Becca smirked then leaned in again. "Can you promise to keep a secret?"

"I think so," Meredith replied, leaning in as well.

"I have an idea of how I could get mom to come back to Chilton for her last year. She never says it but I think deep down inside she wishes she had been able to finish her degree and play her last year of basketball. But I need to know some things first."

Meredith looked over the rim of her glasses at Becca.

"Liz Elliott was an outstanding student and she was one of the best woman athletes to ever play for Chilton. I remember going to the games. Her junior year they won the conference championship right here in our own gymnasium. I think she scored twenty points, maybe more. It was a real shame she couldn't play her senior year." Meredith shook her head reflectively.

"Please," Becca pleaded. "I can't do this alone. I need your help."

"Honey, Chilton College has a long tradition of respecting a student's privacy. It is one of the cornerstones on which this institution was founded one hundred and twenty-five years ago." As Meredith lectured Becca her fingers were busy at her computer, bringing up Liz's records and printing them off. She winked at Becca then exited the archives data files. "What good is it to work for a college if you can't help a student from time to time? Let's see what we have here. It looks like Liz took some summer classes a few years back so she only needs fifteen credits for her bachelor's of science in business administration. She had a Dartmouth Hilliard Scholarship. Wow. That was a feather in her cap. They only give out one of those a year, you know."

"It wasn't an athletic scholarship?" Becca asked, looking at the printout.

"No, it was an academic scholarship. In fact, it was a little different from the ones they award now. This one allows for up to four years to complete the degree but it doesn't have a running date."

"What does that mean?"

"It means she could take a year now and a year later, whatever she wants to do. It was originally written that way back during World War I in case a man won it and was called away to war. He could serve his country then return and pick up where he left off. They decided it worked equally well for women too so they left it that way."

"You mean it is still there? She could still use it to finish her last year?"

"Yes, that's just what it means. All she would have to do is register for classes and it would automatically reactivate. What's great about a Dartmouth Hilliard Scholarship is that it is for degree fulfillment, whatever the cost of her classes. It doesn't have a financial limit. Tuition is significantly higher now than twenty years ago when she started. There is a limit on the room and board but the classes, books and student fees would still be covered." Meredith looked around the room of desks nonchalantly then looked at Becca. "How are you going to convince her to come back to school?"

"I don't know yet," she replied with a small mischievous smile.

"Your mother was a deserving student. It was a real shame she couldn't finish. Do you think she'll do it?"

"Oh, I think I can find a way." Becca flashed her dark eyes.

Meredith smiled fondly at her.

"You are a good daughter, Becca Elliott. You tell your mother I said hi, okay? But don't you dare tell anyone where you got this information." She cast a caustic stare at Becca.

"I won't. Thanks."

Chapter 3

Liz stood at one of the big stainless steel sinks washing and sorting tomatoes. Some would be sliced, some chopped for salads and some would be cored to hold chicken salad. Becca hobbled over and leaned on her crutches, waiting for her mother's attention.

"Pauline said you wanted to see me," Becca offered as she popped one of the cherry tomatoes in her mouth.

"Don't eat those. I haven't washed them yet. Here," Liz said, handing her one from the strainer.

"What did you want?" she asked, eating that one as well.

"Did you get enrolled?"

"No," Becca replied distractedly as she searched for one more tomato.

"As soon as I finish here I'll give you a ride to the registrar's office," Liz advised as she poured the last crate of tomatoes into the ice water bath.

"That's okay."

Liz gave Becca a curious look.

"When are you going to turn it in? You just have this week."

Becca didn't say anything.

"Becca?" Liz asked carefully, seeing something strange in her daughter's behavior.

Becca shrugged indifferently.

Liz turned to face her and studied her intently.

"You are going to enroll, aren't you?"

"I don't think so," she replied, keeping her eyes lowered. "I think I'll stay out this year. I can't play ball this season anyway. So why should I attend classes?"

"Your coach talked with you about that. You can be redshirted this year then still play three more years, as long as you enroll as a full-time student. Your scholarship will still cover your expenses for this year, too."

Becca shrugged again.

"Sweetheart, I know you want to play basketball. But don't quit college just because you have to wait a year. College is important for your future. Not everyone gets a chance for a college education. You have a talent to play basketball and that won you a scholarship. Don't throw it away. Don't give up so easily. If you don't finish you'll always regret it." Liz rubbed Becca's arm warmly. Her words were ringing in her own ears, a reminder of what might have been years ago. "Believe me, you will."

"You didn't finish. You didn't go back," Becca replied defensively.

Liz took a deep breath. She didn't say anything. She hadn't expected her daughter to challenge the choices she made twenty years ago.

"You dropped out and went to work. Why can't I?" Becca stared defiantly. "You had a scholarship and only used three years of it. You could have played your last year."

Liz smiled at her tenderly.

"Honey, I was pregnant with you. And for me, having a beautiful baby was far more important than playing basketball or getting a degree in business administration."

"Why didn't you go back the next year? You could have. You had a scholarship for ten semesters. You could have redshirted the year you had me then gone back."

For a brief moment Becca's words echoed through Liz's mind, just as the same arguments had done when the coach pleaded with Liz to return after Becca was born.

"Why Mom?"

Liz looked away. The cold reality of the question slapped her across the face.

"I had a baby to raise. I had to work to keep a roof over our heads and food on the table. That's why."

"If it's good enough for you, it's good enough for me," Becca stated dryly.

Liz snapped a look at Becca and gasped.

"Are you pregnant?" she asked in a hushed voice.

Becca laughed and gave a wry smile.

"God, no."

"Thank goodness," Liz replied with a relieved groan.

"What if I was? What would you say about going back to college if I was?" she asked as if testing her mother's response.

"If you were, and I am glad you aren't, I'd say if you decide to have the baby then we'll work something out so you can go back and finish your degree and play your four years of eligibility. You have to play to keep your scholarship."

Becca smiled coyly.

"You didn't go back. And don't give me that stuff about getting a job. You could have found a way if you really wanted to. How about grandpa? Couldn't he have helped?"

Liz shook her head.

"Grandpa was busy with the farm. That's when grandmother was so sick. He couldn't help. And if you want to know if I wish I had gone back to finish my degree and play my last year at Chilton, the answer is yes. I do. I have no regrets about the decisions I made. But yes, finishing what you start is always important. That's why I want you to finish, Becca. You'll wish you had." Liz looked deep into her daughter's eyes, the importance of her message clearly visible on her face.

"Tell you what," Becca started then stiffened her posture. "I will if you will."

"You will if I will what?" she asked curiously.

"I will go back to college, finish my degree and play basketball after my leg heals if you will go back and finish your degree and play your last year of eligibility for Chilton College this year." Becca said it as if she had prepared the declaration and had practiced it.

Liz laughed and shook her head at the suggestion.

"That's funny," she scoffed then set the bowls of sorted tomatoes in the refrigerator. She took out a crate of onions and began washing them for peeling. Becca leaned on her crutches and watched, her face stone cold serious.

"I mean it," she added. "I'm not going back unless you do. I'll quit college and join the army. I hear they are offering a forty-thousand-dollar signing bonus."

"Don't be ridiculous," Liz frowned as she worked in the sink.

"I'm old enough to join, Mom. Karen Miller joined. She's going to boot camp next week."

"Becca Elliott," Liz scowled. "You'll do no such thing. Besides, you could never be a soldier. You could never get up at the crack of dawn." Liz laughed to herself remembering how many times Becca was late for classes in high school.

Becca didn't reply. She continued to stare at her mother, a small devious glint sparkled in her eye.

"Becca, I mean it. I don't want to hear another word about you joining the army. Or the navy or any other branch of the military." Liz met Becca's stare with one of her own.

Slowly Becca pulled a folded paper from her backpack. She opened it and held it up. It was an army application, filled out with everything but the date. Liz dropped her knife in the sink and grabbed for the paper but Becca pulled it away.

"Oh my God, Becca. You didn't?" Liz gasped in horror.

"Not yet," she replied coyly.

"Sweetheart, please! Think what you are giving up." Liz spoke as if she was coaxing her down from a ledge. "You have a full scholarship. You are a good basketball player. For God's sake, Becca. You could end up in Iraq or Afghanistan or who knows where. Women are right there on the front lines being killed right along with our brave young men." A small tear filled Liz's eye and threatened to spill out. She looked away then back at her daughter. "I couldn't stand it if I thought you were in danger or hurt." The words choked in her throat. "Please," she pleaded, holding Becca's face in her hands tenderly.

Becca reached back into her backpack and took out another paper. She unfolded it and handed it to her mother.

"If you don't want me to join up you have to agree to this."

"What's this?" Liz scanned the paper.

"It's a contract. And it's all legal. Mark is pre-law at Harvard and he helped me write it."

"Contract for what?" Her eyes stopped halfway down the page. "You're kidding. You have to be kidding. Becca?" She looked up at her daughter skeptically. "This says I agree to return to Chilton College and complete my bachelor's degree in business administration and go out for the basketball team."

"No, it says you have to *play* for the basketball team," Becca corrected.

"Are you crazy? I have a business to run. I can't be taking time out to go back to college much less play basketball." She chuckled and perched her hands on her hips. "I'm thirty-nine years old, you know."

Becca started to say something but Liz held up her hand.

"And don't tell me Michael Jordan did it. That was completely different. He was a superstar in the NBA and he was still in good shape when he decided to make a comeback."

"You are in good shape, too. You've got great buns, mom, if I do say so myself."

"Great buns won't make up for aging legs."

"What about all that running you do?"

"That isn't the same," Liz warned. "I haven't shot a basketball since—"

"Since last fall when we played one-on-one in the driveway."

"And you won big time," Liz admonished.

"Yeah, but you won when we played horse. Twice. You've still got a decent shot, Mom. I wish I had inherited your three-pointer from the baseline."

"I'll teach it to you. But I can't play again." Liz laughed. "I can just see me trying to run a fast break. It would look like slow motion." She smirked at the thought. "I'd need oxygen by the end of the first half."

"I doubt it." Becca narrowed her eyes at her mother. "You can't stand there and tell me somewhere deep down inside you haven't imagined yourself playing that last year. God Mom! All you needed was two hundred points to set a school career record."

"Two-twelve," Liz said with lowered eyes. "And I'm sure that record was broken a long time ago. Probably many times over." Liz went back to work on the onions.

Becca slowly but adamantly shook her head.

"Nope, not even close," she declared.

Liz smiled over at her proudly.

"You'll break it, sweetheart. I'm sure you will." Liz patted her arm.

"That's up to you," Becca declared, waving the two papers in front of Liz. "You sign the contract with me or I will sign up for the army."

"Becca, if you sign up for the military, it is for six years. You can't get out of it. You can't say I was just kidding. I didn't mean it."

"I know." She waved the papers tauntingly.

"College is expensive, honey. You have a scholarship. I can't afford to just take time off from the restaurant and pay all that money for tuition and books and fees."

"You have a scholarship, too. A full boat."

"I *had* a scholarship, sweetheart. That was twenty years ago."

"It is still good." Becca had a smug look on her face.

"No, honey. They expire. That money is long gone. That's why I keep telling you not to wait too long or you will lose yours."

"I checked and yours is still good."

"How did you find that out about my scholarship?"

"Never mind how I found out. But it's still there. Two semesters of tuition, books, fees, room and board, athletic equipment—you can even get a room in the dorm if you want it," she giggled. "You know, all-night gab fests, panty raids, sneaking in after hours."

"Very funny."

"I'm serious Mom. Your Dartmouth Hilliard Scholarship is still there. I also found out since you took those summer classes you only need fifteen hours to graduate. You can check all this stuff online. You'll even have the same student ID number."

"*Only* fifteen hours?" Liz laughed. "Might as well be a million."

"Fifteen hours spread over two semesters. That's just five classes, four if you take a class with a lab. You could take a couple computer classes since they didn't require them back when you went before. You could take introduction to computer use and computer applications." Becca took a class catalog from her backpack and opened it to the paperclip.

"I don't need to take a computer class. I have been using them for years, sweetheart."

"Exactly. You'd ace that. Maybe you could take something like business computer theory, too. There's nine hours right there."

"And what about the other six, miss smarty-pants?" Liz turned and leaned against the sink with her arms crossed.

"I figure you could take speech. That would be easy for you. You're always ordering people around."

"Becca!"

"And maybe business applications or business purchasing basics. Each is three hours and you haven't taken them yet. I checked." She grinned knowingly.

"You have been busy, haven't you?"

"Yes. And if you spread out your classes, you would still have plenty of time to help us run The Sugar Bush as well as time for the practice and the games."

"Help who run The Sugar Bush?" Liz asked skeptically.

"Me and Pauline and Georgia and the rest of the employees. Mark said he'd help when he is home on vacations. It would only be for thirty-two weeks when you take out the vacations."

Liz glanced over at Pauline and Georgia who were eavesdropping from the other side of the kitchen. They both nodded and smiled encouragingly.

"You seem to have done a lot of thinking and planning about this."

"I figure those classes won't have a lot of homework for you because you already know the stuff," Becca added.

"Don't count on it."

"And you know what they say about nontraditional students, Mom."

"Nontraditional?"

"Yeah. Old people who come back to college instead of going straight in from high school."

"What is that? They're crazy."

"Nontraditional students have a higher GPA, a better attendance record and they have a better graduation percentage."

"Oh, they do?" Liz asked smugly.

"Yep. I learned that at freshmen orientation last year. Aren't you glad I paid attention?"

Liz took a deep breath then laughed out loud.

"This has got to be the most harebrained scheme I have ever heard. Going back to college and what's more, playing basketball at age thirty-nine. Becca?" She stared doubtfully at her daughter.

"I don't think so, Mom." She took a pen from her pocket and held it out to Liz as she spread the contract on the counter.

"Wait a minute. I have to think about this."

"Don't think. Just sign it, Mom. You know you have always wanted to do this. You even said so." She wiggled the pen at her.

"But I'm not at all sure that scholarship would still be good."

"It is, but the contract says right here, it is contingent upon the scholarship being available." Becca pointed to the appropriate paragraph.

"And what do you agree to?"

"It says I agree not to join the military. I also agree to return to Chilton this year and I agree to finish my degree. You never know. I may major in business and become your partner. Someday we can convert The Sugar Bush into a beer and pizza place."

"Lord, help us all," she scoffed as she read the paragraphs.

"College. Basketball." Becca whispered the words as if they were bits of chocolate she was waving in Liz's face. "You know you have always wanted to do this, Mom. You always told me never say can't."

Liz took the pen nervously.

"You'll go back to college?" Liz asked.

Becca nodded.

"And no army?" Liz added sternly.

"Nope."

Liz prepared to sign then threw her head back and ran her hand through her hair.

"What am I doing here?" she muttered.

"Fulfilling a dream," Becca whispered over her mother's shoulder.

Liz looked at her daughter with both fear and nervous excitement in her eyes. She took a long preparatory breath and looked down at the contract. She closed her eyes and exhaled. She reached over and took Becca's hand then signed on the line below Becca's signature. She studied the signature for a moment, surprised at how quickly she had committed herself to this lunacy. She suddenly reached down as if to wad up the contract she had just signed but Becca snatched it away and held it out of reach.

"Here," Becca said, handing her mother the army application. "This is for you."

Liz immediately tore it into tiny pieces and stuffed it in the trash. They smiled at each for a long moment. Liz's smile melted into a terrified look.

"What have I just gotten myself into?"

Becca hugged her mother tightly.

"Want to join my sorority, Mom?" she teased.

Liz laughed and held her daughter in her arms as tears welled up in her eyes, tears of joy and of apprehension.

Chapter 4

Liz's curiosity over whether she could still shoot a basketball nagged at her all day. She knew she could horse around in the driveway with Becca and occasionally sink a shot or two but shooting a jumper at the buzzer or sinking a pressure free throw with the game on the line was a different matter altogether. After The Sugar Bush closed at three she drove to the Chilton campus. The gymnasium was open but empty. She had brought Becca's basketball and was determined to find out how much she had to do to repair her shooting technique.

Liz stood at the free throw line and stared at the basket as if it were a mile away. She bounced the ball once then rubbed her palms against the textured surface. It felt foreign to her. Something she had spent four years in high school and three years in college holding, dribbling, passing, shooting and carrying now seemed as strange as a moon rock. She bounced it again and heaved a deep relaxing breath. She bent her knees and positioned the ball in her line of sight. After a long pause of concentration, Liz shot the ball. It arched toward the rim but fell well short of its target. She stood with a stunned look on her face. She used the same technique that had been so successful for her before but it wasn't even close. As a ninety-percent shooter from the charity stripe, she felt this was the one thing she could still do. But unless the distance from the line to the rim had increased drastically over the past nineteen years, she didn't even have this in her arsenal of skills.

She ran the ball down and returned to the line to try again. She set her feet, bounced the ball once, rubbed it with her palms then held it at the ready position. She expelled her breath then shot the ball, this time with a small groan as she released it. The ball traveled further but still fell well short. She tried again and again but only succeeded in raising a sweat.

"Dammit!" she muttered disgustedly. The ball bounced back to her and she slapped at it. This was her specialty. This was her domain. During her three years at Chilton as point guard her teammates considered Liz the shot doctor when it came to free throws. She was the player who was called upon to shoot when the other team was called for a technical foul. She was the one who no team wanted to foul in the last few minutes of the game for fear her free throws were nearly automatic. But now she couldn't even reach the rim. What had she gotten herself into? What had Becca cajoled her into doing? Determined to bang the rim at least once, Liz set herself and shot again, this time with clenched teeth and narrowed eyes. Again she missed. Finally she flung the ball at the basket in disgust. It hit the rim awkwardly and bounced away, sending a loud twang echoing across the empty gymnasium. She grabbed the ball as it rolled back to her and threw it against the end wall, yelling a curse word. She flopped down on the floor, lying spread eagle and pounding her fists like a child having a temper tantrum. For the moment, it seemed like an acceptable release of her frustrations. She didn't want to accept her shortcoming and she certainly didn't want to admit she had agreed to something beyond her capabilities. She would have to try harder.

She was not giving in to defeat. She was not. She lay on the floor, staring up at the rafters. She took a calming breath then closed her eyes to regain her composure and reaffirm her dedication to getting at least one ball through the net. When she opened her eyes, Sheridan was standing over her, looking down suspiciously.

"Are you having a problem?" she asked, frowning at Liz.

Liz groaned and rolled her eyes at being found in such an embarrassing position.

"No," she replied, gazing up at Sheridan. "I didn't know anyone was here." Liz scrambled to her feet.

"You're Becca's mother," Sheridan said, looking her up and down. "What brings you to the gymnasium?"

Liz hesitated, not sure if this was the right time to admit her motives.

"Bringing back old memories?" Sheridan suggested. "I saw your name on one of the trophies in the case. You were on the Connecticut Valley Conference Championship team the last time Chilton won the title."

Liz nodded at the memory.

"Seems like centuries ago," she said reflectively.

"Point guard, right?"

"Yes, and occasionally a forward," Liz replied, realizing her five-eight stature didn't bestow confidence as a big power forward.

"Forward?" Coach Ross raised her eyebrows skeptically.

"Yes, I know. I'm too short to play inside. I guess my coach thought I could dribble between their legs or something. Actually that only lasted one year. By the time I was a sophomore she kept me playing outside."

"I saw you had pretty impressive numbers. Scoring leader on the team and on the conference, free throw percentage leader two years running, most minutes played in a season, just two hundred and twelve points shy of a Chilton career scoring record. Not bad." Sheridan rattled off Liz's statistics as if she was reading a scouting report. Liz lowered her eyes and smiled to herself, both embarrassed at the listing and pleased someone had noticed. It had been a long time since the details of her career as a Chilton Stinger had been paraded in front of her.

"Thank you," she replied and tugged at her ear as if trying to stop the blush that shot over her face.

"Do you mind if I ask a personal question?" Sheridan stated.

Liz knew the question before it left her lips. She wanted to know why she didn't play her senior year. As much as she thought it was none of her business Liz also knew the subject would have to be addressed if she expected to try out for the team.

"You want to know why I didn't play my fourth year, right?" she asked stoically.

"You must admit. It's a logical query."

"I don't know about you, Coach, but I find it difficult to dribble a basketball when I'm six months pregnant," Liz stated defensively.

"Why don't you call me Sheridan," she offered. "And yes, I can see how that would be a problem." She crossed her arms and studied Liz pensively. "Timing is everything."

"I beg your pardon," Liz replied.

"Becca told me you had her instead of playing your last year."

"Yes. Sometimes things happen and we just have no control over them. But sometimes things happen for the best."

"I think we always have control, one way or another," Sheridan proclaimed.

"You've never had your life turned upside down without your consent, have you?"

"No. I like to keep my feet under me at all times."

"Lucky you." Liz wasn't impressed with the coach's abrasive or arrogant remarks. She had her reasons for the choices she made and it was none of this woman's business when or why she had a baby.

They stood staring at one another, their eyes dueling in silence.

"So you came in to see if you can still hit the rim," Sheridan said finally, seeming to realize she was making Liz uncomfortable.

"I was hoping I could still sink one, not just hit the rim." Liz looked up at the backboard.

"Try it again. Let's see what happens." Sheridan tossed her the ball.

Liz took her stance. She bounced the ball once, flexed her knees and rubbed the ball with her palms. She brought the ball up and shot. It hit the front of the rim and bounced back to her.

"Damn," she muttered.

"Okay, not bad form but you aren't cocking the shot." Sheridan stood next to her. "Try it again."

Liz went through her preparation again and just as she was about to shoot, the coach pressed back on her forearms. She held them there, the ball just inches from her face.

"Bring it to this point before you release." Sheridan released her arms.

Liz started again and did as she suggested. This time the ball made a longer arc and bounced off the back of the rim but still didn't go in. Sheridan ran the ball down and brought it back.

"Once more," she said, taking a position behind Liz. As she brought the ball back to shoot, Sheridan wrapped her arms around her and pulled her elbows in slightly. It wasn't enough to stop her shot but it was enough to send the ball in a steeper arc and it dropped neatly through the net.

"Hey, what do you know? The basket doesn't have a lid on it after all," Liz joked.

Sheridan retrieved the ball and pointed for her to try again. She stood behind her again, waiting for her to set herself. Liz could feel Sheridan's breath on the back of her neck. As she brought the ball up to shoot, Liz could also feel Sheridan's body pressing against her. Sheridan's arms around her and the touch of her body made concentrating on the shot impossible. This time the ball went sailing over the backboard, striking the wall.

"Oops!" she said and went to get it. She suddenly couldn't think clearly. She needed to move away from Sheridan. She needed some fresh air.

"Well, you made one," Sheridan teased.

"Better than none, right?" Liz looked up at the clock on the wall. "I better go. I've got deliveries coming this afternoon." She smiled nervously, her body wishing she would return to Sheridan's arms and stand against her again. "Thanks for the help."

"Glad to be of service." Sheridan watched as she collected her keys and headed for the door. "Tell Becca I said take care of that leg," she called.

"I will but you could come by The Sugar Bush sometime and tell her yourself," Liz offered. "She's there most mornings." Liz was surprised to hear herself say that. After all, this woman was arrogant and opinionated just three minutes ago. Now Liz found herself wishing she would show up at her restaurant.

"I just might do that," Sheridan replied, still watching Liz intently.

Chapter 5

Robin Harrison, Sheridan's handpicked assistant coach, knocked on Sheridan's open office door then stepped in. Robin had been the second assistant last year. She was the only addition to the staff Coach Hanley allowed Sheridan to make. She was wearing tan shorts and a yellow polo shirt with a Chilton College logo above the chest pocket and an angry looking bumblebee embroidered on the pocket. The students joked that Bart the Bumblebee looked like he was on steroids and PMSing all at the same time. This was the Chilton coaching apparel. When the weather cooled, khaki slacks were substituted for the shorts. All of Chilton's women's and men's coaches wore similar outfits for practice, some because Chilton supplied them, others because of the sense of authority they represented. Sheridan wore them because they were comfortable and meant she and her two assistants were easily recognizable while they worked with the players on the court. Robin placed a list of names on the desk.

"Official player tryout list," she reported.

Sheridan scanned the list casually then returned to her computer screen. She knew who was on her team. She knew who graduated, who transferred out and who was returning. The official list that was generated by the athletic department was a pure formality. After a moment, she frowned and slowly looked back at the list.

"I thought you'd give that a second look," Robin chuckled.

"Is that a typo?" Sheridan asked skeptically.

Robin shook her head.

"Got to be."

Robin shook her head again.

"Liz Elliott? That's Becca's mother." Sheridan looked closer at the name and the information. "She's a senior? You've got to be kidding." She leaned back in her chair and frowned up at Robin. "She's not trying out for my team, is she?"

Robin changed her headshake to an emphatic nod.

"Yes, she is, Coach."

"Liz Elliott wants to play basketball for the Chilton College women's basketball team? Whose joke is this? Is this one of Dean Carlton's crazy ideas on how to boost ticket sales?"

"It's no joke. She came in and signed up to tryout for the team. I checked. She still has two semesters of eligibility left and she's enrolled in classes. She even has one more year on a Dartmouth Hilliard Scholarship." Robin pointed to the statistics on the sheet. "She has damn near perfect grade point average, too. Three-point-nine is pretty damn good."

"Majoring in what?" Sheridan asked cynically. "Mothering?"

"Business management. She's already taken all the heavy stuff. All she needs is fifteen credit hours to graduate."

"She's thirty-nine. *Thirty-nine!*" Sheridan declared, pointing to the sheet.

"Now, now. Let's not be prejudice. You were thirty-nine a few years back." Robin snickered.

"But I'm not playing ball. I'm coaching. There's a big difference."

"I understand all she needs is something like two hundred points to set a record. And look at her assist-to-turnover ratio. You've always said that is the tell-all stat for a point guard." Robin tapped the paper persistently.

"She's thirty-nine, Robin." Sheridan scowled at her.

"She shot over ninety percent from the line when she played nineteen years ago."

"Twenty years ago," Sheridan corrected. "Some of the players weren't even born the last time she put on a uniform. In fact, they still wore shorts the last time she played, not these culottes they wear now. The first years she played they didn't even have the three-point line."

"All the more amazing when you think all her points were two pointers or from the free throw line. Maybe she can still play." Robin raised her eyebrows.

"My mother knows how to ride a bike but she isn't entering the Tour de France." There was an unmistakable bitterness in Sheridan's voice. "I don't want any loose cannons on the end of my bench."

"I think she has a right to try out, Sheridan," Robin said, sitting on the edge of her desk and trying to sound diplomatic.

"I don't give a shit what she does but how serious do you think the rest of the team will be if I allow someone twice their age to join the practice?"

"How serious will they be if you deny her a chance? Most of them know Becca and they know how much she has suffered with that broken leg. Do you want to tell Liz she can't even attend one practice? You'll look like the Wicked Witch of the East. By the way, that might be considered age discrimination."

"Oh, please," Sheridan scoffed.

"What will it hurt? One practice. You'll probably know by then if she can keep up." Robin headed out the door then turned back. "Just think. When she collapses at midcourt from exhaustion you can say I told you so." Robin grinned then left Sheridan scowling at the list.

Sheridan was about to make a smart-aleck retort just as the telephone rang.

"Hello," she snapped.

"Well, God damn, daughter. It can't be that bad." A man on the other end chuckled loudly.

"Hi, Dad," Sheridan replied, regaining her composure. "How are things in Springfield?"

"You'd be proud of your brother," he advised.

"Oh? What's going on with Marty?"

"His wrestling team won the Southern Illinois High School Fall Invitational Tournament last weekend. He also had four individual weight class winners."

"Wow. That is something. Tell him I'm very pleased for him. He's a good coach." Sheridan had always been proud of her younger brother's accomplishments.

"He needs to be at a four- or five-A school. You can't get noticed at the three-A level. I think he's looking at Springfield Central. They are looking for a new coach. It would be great if he could land head coach at Central."

"How's Mom? Is she over the flu?" Sheridan asked, diplomatically steering the conversation away from where she knew her father was headed.

"She's fine. By the way Sheridan," he quickly inserted. "Talking about jobs."

"Were we talking about jobs?" She chuckled to herself, knowing full well whatever came next was the sole purpose for her father's call.

"Yeah, you know, moving up to bigger schools. Anyway, did you send in those applications yet? Sheridan, don't wait too long to get them sent off. Get them postmarked before the season starts so they can be following your schedule. It wouldn't hurt to pay the schools a visit sometime. You know, face-to-face, handshake-to-handshake."

Sheridan leaned back in her chair and let him finish his fatherly advice. He had certain points he wanted to make and nothing would stop him from completing his oration. She had learned to nod politely and give in to his lecture. It was easier than to interrupt and suffer his wrath. As Sheridan's achievements grew, so did her father's interest in her career. When she graduated from college and announced she wanted to coach a Division I university, he took on the mantle of responsibility as if it was his own goal. She knew his drive and enthusiasm came from the heart even if it was occasionally overbearing.

Martin and Amelia Ross had been married for forty-six years and had two children, Sheridan and her younger brother Martin Junior, or Marty as he was known. Martin had been a multi-sport athlete in high school and an average basketball player at the University of Illinois. He had gone on to become an assistant then a head coach with the Springfield, Illinois school system with only marginal success. His aspirations and intentions far outweighed his abilities. But he loved coaching and was well-liked by his players right up to his retirement last year. Sheridan's mother, Amelia, was a part-time real estate agent, a part-time substitute teacher and a full-time wife and mother. She was a tall woman with willowy features and a thin face. Her hair had turned completely white by the time she was fifty and it gave her a wise yet serene quality. Martin was also tall with broad shoulders and deep-set eyes that narrowed menacingly when he was crossed but flashed angelically when he was happy.

"Dad, I'll take care of it. Relax. I've got it covered." She smiled to herself, imagining the vein popping out on his forehead as he got wound up in his tirade.

"Don't worry about your contract for next year there at Chilton. I talked to Rick Moody. He's sure he can find a loophole in that contract. Just let me know when you want him to go to work on it."

"Dad," she interrupted.

"When's your first game, Sheridan?" he asked, determined to drive the conversation.

"November third against Central Vermont. They won the con-

44

ference last season. Should be a tough opponent. They didn't graduate anyone out."

"Listen, babe. I have to go. Your mother has breakfast on the table. Talk with you soon. And don't forget those applications," he said, then hung up before Sheridan could reply.

"Coach, one of the players is here to see you. Have you got a minute?" Mary Lou said over the intercom.

"Sure. Send her in," Sheridan replied, hanging up the telephone.

Liz stood in the doorway, waiting for Sheridan to finish digging in the bottom desk drawer.

"Come on in," Sheridan said, still looking through the files and unaware who was in her office.

"Am I interrupting something?" Liz said, trying to get her attention.

Sheridan instantly stopped what she was doing and stared up at her.

"I guess I should have said something the other day in the gym, huh?" Liz said nervously, trying to read the coach's mood.

Sheridan slowly straightened in her chair but didn't reply. She drew a deep breath as if calming herself and deciding how to proceed.

"Why didn't you?" she asked stiffly.

"I have no idea. I guess I was waiting for the right moment."

Sheridan looked down at the player list Robin had put on her desk.

"You're a little late. It seems you made a decision without checking with the head coach." Sheridan's voice was cold and accusatory.

"I am sorry I didn't explain why I was shooting. I just had to see how much work I had to do before practice began in October."

"How many shots did you try?"

"I don't know. Maybe a dozen, fifteen tops," Liz replied.

"And how many did you make?"

"Just that one you saw," Liz said, trying to smile.

"So one out of fifteen?" Sheridan persisted.

Liz nodded.

Sheridan leaned back in her chair and folded her hands behind her head smugly.

"Let's see. According to modern statistical calculations, that would equal a little over six percent. If we give you the benefit of the doubt and say you only shot twelve times that would be one out of twelve or eight percent."

Liz lowered her eyes, knowing how ridiculous it sounded.

"I know. It was a little disappointing," Liz admitted.

"That's okay. By the end of the season maybe you can work up to ten percent."

"I don't think it will take that long," Liz joked, uneasy with Coach Ross's sarcasm. "Maybe I could be up to ten percent by Christmas."

Sheridan dropped her hands to her desk and leaned forward in her chair. "This is not child's play, Mrs. Elliott. I take this very seriously. Ever since my first day as an assistant, I have coached to win." Her eyes gleamed with professionalism and dedication. "You have a right to try out for the team. I can't stop you from doing that. But if you can't play up to my standards, you won't be around long enough to work up a sweat." She stared decisively at Liz.

Liz nodded and turned for the door. She hesitated a moment then turned back, fixing Sheridan with a determined stare of her own.

"If you didn't demand all the players perform to a higher standard I wouldn't want to play for you. I have a successful business to run. My days of playing life fast and free are long gone. I'm here for two reasons and two reasons only; to obtain my degree and to play my last year of eligibility. I take this seriously. I don't have time to waste, Coach." Liz narrowed her eyes at Sheridan. "Don't let my age fool you. I'm young enough to remember how carefree I thought college was but old enough to know better. If I play, I play to win."

"Do you bring this kind of feistiness with you when you step on the court?" Sheridan asked, studying Liz's defiant posture.

"You ain't seen nothing yet. Like I said, I play to win or I don't play."

"I'll be watching, Mrs. Elliott. I'll be watching."

"It's Ms. Elliott," Liz corrected sternly, then walked out the door.

Chapter 6

Liz was surprised at how easy it was to access her scholarship information online. She was able to check her transcript, select classes, activate her student business account and pay her fees all from her computer.

"Easy, huh?" Becca said, looking over her shoulder.

"What happened to standing in lines and running all over campus to get class cards signed?" Liz joked.

"You still have to go to the bookstore and there will probably be a long line if you wait until everyone moves into the dorms," Becca advised, typing in her own student ID number and accessing her records.

"Good for you," Liz said with a proud grin as Becca's class schedule popped onto the screen. "Why are you only taking twelve hours, though?"

"I figured you'll need me here at the restaurant quite a bit.

Besides, that calculus class will be a bear. I hear that professor uses two textbooks and loves to give pop tests."

"I thought you loved math. You always got A's in high school."

"I want an A in calc, too. Since Professor Berkman's wife just reamed him a new asshole in their divorce settlement, he'll act like he's got a cob up his butt."

"Becca!" Liz smirked at her.

"He will. Men always try to get even when they are embarrassed in public. You watch, he'll have one of those tests with subjective answers so he can give the girls in class lower grades. Men do that, you know. They take out their frustrations on women."

Becca hadn't noticed Liz's face. Something in what she had said sent Liz into a trance, staring blankly at the wall. She sat motionless until the tiniest quiver pulled at her chin. Becca couldn't see the image in her mother's mind, the image of hands clutched at her throat.

"Mom," Becca said, frowning at her distant look. "Did you hear me?"

"Yes, sweetheart." Liz replied, returning to reality. "What do I need to do now? Am I all enrolled?"

"Yep."

Becca printed their class lists and handed Liz hers.

"Deb is coming by this afternoon to give me a ride. We're going to get our books. Do you want to go with us?"

"Thank you, honey but I have some orders to make and I need to finish next month's work schedule. That was nice of you to ask, though." She rubbed Becca's arm and smiled at her, the memories from the past still scratching at the corner of her mind. "You have fun and watch the leg," Liz said, stroking her cast.

"That's why Deb is driving. She has her dad's big SUV. By the way, is it okay if I let her eat lunch?" she asked as she hobbled out of Liz's office.

"Sure, honey." Liz appreciated that Becca would always ask before feeding friends at her expense.

"I can't wait to tell Deb you will be her teammate." Becca looked back and smiled devilishly.

"For Pete's sake, don't scare her. I don't want anyone quitting the team on my account." Liz followed her into the kitchen.

"Deb would never quit. She loves basketball. She fantasizes about playing one-on-one with Diana Tarausi and being coached by Pat Summitt from Tennessee."

"It's good to have lofty aspirations."

"Who was your idol when you played?" Becca asked, pushing the swinging door to the dining room open with her crutch. Liz grabbed it and held it for her.

"Ann Meyers," Liz replied instantly then winked. "Cute, too!"

"Tarausi is cuter, at least according to Deb she is." Deb was just walking in the front door as they entered the dining room. She waved and came to hug Becca and Liz. Deb Morrow was Becca's best friend. They had been buddies since junior high school. When her parents moved to Portland, Maine, three years ago they continued a long-distance friendship. Deb came to grips with her homosexuality when she was a freshman in high school. She credited Becca's friendship and understanding in her being able to live the life she was meant to live. It took her parents several years to accept their daughter's lifestyle and they still occasionally anguished over her choices. Liz had once overheard Deb telling them that Becca was her best friend and she was straight. If she accepted her as a lesbian then why couldn't they?

"Are you moved into the dorm yet?" Becca asked Deb.

"Yeah, almost. I dumped the boxes in my room," she joked.

"Mom's buying us lunch. You want a hamburger or cheeseburger?" Becca asked leading the way to a table.

"Hamburger, thanks," Deb replied, holding the chair for her.

"Coke, right?" Liz asked as she turned to place the orders.

"Could I have milk?" Deb asked politely.

"Sure," Liz replied with a broad grin. "Talk that one into drinking milk occasionally." Liz pointed at her daughter. "I suppose you two want fries or would you like a salad?" she asked before heading into the kitchen.

"Fries, please." Deb was polite with a big grin that Liz knew would melt hearts someday if it didn't already. She was like a second daughter. Becca gave some thought to offering to share the apartment with her but she knew they each needed their own space. Liz knew Becca and Deb confided everything to each other so whatever happened at practice, Becca would know about it almost immediately.

Liz's apprehension about returning to classwork was misplaced. It took no time at all for her to fit in with the students half her age. She was accepted by her classmates and professors alike. After three sessions of her business management class, Professor Ellersby realized Liz knew far more about running a business than the class would cover. She offered Liz an option to take the midterm and final exams with whatever grade she made on them being her final grade for the semester. Liz didn't want any special favors but she took Professor Ellersby up on her offer, freeing additional time for work at The Sugar Bush. Liz passed with flying colors, using her own financial spreadsheet as a model for her final exam. The professor even encouraged the other students to stop by Liz's restaurant to see how business management skills had been adapted to a small business. Becca teased her mother about testing out of the class, calling her a teacher's pet and a brownnoser. Liz only grinned, saying an A was an A. It meant Liz now needed just twelve credit hours to graduate. With the computer applications and speech classes she was taking in the fall semester, she would only need two classes during the spring semester.

The first week of October brought the first leaf-peepers to northern Vermont. They would slowly migrate southward, filling the hotels, inns, bed and breakfasts, campgrounds, hiking trails, restaurants and towns with four to six weeks worth of tourists— camera-toting, money-spending, hungry tourists. The flood of visitors to Ashton would keep The Sugar Bush full from morning to night. The foliage season was the only time of year Liz opened seven a.m. to nine p.m. It was a bustling, hectic month, with every employee working long hours and reaping the benefits of steady crowds and generous tippers. Tia Sanders, the previous owner of the restaurant, came out of retirement to help out. She was wonderful with the customers and used the extra money to buy herself a winter cruise to some warm destination. Even Pauline's girlfriend lent a hand on busy peak days. The employees didn't mind the hectic tourist season since they knew the long cold winter months weren't as profitable. Skiers were usually younger and didn't tip as well. Once a chill fell over the New England countryside, Liz changed her menu. Instead of fresh fruit plates and light salads for the seasonal entrees, The Sugar Bush specialized in hearty soups, stews, pot roasts and grilled items that warmed the body and satisfied the hungry tourists and locals alike.

Liz had been promising herself an afternoon run for days but her schedule was too tight to allow it. Finally, she was able to slip away for an hour just before sunset. She headed out of town and followed the river road for two miles before crossing the covered bridge at Stoutman's Crossing. She could have crossed the river on the new bridge but she much preferred to use the historic wooden one. She loved the way her running shoes patted out a rhythm as she crossed. The road narrowed to one lane and wound around the hills that the locals called biscuit ridge because they resembled a row of buttermilk biscuits. She crossed back into Ashton just as the last glimmers of light were fading in the evening sky. It had been a nice run, a little over four miles of quiet solitude with Vermont's spectacular beauty leading the way. She had worked up a satisfying sweat. As she climbed the front steps, Becca opened the door and scowled down at her.

"It's dark, Mom," she declared harshly.

"So," Liz replied, gasping to catch her breath.

"I told you not to run in the dark unless you are wearing that reflective vest I got you. Where is it?" Becca perched a hand on her hip and leered at her. Liz thought it was cute when Becca acted protective and parental.

"The dog ate my homework," Liz teased and slid past her.

"I wish you wouldn't run after dark at all," she added.

"I appreciate your concern, sweetie, but it isn't dark. It is just dusk." Liz pulled her sweaty shirt over her head and blotted her face and neck with it. Becca followed her as she trotted up the stairs to shower. "How are your classes going?" Liz asked as she stripped out of her shorts and underwear.

"I think Professor Gibson is gay," Becca stated, rummaging through Liz's makeup drawer.

"What class does he teach?" Liz asked, as she stepped into the shower.

"World lit," Becca called over the noise of the water. "He wears bright colored socks with khaki slacks." She tried out one of her mother's lipsticks.

"That doesn't necessarily mean he's gay."

"He also wears a necklace with two little interlocking symbols for Mars," she added.

Liz stuck her head out from behind the shower curtain.

"Then Professor Gibson is probably gay," she declared then smiled. "Does it bother you?" she asked carefully.

"No, but I wish he wouldn't flirt with the guys in class. That gives me the creeps." Becca shivered deliberately. "He isn't even cute, Mom. He's skanky looking."

"You should be glad he isn't flirting with you then." Liz went back to showering.

"Speaking of skanky, you had a phone call this evening," Becca offered, dabbing on some eye shadow.

"Who from?"

"Sheila." Becca made it sound as nasty as possible.

"Becca, that isn't nice. What did she want?"

"I have no idea but I can guess." Becca stuck her tongue out as if she was gagging.

"Becca, what did she say?" Liz asked, looking out again, shampoo running down her face.

"She wanted to know if you would be available for dinner on Thursday." Becca turned to her mother and smiled. "I told her you were married to a football player and moved to Baltimore."

Liz smirked at her. "You did not." Liz finished her shower and stepped out.

"Please tell me you aren't still dating her."

"No, I'm not, but what business is it of yours, Miss Nosy." Liz dried off and went into the bedroom to dress. Becca flopped down on the bed.

"Sheila grunts when she eats and she rides a Harley. Need I say more?"

"Sheila is a gentle, caring person."

Becca pulled a pillow over her face and screamed into it.

"She is too weird for you, Mom. How about that woman from Brattleboro you were seeing a couple years ago? What happened to her?"

"Marilyn Ramsour? She moved to Cleveland." Liz stood in the closet in her panties and bra, deciding what to wear. "Now *she* was weird." She looked back at Becca and made a ghastly face. "She liked some strange stuff in bed."

"I do *not* want to hear it."

"Me, either. Plus she wasn't even that good looking." They laughed.

"How about Coach Ross?" Becca suggested. "She's good looking, for a coach."

"Yes, she is better looking than Marilyn."

"Better than Sheila too," Becca added.

"Yes, she probably is." Liz stepped into a pair of tight jeans, hopping up and down to get them on. "I need to throw these out. They didn't fit when I bought them and they still don't fit."

"Camel toe," Becca replied nonchalantly.

"What?"

"When jeans fit like that in the front, they call it camel toe," Becca advised.

Liz looked in the mirror at the way the jeans hugged her crotch.

"God, you're right. I never heard that expression before." She stepped out of them and tossed them over the chair then went back to the closet for another pair.

"You should wear those when you go to your first practice. Let Coach Ross see you in those." Becca raised her eyebrows. "And a tight fitting top. Maybe a push-up bra," Becca teased, pushing her arms together to make her own breasts seem larger.

"I will not. I have some dignity and decorum left."

"Screw dignity and decorum, Mom. When you see what you want, go for it."

"I am not that desperate, daughter."

"You know you're interested in Coach Ross. I saw you looking at her when she came to talk with me at The Sugar Bush. And last year during my ball games, every time I looked up into the stands you were looking at the bench. You couldn't take your eyes off of her." Becca laughed at her.

"I did not," Liz said vehemently. "I have done nothing of the kind."

"She's pretty hot looking, Mom." Becca stood up and mimicked Sheridan's sideline stances.

"Oh you think so?"

"And what's more, I saw the way she looked at you in the restaurant. I saw her eyes following you."

"You're crazy." Liz went downstairs. Becca followed.

"Do you want me to find out if she is available?" Becca asked with a sassy grin.

"No, I do not." Liz turned around and scowled at her. "Now drop it. Coach Ross is just that, my coach. You stay out of this." She pointed a disciplinary finger at her daughter.

"She's a lesbian, Mom," Becca whispered.

For a brief instant Liz felt herself wondering if that was true.

"Mark and I saw her at a restaurant in Rutland last year over spring break. She was with this hot looking babe and believe me, she was doing more than scouting a basketball player." Becca winked.

Liz went into the kitchen and held the back door open for Becca.

"Go do your homework or something," she said.

"Aren't you going to offer me dinner?" Becca asked with an artificial pout.

"No. I'm going to call Sheila and tell her I'm back from Baltimore."

"Oh gross! Stick with Coach Ross. She even smells better than Sheila."

Becca smiled broadly as she sashayed out the door. Liz swatted her rear as she passed. As much as Liz wanted to ignore Becca's teasing, she had to admit Coach Sheridan Ross was indeed a good looking woman. It was a week before the team's first practice and knowing she was gay only added to the intrigue. Liz fixed herself a salad for dinner and went to work on a speech she needed to prepare. She decided to call Sheila another day.

Chapter 7

"Hi. Are you one of the new coaches?" asked a tall, dark-haired girl as she tossed up an awkward shot that went long and struck the backboard then bounced away. She seemed unconcerned at her errant attempt.

"No," Liz replied as she too released a shot. It might have gone in had it not collided with another player's attempt.

"She's Becca's mom, Trish," Deb remarked then smiled at Liz. "Hi, Miss Elliott."

"Hi, Deb," Liz replied. "I haven't seen you around lately. How have you been?"

"I'm taking quant phys this semester so I'm pretty much a bookworm."

"Wow. Quantum physics? I'm impressed."

"Don't be. I may flunk it and have to take it again." Deb frowned and set her feet for a long shot.

"It can't be worse than probability and statistics," offered Trish as she retrieved her ball and tried again. This shot was also off target. "The freaking textbook weighs twenty pounds."

"Becca told me you were coming back to finish your degree, Miss Elliott. What classes are you taking?" Deb asked.

"Computer applications, business management and speech theory."

"Com app is easy. Didn't you take that as a frosh?" Trish asked, practicing her between-the-legs dribble.

Liz smiled reflectively. "They didn't have computer classes when I was a frosh."

Trish grimaced as if realizing how old Liz really was.

"And you can call me Liz," she added. "If I'm going to be a teammate, we better be on a first-name basis."

"Did coach tell you that you made the team?" Deb asked.

"Not exactly," Liz muttered.

"You're a walk-on?"

Liz nodded discreetly.

Deb gave a wry smile and went to retrieve her ball.

"Ladies," Robin shouted after blowing several toots on her whistle. "Let's bring it to the hive, ladies."

Liz wasn't sure where the euphemism originated but when a coach called to come to the hive, it was a call to huddle up and listen. She and the other players placed the balls in the rack and gathered around Sheridan who was checking through a stack of papers on a clipboard. She was dressed in khaki slacks and a three-button polo shirt tucked neatly into her slacks. Both fit her perfectly and showed off her statuesque body. She wore white Nike sneakers that looked new. She set the clipboard on a chair and scanned the group of twelve players. The returning starters included Deb, a six-five center; Miriam, a six-foot forward with neatly braided cornrows and a fiery temperament; Jen, a five-ten utility player with a deadly three-point shot and a quiet disposition; and four bench players with hope that this would be their year to start. The rest of the team included three freshmen, a junior college transfer and Liz, the solo walk-on. As Liz scanned her fellow players she suddenly felt much older than her thirty-nine years. One of the freshmen looked like Becca when she was in high school with a baby face and innocent but mischievous eyes.

"Good afternoon, ladies," Sheridan announced. She looked at her watch and scowled. "Do you know what time it is?" Everyone scanned the gymnasium for a clock and then muttered four o'clock. "Right. Four o'clock," she acknowledged. The players looked at each other as if to make sure they hadn't misunderstood the practice time.

"Practice was supposed to be four, wasn't it Coach?" Trish asked.

"Yes. You were supposed to be here October fifteenth at four o'clock ready to start team practice," Sheridan replied, crossing her arms. "Ready to start team practice," she repeated loudly. "*Ready* to start." She scanned the group, fixing each player with a determined stare. "Each of you should be ready to be a Chilton College basketball player. Do you know what that means?" She left an awkward pause and waited for someone to fill it.

"It means we show up on time dressed for practice," offered one of the new players, happy with herself for the reply.

Liz smiled softly and looked at the floor. She knew that wasn't what Coach Ross meant. That might be what a high school coach wanted but at this level more, much more was expected. College basketball was more than a game. It was a job, a career, a means of producing revenue for the school, a vehicle for students to hone their craft so they might go on to teach other players, it was entertainment for the community and it was competition at the highest level since most players at the Division II level would end their playing career after graduation. She knew Sheridan was about to present her philosophy as a coach and outline what she expected from the players. Liz remembered this poignant moment from her freshman year when her coach removed her bifocals and scowled at the team, hoping to make a lasting impression.

"The operative word here is ready, ladies. Ready!" she stated clearly. "I don't expect you to just arrive on time and neither should you. We have twenty-six games to play this season and if you expect to show up for our first practice then get yourself ready to play, it is going to be a very long season for all of us. I expect— no, I demand that at four o'clock you show up in this gymnasium with your game face on and your shooting skills in game condition. I have seen some pretty sloppy shooting today. The time before practice should be used to set your range and warm up your rhythm, not just lob up any old attempt. I saw some of you shooting with your off hand simply because it was easier than moving away from who you were visiting with. I saw three-point shots taken with both feet on the line. That's the worse shot in basketball. I saw free throws taken as lazy jump shots. I saw some of you too winded to run the length of the floor for a fast break. This isn't high school anymore. I don't have time to get you into shape, into game condition. My job is to combine your basketball abilities into a team capable of winning games in one of the toughest conferences in Division II. I have to keep five players on the court at all times who have the best chance to find victory. If you are on this team, I expect you to arrive for practice with the skills necessary, the attitude necessary and the determination necessary to be a keeper. This is not Coach Hanley's team anymore. This is Coach Sheridan Ross's team now. If you sit on my bench, you will ultimately play for me. There are no free rides. That is my promise. As a coach I know it takes every player and every assistant coach to turn this year into a winning season. This means there will be no deadwood on my bench. I only offer uniforms to players with a winning mind-set. As you all are aware, we lost some terrific players to graduation. We also lost two to other schools and I wish them all the success in the world. But I have news for you. That does not mean we are planning a rebuilding year. A rebuilding year means we plan on losing some games. But ladies, I do not plan on losing even one game. Not one. Do I make myself clear? When we reach the end of this season, I don't want even one of you to say you had any regrets about your season. So, this is the game plan. First, you bring the best of your talents to every practice and every game. Second, we coaches promise to provide the best of our coaching experiences. Third, you accept that this is the greatest team you have ever played on. Those are the three proverbs we will live by from this minute until the horn blows at the end of our last game. Just like churning milk into butter, it takes a lot of elbow grease, sweat and dedication to bring the cream to the top. But if you keep your eye on the target and your hands working, I guarantee the cream will rise, ladies. And believe me—victory is just as sweet and just as smooth as butter." Sheridan pulled a slow smile across her face as she spoke. "It is sweet, ladies."

She looked around at the group of players hanging on her every word. "I like to win, ladies. I like to win." She rolled the basketball at her feet with the toe of her shoe then flipped it up in the air and caught it. "When you prepare to take a shot, even in practice, I expect your best effort. Set your feet and square up to the basket. When you pass the ball, even in practice, I expect a crisp, no-nonsense pass. If I or one of the other coaches can intercept a pass or block a shot, you damn well better believe the other team can too."

She made a hard two-handed pass to Liz without looking at her. Liz was startled and caught the ball awkwardly. Sheridan held out her hands for a return pass while still looking away. Liz tossed it back lazily. Sheridan immediately fixed her with a fierce glare and passed it back to Liz even harder. Liz caught it with both hands and snapped it back to Sheridan with a firm pass. Sheridan received the ball and quickly flipped it to another player who also caught it and tossed it back firmly. She continued to make firm passes randomly around the circle as she spoke, expecting an equally firm return pass even though she never looked at the player receiving the ball. Soon the players were on the balls of their feet, their eyes watching her every move, ready to receive the ball if it came their way. The passes continued around the group until she pointed for the girl with the ball to toss it to someone else in the group. The snap passes went back and forth, each player taking her turn at catching and releasing a pass. Sheridan picked up another ball and introduced it into the circle as well. Now two basketballs were being passed across the circle, the players being careful not to allow them to collide in midair. One at a time Sheridan added a third, a fourth and finally a fifth basketball into the circle of passes. Sweat formed on the players' brows as they worked frantically to keep all the basketballs moving back and forth across the circle with crisp, rapid passes without hitting each other. Sheridan circled behind them, clapping encouragement. When one of the balls hit the ground or bounced away from the group a player would quickly scramble to retrieve it and get it back into play.

"Good passes now. Snap it in there. Keep them moving." Sheridan watched intently as the players worked to increase their efficiency. "Keep them moving, ladies. Keep them going but everyone take one step backward." They did as she instructed, making the circle larger so the passes required more force to travel from one player to another. "Come on, Trish. Straight passes. Don't flop it over there. Two hands, Megan. Two-hand, crisp passes." Sheridan stood behind one of the freshmen and waited for her to receive another pass. When she did, she lowered her hands before passing it away. At that moment Sheridan stuck her hand in from the side and knocked the ball away. "If you pull the ball down like that before every pass you might as well kiss it good-bye, Lori. The other team is going to have you for lunch, kid."

Lori raced to the ball and brought it back into the circle. She passed again, her forehead furrowed as she waited for another pass to come her way. This time she got the ball and passed it away in a quick, flawless motion. Sheridan didn't say anything as if she expected this simple technique to be second nature to her players and it didn't require praise.

"One more step backward, ladies. Don't let those passes hit the ground. Keep them crisp and clean."

It was obvious the players were getting tired as sweat dripped and breaths became gasps. Sheridan didn't relinquish. She kept clapping and encouraging the players. When it seemed their arms were too tired to receive or pass another ball, she introduced a sixth basketball into the circle. The sounds of small groans began to accompany each pass but they continued to pass the six balls. The occasional collision of balls and errant throws became more frequent. Sheridan circled behind them and watched the determined faces of her players for signs of surrender. Liz was dripping with sweat. Her arms felt like rubber. Her throat burned as she breathed through her mouth and gasped for breath with each pass. Finally, the coach walked into the center of the circle and caught one of the balls and held up her hand. The players stopped passing and hung their arms at their sides like limp rags, gasping for breath. Some leaned over and gripped the hem of their shorts, resting their hands on their knees as they recovered.

"Now," Sheridan announced calmly. "Everyone takes free throw practice." She bounced one of the balls to Liz. "Get a partner and alternate. Twenty-five shots each." There was a group groan from the players. Sheridan scowled harshly. "Why should you shoot them now?" she asked, looking around for someone to offer a reason. One of the players mumbled something inaudible. "What was that?" she asked loudly in the direction of the voice.

"Because you are trying to see who's out of shape," repeated one of the players.

Sheridan laughed and shook her head. "That's self-evident, Miriam. And no, that isn't the reason. Why shoot them now? Come on. Someone. Anyone."

"The important free throws are shot late in the game when you are tired and exhausted," Liz said quietly after no one else offered an answer.

"Right," Sheridan yelled. "You have to make the shots when your arms are sore and you feel like you're going to collapse. Anyone can shoot and make free throws in the first minute of the game. I want you to be able to shoot and make them in the last minute of the game. Partner up, ladies." She gave Liz an acknowledging glance.

The players shot at the baskets around the gymnasium's perimeter. Most of the first few attempts were well off their mark as the girls felt the fatigue gripping their arm muscles. Sheridan and the other coaches roamed the floor, watching the shooting techniques and giving advice for improvement.

Liz set herself at the line with the calm and deliberate stance she had always used. She bounced the ball once, rubbed her palms over it then took a deep breath. To her surprise, her first shot dropped through the net cleanly making a leather on rope sound as it swished through the rim. After Deb tried a shot, Liz repeated her technique and again the ball hit nothing but net as it fell through. The pairs alternated shooting and rebounding until they had each completed twenty-five shots. Liz made twenty one, surprising not only herself and her partner, but attracting the attention of everyone on the team. She blushed and smiled shyly as she sank her last shot, the rest of the team cheering her effort. Deb made only eight, similar to the other players' poor performances.

"Not bad, ladies. I will schedule an exhibition game with the Ashton High School women's team. But shooting thirty-five percent from the line won't cut it against the teams in the Connecticut Valley Conference this season. I need much better than that. Eighty percent. I need every bit of eighty percent." She looked at Liz and nodded. "Nice job," she said calmly then turned her attention to her clipboard. "Let's get started. We've got a lot of work to do before our first game."

Sheridan divided the players into two teams and explained the first offensive play. The returning players had little advantage over the new players since they were all learning Coach Ross's system together. Coach Hanley hadn't allowed Sheridan to introduce any new plays during her first year as assistant. He was happy to finish out his career with the same simple plays he had been using for the last ten years.

The players gave the coaches their full attention as the first three offensive plays were diagrammed then run through for the first time. After the plays were introduced and practiced several times, they spent an hour running the plays, each team trying to outplay the other.

Liz felt Sheridan's eyes on her as if challenging her right to be there. Sheridan's riveting stare seemed unyielding. Even through her sweat, Liz felt a shiver crawl up her back as the coach scrutinized her every move. The more she stared the more determined Liz became. If this coach was trying to intimidate her into running off the court in shame, she was staring up the wrong tree.

"That's it, ladies," Sheridan called finally, clapping her hands to get their attention. "Good job. Catch a shower and we'll see you tomorrow, four o'clock." She offered words of encouragement as the players funneled toward the locker room, tired and sweaty from two hours of intense practice.

Liz showered, standing under the soothing spray for a long time. Through the shampoo and soap, she could see Sheridan looking across the shower room at her with the same critical eyes that followed her up and down the court. It was a brief glance, but an obvious one.

"How you doing?" Deb asked, shampooing her hair under the next shower head.

"Okay. How about you?" Liz let the hot water run down her back and legs.

"First practice is always hard. I'm going home and crash. I'll probably sleep until noon tomorrow." Deb rinsed her hair and towel dried it while she dripped back to her locker. Her body was lean and young. Her breasts were small, firm and round, like most of the girls on the team. Liz's breasts were full and round but the results of gravity and motherhood had settled them slightly, something she knew would eventually be the brunt of someone's joke as soon as everyone got to know one another. Deb didn't seem to have any modesty or at least not enough to cover up while she dried her hair and combed out the tangles.

Liz returned to her locker with a towel wrapped around her. She noticed locker room customs hadn't changed since she played twenty years ago. A few players, usually the freshmen or the girls on their period, were extremely modest, showering, changing and dressing in the stalls with the curtains. Some girls kept their eyes lowered while they were exposed. And there were always a few like

Deb who flaunted their bodies as if there was nothing unusual about it. Liz was somewhere in the middle. She showered in the common shower that had six shower heads around the C-shaped room but covered herself afterward. Once her panties and bra were on she felt comfortable to visit and joke with the other girls. The typical locker room chatter hadn't changed either. It covered everything from how much homework they had to where they were going to eat after practice. The college cafeteria menu was always the object of criticism. The Sugar Bush collected some business but since it closed at three in the afternoon for most of the year, post-practice and game gatherings were usually at the Pizza Barn or at McDonald's. At least that's what Becca had reported.

"We're going for pizza. Becca is meeting us," Deb announced, stepping into her bikini underwear. "You're coming, aren't you?"

"Thanks for including me but I think I'll go home. I've got homework and a mountain of laundry to do." Liz pulled on her sweatpants and sweatshirt, glad she had brought something easy to wear since her muscles were starting to cramp. "See you all tomorrow," she said, stuffing her dirty shorts and T-shirt in a tote bag. By the time she reached her car, her body was screaming at her. She sunk into the driver's seat with a gasp and leaned back, closing her eyes. "And this is just the first practice," she muttered. "What have I gotten myself into?" She sat motionless for a long minute, wishing she was already home and in bed. She drove home and pulled into the drive, moaning at the thought she would have to climb the front steps with her stiffening legs and back. She placed the key in the lock and tried to open the front door but the rainy weather had swollen the wood. She knew the hip bump she would have to administer to coax it open was going to be painful, and it was.

"Oh, please," she winced when it didn't open with the first bump. "Have a heart," she groaned and gave the door another full butt shot. The door flew open and Liz stumbled inside. She dropped her tote bag and keys on the dining room table on her way to the kitchen, every step agony. She opened the refrigerator and peered in, supporting herself on the frame. Dinner seemed like too much effort. She retrieved a carrot stick from the bin then let the door swing shut, too tired to wrestle with anything else. Her textbook and notes were spread across the kitchen table but she stuck her tongue out at them as she made her way back into the living room. Just as she was about to start up the stairs the telephone rang. It took her three rings to cross the room and answer it.

"Hello," she said, leaning against the wall heavily.

"Hey, Mom." Becca said happily. "How was your first practice?"

"Becca Elliott, you are grounded. How dare you talk me into doing this?" she replied, then groaned as she shifted her weight.

Becca chuckled.

"Deb said you did okay. She said Coach Ross was riding you pretty hard but you kept up."

"She was riding everyone."

"She isn't anything like Coach Hanley," Becca declared. "She acts like she really cares what happens."

"How's your leg, honey? Are you being careful with it?"

"It's fine. A little stiff but I'm doing okay."

"Be careful. You've only had the cast off a short while. Remember the doctor told you it will be weak for a few weeks. Use the cane. I wish you would have agreed to use the walker."

"Yeah, right, Mom. Like I'm going to drag that freaking thing around with me. Get real. Got to go. Pizza is coming. By the way, the Ben Gay is in the half bath under the sink." Becca laughed and hung up.

"Very funny," Liz said as she pushed herself off the wall and went to the stairs. "I need a nap so bad," she declared as she looked up the steep stairs. She maneuvered one step, leaning heavily on the railing as her thigh muscles throbbed. "No, I need a crane." She looked up the stairs then back at the couch in the living room. "I wasn't this stiff after the Boston Marathon. Yes, I was. But at least I got a certificate when I was finished."

She continued to mutter to herself as she eased her body onto the couch and pulled the comforter down from the back. Within two minutes she was snoring, her shoes still on her feet. She awoke just before midnight and tried to make the trip up the stairs to her bed but her aching muscles wouldn't hear of it. She spent the night on the couch.

"Mom," Becca called, patting her mother's shoulder. "Mom!"

Liz opened one eye and looked up.

"It's almost eight o'clock. Don't you have a class in thirty minutes?" Becca asked with a frown. "I was going to ride with you this morning. I'm low on gas."

Liz blinked herself awake and tried to sit up.

"Oh, God," she groaned.

"Are you hung over?"

"No. But I wish I was. I might not hurt as bad."

"What happened?"

"Don't get cute with me, Miss Contract. Miss You Really Want To Do This, Don't You, Mom. You know good and well what happened. Every muscle in my body hurts. Even my fingernails hurt. My hair hurts." Liz continued to list her ailments as she pulled the comforter over her head.

"Come on, Mom. Get a grip. It isn't that bad." Becca pulled the comforter from her mother's grasp then pulled her to her feet. Liz groaned all the way up. "Are you going to class or not?"

"No," Liz gasped, steadying herself on the back of the couch. "Yes. I'm going. We're receiving notes for our midterms. Give me a couple minutes in the bathroom. Go eat a bowl of granola or something," she said as she headed for the half bath off the kitchen. She grabbed the Chilton sweatshirt and jeans from the hanger in the laundry room, too sore to look for something nicer. She emerged from the bathroom in the jeans and carrying the sweatshirt.

"You ready?" Becca asked, waiting by the kitchen door.

"I can't wear this sweatshirt. It has a stain on it," Liz replied, pointing to a tiny spot.

"That isn't a stain. It's a flaw, Mom." She held the sweatshirt open and pulled it over Liz's head. "Come on."

"You sound like me," Liz laughed as she gathered her notebook and tote bag from the table. "Okay, I'm ready but you are driving." She tossed Becca her keys. "I'll do some damage control with the makeup on the way."

"You sound like me." Becca laughed.

Practice that afternoon hit Liz like a sledge hammer. Her muscles were still recovering from the first practice when she took the floor and began her warm-up shots. The floor seemed tilted uphill as she trotted up the court for a layup, making every stride agony. She wondered how stiff she would have been had she not been a runner.

Coach Ross started the practice with a series of wind sprints up and down the floor to develop the players' stamina. Since the Stingers were a relatively short team compared to other teams in the conference, without bulk or height in the forwards or centers, she decided their best offense was a quick one.

"We are going to run the ball, ladies. And I mean hard, all game long. We're going to run our opponents up and down the floor until they drop. Several of the teams in the conference have big players. *Big* players. We don't. So get on your horse. Even you freshmen. All my players will be used. There is no pass for the bench players. We are twelve players deep and I guarantee you *will* be called upon to contribute. We are going to conquer Goliath by running him to death."

And run the players she did. She clapped and yelled encouragement as the players struggled across the line, gasping for breath. After fifteen minutes of hard wind sprints, everyone on the team was doubled over, grabbing their shorts for support. Liz had a small advantage when it came to running. She was able to stay with the younger players and she recovered her breath much faster. The rest of the practice was just as rigorous. There wasn't time to be stiff or sore. There were new plays to learn and techniques to be refined. Sheridan and her assistants were out on the floor, directing the plays, pointing out missed opportunities and yelling at slackers.

"Square up, Deb," Sheridan yelled as Deb received a pass and took a lazy shot. "This isn't playground ball." Sheridan took the defender's place and ran the play again. This time she muscled Deb out of the lane as she received the ball, preventing her shot. "Use your body. Lean in on the defender," she ordered, scowling at her. "Come on, Deb. Push in on me. Run that play again, Liz," she ordered, tossing the ball out to her.

Liz dribbled then passed the ball in to Deb. This time she responded to Sheridan's shoving by stepping back into her and going up strong for a shot. Sheridan timed her jump perfectly and went up with her, trying to block the shot. They both extended as far as they could reach. At the last moment Sheridan swatted at the ball and sent it over the glass. Sheridan's shirt had come loose from her slacks and Liz could see her smooth and lean abdomen as she stretched for the ball. Liz found it hard not to stare at Sheridan's exposed midriff.

"If you hold the ball out like that they'll block it every time," Sheridan advised. "Release it quicker." She waved the defender back into play. As she stepped off the floor, straightening her shirt, all the returning players were thinking the exact same thing. Coach Hanley never came on the floor to demonstrate a play. He was a couch potato coach, content to sit on the sidelines and yell. Sheridan had just won a huge measure of respect from her players. Throughout the practice she took a hands-on approach to her coaching. She wasn't adverse to giving or taking a push or bump to make her point. By the end of the practice Sheridan, Robin and Jasmine were as sweaty and tired as the players. Everyone was consumed with their work.

"Okay, ladies, that's it for today. Take twenty-five free throws then catch a shower," Sheridan announced, wiping a towel across her forehead.

Liz was impressed with her dedicated yet respectful approach to coaching. She was slowly improving her opinion of the coach over the awkward start they had in her office.

Each practice was filled with obstacles for Liz as she learned new plays while trying to overcome the coach's critical eye. As the shortest player on the team she was relegated to guard positions which meant she handled the ball often. She had to renew her ball handling skills. It took several practices before she felt comfortable dribbling with either hand, dribbling between her legs, passing without looking at her teammate and timing her breaks to the basket. But it was returning, slowly but steadily. Her ability to read where her teammates would be on the court and recognizing their habits was also returning. Twenty years ago she had a sixth sense about who would be where on the court and her passing was deadly accurate. It was one of the things she would have to rely on to make up for the half step she had lost in quickness.

Sheridan hadn't stopped scrutinizing her every move and every shot but Liz had learned to accept her watchful eyes. She told herself the coach was doing the same for all the players, not just her. Liz found herself playing more and more minutes during practice, often as point guard. Becca occasionally came to the gymnasium and watched from the bleachers, hoping to keep up with Coach Ross's practice routine and game plan. She would cheer and applaud at her mother's achievements, goading her into trying harder. Sheridan didn't mind, knowing Becca desperately missed not being able to play herself.

"Take it to the hoop, Mom," Becca yelled as Liz dribbled past one of her teammates. Deb was playing defense and was well outside the lane. Liz saw the opportunity and exploded down the lane, going straight in for a layup. Deb was late in getting back to defend the shot and instead grabbed Liz's shorts, pulling them down to her knees. Everyone laughed, both at Liz's lowered shorts and at her catching Deb out of position.

"Take that, you traitor," Deb joked, bumping Liz playfully.

Sheridan chuckled as well, noticing Liz's bikini panties.

"Mom," Becca shouted. "A word of advice. Biker shorts."

Liz blushed and pulled her shorts up as far as they would go. She grabbed Deb's arm and gave her a swat on the butt.

"Okay, okay. Catch a drink and take five, ladies." Sheridan was still chuckling as Liz walked off the floor.

"I think that was a foul, Coach," Liz said, smirking at her.

"No harm, no foul," Sheridan teased. "Good cut to the basket though. Becca is right. You might think about wearing spandex shorts under your practice and uniform shorts. They seem to help with muscle strain and it isn't inconceivable an opposing player might try the same thing to defend your shot."

"I thought those things were just a fad," Liz replied. "Like the long shorts."

"Actually the long shorts do have a function. When you are tired and want to catch your breath, you can grab your shorts to keep your hands from sliding off your sweaty knees."

"I still think they are too long. There must be three yards of material in them. And when they are soaking wet with sweat they weigh a ton."

Sheridan nodded. "Coaches put up with them because the players like them. It is a small sacrifice to keep them happy. By the way, take that jumper at the baseline if they are going to give you the corner. I want them to see they can't sag off the corners that much."

"Okay. Maybe I can manage my eight percent shooting from outside," she teased.

"Go get a drink," Sheridan smirked then smiled coyly. "I do like that color though," she added quietly.

"That color what?" Liz asked before going to the drinking fountain.

"Panties. I like lavender."

Liz took a deep breath as another blush shot up over her face. At first she was furious with Deb for pantsing her in front of everyone but it suddenly became less of a tragedy knowing Coach Ross had noticed. Liz fought the urge to admit her sports bra matched her panties.

Chapter 8

Liz hit the print key and leaned back in her chair as a copy of her speech rolled out of the printer. She reread it carefully, looking for typos and incorrect usage. She was determined to have an accurate clean copy for class.

"Someone is here to see you," Pauline said, leaning in the office door.

"One minute," she muttered as she finished reading the last paragraph.

"Is this where you hide from customers?" Sheridan said from the doorway, waiting for Liz to finish reading.

Liz snapped around. She looked up at Sheridan's serious expression.

"I'm sorry. I was printing something."

Sheridan's stern look began to melt.

"I'll bet you're just playing computer games," she teased.

"Actually, I was finishing my homework," Liz admitted.

"What class?" Sheridan asked, sitting down in the chair next the desk.

"Speech. I have to give a demonstration speech tomorrow." She rolled her eyes as if it was a nightmare waiting to happen.

"That shouldn't be a problem, should it?"

"I didn't think so. We all had to submit our topics last week. Then the professor threw us a curve. He put them all in a hat and we each drew one out. What we drew was the topic for our speech."

"You mean you don't do a speech on what you submitted?"

Liz shook her head adamantly. Sheridan chuckled at the thought.

"I've never heard of that before. What topic did you draw?"

"Knitting!" Liz smirked and heaved a heavy sigh. "Can you believe it? Knitting. I've never knitted in my life. My mother used to knit years and years ago but I never paid any attention. I didn't know a knitting needle from a sewing needle. At least I didn't until this week."

Sheridan laughed heartily as Liz explained the painful process of learning to knit.

"But I did it. I can cast on. See!" Liz gloated as she produced a yellow ear warmer. It was a two inch wide band with a few dropped stitches and a variety of stitch sizes, but Liz was proud of it. She pulled it on over her head, carefully covering her ears. "What do you think?"

"Looks like an A to me," Sheridan replied, adjusting a few locks of Liz's hair around the headband.

"I hope so." Liz pulled the tight thing off her head and stuffed it in her tote bag.

"What topic did you submit?"

"I wasn't very imaginative. I submitted free throw shooting. I was going to use a small beach ball and put a wastebasket on a desk."

"That would have been easy for you. Do you know who has to do yours?"

Liz threw her head back and laughed.

"Yes. His name is Nigel and he is from Great Britain. He is a computer nerd working on his master's. He's never played a sport in his life."

"That should be fun to watch," Sheridan offered.

"If you see a skinny guy with glasses, a heavy British accent and a severe uni-brow wandering around the gym, don't help him. We are on our honor to do this project by ourselves."

"I wouldn't dream of it," she replied, holding up a hand as if making a solemn promise. "Speaking of the gym, that's why I came over. Team pictures are being taken on Friday. I wanted to ask if you would like to wear number twenty-three this year."

Liz hadn't thought about it. She assumed the returning players had first dibs on uniform numbers. She and the other freshmen would be assigned whatever was left. She never dreamed her old number would be available to her. She looked at Sheridan with a growing smile.

"Yes, I would like that," she replied. "I'd like that very much."

"I thought so. After all, it will make it easier for the scorekeepers to keep track when you set the career scoring record."

"Don't even go there," she declared. "I may be lucky to score ten points all year. I didn't do very well in practice yesterday."

"You did pretty well considering I threw four new plays at you."

"I think we need to scrap that last one," Liz said with a smirk.

"Which play? The one-flex?" Sheridan asked with a serious expression.

"Yes."

"No way. That will be one of our bread-and-butter plays."

"But it has me setting a pick and then going inside. I'm too short and too slow for that," Liz argued vehemently.

"But you may pull their big players to you and then Deb or Jen will be open. You have a deadly pass and I want to use it." Sheridan pointed a finger at her. "That will be your play. You wait and see. You'll be calling it a lot." Sheridan had a warm kindness to her eyes as she spoke to Liz. She leaned in to her, resting her arms on the desk. "That is another reason I came by today. I have decided to make you point guard. I need a consistent player with experience to handle the ball and steady the team on the floor."

Liz leaned back in her chair and stared at Sheridan.

"You are kidding," she gasped. "Me?"

Sheridan nodded.

"Me? Good old eight-percent shooter?" Liz asked, unable to resist the temptation to remind the coach of her first opinion of her shooting skills.

"Yes," Sheridan replied, knowing Liz was going to rub it in. "I admit it. I was a bit hasty in my appraisal of your shooting but you have to agree, that day you came to the gym was less than inspiring."

"I don't know. I liked my technique when I had the fit on the floor," Liz said with a dead serious expression.

"You're right. I'm sorry. You did have good arm and leg action. I should have noticed that." Sheridan stared back. "I'll watch for that next time." She couldn't keep from laughing.

"Thank you for having the confidence to make me point guard." Liz eyes's caught Sheridan's and was locked in her gaze.

"I'm sure you can handle it." Sheridan sat calmly staring into Liz's blue eyes.

They both were at ease with each other, talking about the practices and joking about that first day in the gym. Finally Sheridan stood up and moved to the doorway.

"See you at practice. By the way, you can leave the knitting needles at home." She grinned broadly. "I wouldn't want you to hurt yourself."

"I'll send Nigel over in my place," Liz teased.

Sheridan laughed and winked at her then left. Liz found herself going to the window to watch Sheridan cross the parking lot and get in her car. Coach Ross was indeed a gorgeous and caring person she thought as she sighed.

"Get a grip, Liz," she muttered to herself, as she watched her pull away.

"What did you say, hon?" Pauline said, flipping a row of pancakes.

"Nothing," she replied.

Pauline smiled coyly as Liz disappeared into her office.

Practice that afternoon went well. The players were becoming accustomed to the plays and Coach Ross's routine. She required hard work from each and every player but she also offered encouragement and support for solid performances. She was rapidly earning the players respect for her work ethic. They responded to her teaching techniques with hustle and attentive play. She had given them something Coach Hanley never did, self-respect and confidence they could play and play well.

"Ladies," Sheridan called above the locker room noise. "I sent each of you an e-mail just before practice today. It is a ballot. It's time to select a team captain. E-mail me with your choice for this year's captain. Yes, you can vote for yourself," she laughed, looking over at Deb who voted for herself as a freshman. Keep in mind, this is not a popularity contest. You are voting on the person you think best leads the team and symbolizes Chilton College Lady Stinger pride in competition and sportsmanship. If we have a tie, we will have co-captains. I want to receive your ballot by e-mail before tomorrow's practice. I'll announce the winner before we have team pictures."

When the players arrived for practice on Friday afternoon, their uniforms were hanging in their lockers, like badges of honor that they had made the team. They each took a special pride in suiting up for the first time. Even if it wasn't a game, the thrill of wearing the school colors brought a smile to every face. Sheridan, Robin and Jasmine were all dressed in their game attire wearing suits and dress shoes, their hair carefully styled and ready for the team pictures.

Liz opened her locker and saw her jersey hanging on a hanger. It was indeed number twenty-three. She felt a sense of pride and accomplishment at seeing it. As she took it from the hanger, she also noticed a gold letter C embroidered on the front just above the number three. She looked around to see if anyone else had the same C on their jersey. She knew what it meant but she couldn't believe it. It had to be a mistake or perhaps left over from last year.

"Yes, you won," Sheridan said, noticing her puzzled look. "It was eleven to one. One vote for Deb. I guess she voted for herself again."

Liz smiled and lowered her eyes, her face blushed full red.

"I voted for Deb," Liz replied softly.

"You should have voted for yourself," Sheridan said quietly. "Ladies," she announced. "Liz Elliott is your team captain by an overwhelming majority. And I think it is a superb choice." She applauded, smiling at Liz. The other players cheered and applauded as well, coming to hug Liz and offer congratulations.

It took over an hour for the team and individual pictures to be taken. Each player was snapped in several poses, from a formal position to action shots. After the photography session, the players changed into their practice shorts and shirts. Sheridan ran a full drill, running well past seven o'clock before releasing them to shower and go home.

Liz remained behind after everyone had left, unhappy with her shot technique. She stood under the basket, bouncing the ball and facing the far end of the court. She faked a move one way then turned the other and made a jump shot. The ball rolled around the rim but didn't go in. It was her fourth attempt and only one had fallen through the net. She chased the ball down and tried again.

"Damn," she muttered as it too crossed the rim and bounced away. She grabbed the ball with both hands and threw it down hard, making it bounce over her head.

"You aren't squaring up," Sheridan said, leaning against the end of the bleachers.

"How long have you been there?" Liz said with startled eyes.

"Long enough to see you are releasing before your shoulders are square." She set the stack of mail she was carrying on the bottom bench and walked onto the court. "Try it again."

Liz did as she was told. It went in but only after hitting the backboard first.

"Better," Sheridan said, holding out her hands for the ball. Liz tossed it to her. "As you get older you lose half a step in mobility so your release has to be adjusted. Come across the lane," she said.

Liz made a hard move into the lane and Sheridan snapped a pass to her. Liz caught the ball and immediately turned to shoot. The ball went over the top missing the rim entirely. Sheridan retrieved the ball and came to stand next to Liz.

"You're taking one too many steps." Sheridan put the ball in Liz's hands then stood behind her with her hands on Liz's waist. "It has to be all on one count. Receive the ball, square to the basket and shoot in one motion. Try again."

Liz bounced the ball once as if it was a pass then turned to shoot. As she began her move, Sheridan pulled her hips around sharply. The ball went in the net cleanly. Whether it was the expert advice or the surge of excitement from Sheridan's hands pulling at her hips, Liz wished the ball hadn't gone in so she could be shown again.

"Much better," Sheridan declared, applauding and smiling broadly. "When you release, spread your fingers just a touch. You'll get more spin on the ball." Sheridan handed her the ball then wrapped her arms around Liz from the back to show her the technique. She placed her hand over Liz's on the ball, parting her fingers slightly. Liz drew in a breath as Sheridan's hands molded over hers. The pure sensuality of this touch was as soft and intimate as an embrace. Sheridan's body pressed against Liz's back, her breath warm against Liz's neck. "Like this," Sheridan whispered as she guided Liz's hands to shoot the ball. As the ball left her hand, Sheridan's hand remained on Liz's, suspended in midair as the ball arched toward the basket and softly dropped through the net. Sheridan's arms were wrapped around Liz with a commanding yet supportive force. Liz knew how to shoot a basketball. The mechanics of it were second nature to her twenty years ago and were coming back fast. But again she wished the shot had missed so she could stay in Sheridan's arms and be shown again and again.

"You have a wonderful looking shot. You are a pure shooter. I noticed it during the first practice." Sheridan slowly lowered her hands but kept her arms around her. Liz could feel Sheridan's breasts pressing against her back as she breathed in and out. The faint scent of her cologne lingered about them. Liz drank in a long breath of it, closing her eyes at the sweetness. She didn't realize it but she had leaned back into Sheridan. They stood frozen together for a long moment. The only sound in the gymnasium was the final small bounces of the basketball before it came to rest against the bleachers.

"Thank you for showing me," Liz said finally.

"Anytime," she replied softly as she stood supporting Liz. "Anytime." She wrapped her arms across Liz's stomach, enfolding her in a protective embrace.

"Do you give all your players this kind of one-on-one help?" Liz asked discreetly.

"Just the ones who need it." Sheridan's voice was husky with innuendo.

"I'll remember that." Liz lowered her eyes, her mind taking snapshots of the moment for her memory bank. The ceiling of the gymnasium could fall in on them but at that moment neither Liz nor Sheridan would have noticed. Their complete attention was on the touch of Sheridan's hand on Liz's arm. Liz finally stepped away from Sheridan, a warm shudder moving over her body. "I better go. I have some homework to finish." Liz told herself she sounded like a nervous school girl. But then again, she was. Sheridan made her nervous. There was something in her gaze, in her touch that took Liz completely off guard.

"I'll see you tomorrow then," Sheridan said, her expression soft and innocent.

Liz went out into the cool October air, her body still warmed by the coach's touch.

Chapter 9

Liz was so nervous about the first game of the season she couldn't concentrate on work or on classes. The restaurant was full of leaf-peepers all day, enjoying the last dollops of autumn color before winter.

"Come on, Mom," Becca said, waiting at the back door of The Sugar Bush. "You're going to be late." Liz hugged her employees and swallowed hard then followed Becca to the parking lot. "Why are you so nervous?" Becca asked as she drove down Bell's River and turned toward the campus.

"Who's nervous?" Liz replied, her eyes as big as saucers.

"You are." Becca looked over at her mother. "You're going to do okay, you know. I've been watching. You aren't bad, Mom. Really."

"Thank you, sweetheart. But it has been such a long time since I have done this."

"Maybe you'll be better than just okay."

"I'd settle for just being acceptable."

"Naw," Becca scoffed. "You'll be better than that. Of course, everyone will be watching you, you know. And Grandpa said he would be listening. And so will Mark. He can pick up the Chilton station on his shortwave radio. And Pauline and Georgia," Becca continued.

"Honey, please," Liz said, wiping perspiration from her upper lip. "I'm nervous enough without that."

"Sorry," she replied, smiling out her window. Becca pulled up in front of the gymnasium and waited for Liz to get out.

"See you after the game, honey." Liz collected her tote bag and opened the door.

"Mom," Becca said before Liz shut the car door.

"Yes?" she said, looking in.

"I'm proud of you." Becca smiled softly.

Liz smiled back.

"Thank you, sweetheart. But maybe you should wait until after the game to say that."

"I still am," she added.

"I very proud of you too," Liz replied then winked at her daughter. "Later."

Sheridan entered the locker room, dressed in a black suit that accentuated her long legs and lean figure. She wore a tiny gold basketball medallion dangling from a gold necklace. It was a good luck charm given to her by the first team she coached. She hadn't always won while wearing it, but it had become tradition that she wore it during the first game of every season. Sheridan seemed focused and confident as she looked around the room.

"This is it, ladies. Game one. You all know your assignments. You have worked hard and this is your chance to step up to the challenge. I don't want our opponents to take home anything but a healthy respect for our ability. Play smart ladies. Play hard. There are no moral victories. It only counts if you win on the court." Sheridan clapped and nodded her enthusiasm.

The players finished getting ready, added tape to ankles and retied shoes.

Sheridan talked to some of the players, giving last-minute instructions and advice.

"Liz, on the signals, do you remember what the fist is?" she asked, looking over her clipboard.

"Yellow break," Liz replied as she tucked her jersey in her shorts. She was all business when it came to her play but she was still fighting nerves.

"Right. And I have one more for you."

Liz looked at her with a furrowed brow, wondering why she had waited until the beginning of the first game to introduce a new play signal.

"What's that?"

Sheridan pointed to her own shoe.

"What play is that?" Liz asked dutifully.

"It means your shoe in untied," Sheridan replied, trying to relax her point guard.

Liz looked down and chuckled then double knotted them.

"Listen up," Sheridan called. "Central Vermont won the conference championship last year and they have all their starters back. They are tough but I am confident you are ready. Don't play in the past. Play this game as if it is the beginning of a whole new season because it is. This is your season. Now go out there and play it." Sheridan had whipped the team into a frenzy of cheers and hoots. "Let's go sting 'em, ladies," she shouted.

Liz immediately felt a knot form in her stomach. She grabbed her stomach and swallowed back as her Gatorade rose into her throat.

"Are you okay?" Jen asked, noticing Liz's pasty complexion.

"Nerves, I guess."

"You going to hurl?"

"I hope not," Liz said and went to the drinking fountain.

"You all right?" Sheridan asked, placing a hand on Liz's shoulder.

"My stomach is a little tight. You'd think I'd never played a game before." Liz held her hand under the water then patted it across her face and neck.

"You haven't," Sheridan offered. "Not as this Liz Elliott. That was a different person in a different time. That was twenty years ago."

"That's what worries me."

"This Liz Elliott is smarter and more experienced than the one who played back then. I'd take this one any day." Sheridan squeezed her hand reassuringly. "You are my point guard. The game is in your hands."

"Oh, now that helped," Liz replied and dripped more water onto her neck.

"You'll do fine. Come on, hit the floor and show them who's boss."

The team trotted onto the court. The Central Vermont Lady Tigers had already started their warm-up. As Liz emerged from the tunnel she saw the small crowd scattered around the bleachers. Last year's dismal performance had reduced interest in the team to parents, close friends and a few alumni who attended anything open to the public. As soon as she stepped onto the floor a cheer rose from the spectators. Everyone stood and applauded. She assumed it was for the team and the beginning of their season. As she looked up into the stands she could see posters and handmade signs with her name on them. She began to blush. The applause continued until she acknowledged the spectators with a wave and a smile.

"Welcome back, Liz Elliott," the public address announcer said.

Sheridan smiled and gave her a thumbs-up. She crossed her arms and stood watching like a proud parent as the hometown crowd showed Liz their warmhearted support. They hadn't forgotten her.

The Lady Stingers ran through their layup and shot drills while Sheridan shook hands with the opposing coach and checked in with the referees. She gave her starting lineup to the scorer's table and added some last-minute changes. She watched her team practice their shooting with a self-assured posture. Liz and the other freshmen were wrestling with opening game jitters. It took several tries before Liz finally made a three-point shot. When it dropped through the net, the crowd roared. Liz wasn't sure if they were showing genuine enthusiasm or sarcastic support. She shot again and it also dropped through cleanly. The crowd cheered again. The next shot was a miss and the crowd gave a sympathetic groan. It was like that for all her practice shots, cheering successes and groaning the misses. She began to wish they wouldn't pay such close attention since she knew the beginning of the game might be awkward for her.

One of the referees blew his whistle and went to center court to await the teams. Sheridan sent Deb in to jump center. Jen and Miriam were the forwards with Trish one guard and Liz at point guard rounding out the team. The team was balanced with speed to run Sheridan's fast-paced attack. The Lady Tigers were big girls and deadly shooters. Sheridan knew they would have to run hard at them to have any chance at an upset victory.

Liz looked up into the stands where Becca, Pauline, Georgia and some of the other employees were cheering and waving. She took a deep breath as the butterflies in her stomach once again began flying sorties.

"Play smart," she muttered to herself. "Play smart."

Twenty years ago she would have been clapping and exciting her teammates as the ball was about to be tossed up to start the game. But now she was having trouble keeping her knees from buckling. She wiped her clammy hands on her shorts and backed up, taking her position for the start of the game.

"Don't throw up. Please, don't throw up," she whispered.

The crowd came to their feet and cheered. The ball was tossed and the centers went up for it. It was slapped away by the opposing player and went out of bounds. The referee blew his whistle and signaled the possession belonged to Chilton. Sheridan pointed for Liz to throw the ball in and she gave her a hand signal for the play she wanted to run. Liz signaled the players and held the ball, ready to throw it to Trish, who was to cross in front of her. She slapped the ball and Trish broke but it was in the opposite direction. It was too late. Liz had already thrown the inbound pass to where she should have been. The ball struck the referee squarely in the crotch, doubling him over in pain. The crowd roared with laughter as he struggled to the sidelines, holding himself with both hands. Liz blushed bright red. She hadn't meant to hit him and certainly didn't want to hurt him but she had to bite down on her lip to keep from laughing herself. She looked over at the bench. Sheridan was sitting in her seat, her arms resting on her knees and staring at the floor. Liz could see her shoulders shaking as she chuckled at the errant pass. The other referee, a tall woman with a tight ponytail, called a time-out then turned to Liz.

"Lady, I'm giving you a warning. Try that again and I'll call a technical and you'll be out of the game. You hear me?" she scowled.

"Yes, ma'am," Liz replied with a serious expression trying to keep from snickering.

After a few minutes in the locker room with the trainer, the injured referee returned to the game to applause and good-natured teasing from the spectators. He was a good sport about it and told Liz he held no hard feelings. He did call two suspicious fouls on her during the first half that caused her to think differently.

By halftime, the Stingers were down by twelve points. During halftime Liz sat on the bench in the locker room catching her breath and listening to Coach Ross challenge the players to execute better and play up to their potential. She didn't curse or scream at the players. Instead she used precise examples of poor performance to make her points. She turned some of the coaching duties back on her players, asking them what they thought could be done to improve over the first half mistakes. Liz sat quietly watching. She found Sheridan easy to watch with her amicable smile and powerful eyes. There was something else that drew Liz's unwavering attention, something that made Liz's heart race and her eyes sparkle when Sheridan gestured in her direction. Liz couldn't stop her eyes from drifting down over Sheridan's lean athletic body. Her suit jacket was unbuttoned and open as she motioned to her players, the outline of her bra visible beneath her silk top. Liz found herself mesmerized by the imprint of her nipples through the silk. She shifted on the bench then went to get a drink, feeling the need for a distraction.

"Let's hit the floor, ladies," Sheridan ordered finally, following them out of the locker room with long strides of determination.

Sheridan had walked the sidelines, pointing out fouls the referees missed and moving her players around the court. She was totally committed to the game. She worked hard to draw every ounce of talent from her team but with six minutes to go in the game it was obvious the Central Vermont Tigers were bent on more than winning. They seemed bent on nothing short of humiliation. They ran the score up unmercifully. They were like machines with big powerful players racking up points by the dozen. Liz, Deb, Jen and the rest of the Stingers struggled to keep up with them but it was hard not to be discouraged when they trailed by thirty-one points.

As the score went up, the crowd began to disperse. Only the most ardent fans remained to watch the agony. Sheridan called for her last time-out and gave each player an encouraging pat on the back as they gulped drinks and wiped sweat from their faces. She looked over at the opposing bench, expecting to see the coach sending in her second- and third-string players but she kept the starting lineup in the game.

"Damn," Deb said, gasping to catch her breath. "How many points do they need?"

"Good question," Sheridan replied. She pulled Liz aside and whispered something in her ear.

The referee called the teams back onto the floor and signaled the ball belonged to Chilton. Liz stood on the sidelines in front of the bench, ready to throw it in. She looked back at Sheridan for confirmation. Sheridan nodded. Liz slapped the ball as if she was going to throw it in then rolled the ball in-bound to the nearest Central Vermont player. She picked it up, a surprised and dumbfounded look on her face as she received the ball. Sheridan stood up and looked over at the Lady Tigers Coach Riley.

"How many points do you need, Coach? Maybe we can help,"

she yelled. The crowd hushed then began to applaud. Even the Central Vermont supporters seemed to sympathize with the humiliation Chilton was taking and cheered Sheridan's remarks. The opposing coach frowned. If she was embarrassed, she hid it well. She didn't substitute her starting lineup and went on to trounce the Stingers by thirty-five points. As much as Sheridan didn't want to do it, she showed her good sportsmanship and shook the coach's hand.

"Fucking flagger," she muttered as she stormed into the locker room.

"What is a flagger?" one of the freshmen asked Liz as Sheridan strode through to the bathroom.

"A flagger is a coach who runs up the score unnecessarily. You know, run it up the flag pole," Liz replied, peeling off her sweaty jersey. "Twenty or twenty-five is bad. Coach Ross is right. Thirty-five with your first string in is fucking flagging."

Sheridan returned to the locker room, calmed down enough to speak.

"I'm proud of you, ladies. We lost big but you played hard. We've got a lot of work to do. We've got some adjustments to make but it's a start. We can use this loss as a teaching tool. Learn from it and grow stronger." Sheridan seemed to see no point in rubbing in the final score. The damage was done and the best she could hope for was the team learned from their mistakes. She turned to leave the players to their showers and dressing then looked back at Liz. "I did like that pass to the ref, Elliott. Nice strong snap pass." She nodded at Liz then gave a small smile.

The players showered and dressed in quiet. The mood was somber as if each girl had been taken to the woodshed and spanked soundly. They felt betrayed, depressed and humiliated at the stunning defeat. Sheridan had left them to wallow in their self-pity and guilt, a punishment much greater than she could inflict with mere words. She was already focused on the next game and what needed to be done to prepare for it.

Liz met Becca in the hall outside the locker room. They looked at each other with a serious stare then both burst out laughing.

"My God, Mom. Even I didn't suffer a loss that bad. Thirty-five points!" Becca seemed set on rubbing it in.

"Oh stop it. I've never lost that bad before in my life. We did everything wrong. No one was blocking out. No one was rebounding." Liz smirked in disgust.

"I bet Coach Ross is going to ream you all a new one at practice tomorrow," Becca gloated.

"No doubt."

"She must have confidence in you though. You played almost the whole game."

"Maybe too much," Liz replied, rolling her eyes. "I couldn't run a play in the second half to save my life."

"Jen is dyslexic. Don't pass to her left hand. She'll mishandle it every time."

"She is?"

"Yep. She told me that last year. It's a wonder she does so well in her classes," Becca added. "And I think Deb is on the rag. She plays shitty when she is."

"Becca, that isn't nice."

"Well, she does. She's afraid her plug will fall out or something."

"Becca!" Liz scowled then snickered.

The sound of chuckling came from the doorway to the locker room.

"I never thought of that," Sheridan said. "We should blame it all on menstrual periods and PMS." She laughed robustly.

Becca laughed too. Liz frowned at them both, shaking her head in disapproval.

"You two should be ashamed. This is a serious matter. We played miserably. We looked awkward and our timing was way off."

"PMS," Becca offered then smiled at the coach.

"Yep. Got to be, Becca," Sheridan agreed and patted her back.

"Make jokes, go ahead. But I for one am embarrassed at the way we played."

Sheridan stopped laughing and looked over at Liz.

"I know. But don't beat yourself up about it. Yes, we played poorly. Yes, it was a horrific loss. I don't think I have ever lost a game that bad in all my years of coaching. But we can use it. We made a lot of mistakes but we can gain from it." Sheridan gave Liz a positive stare. "You did okay. You were nervous at first but you did some good things. I don't think you realize it but the other players look up to you. They respect your judgment. They'll follow you if you'll lead. You're a good player, Liz. A damn good player. Your age has benefits. You bring maturity to the court some of the players haven't learned yet. Don't you tell her otherwise, Becca." She looked over at Becca and pointed an accusing finger. "You'd do well to watch your mother play. You might learn something."

"Oh really," Becca challenged playfully.

"Really!" Sheridan patted her cheek.

"We're going for coffee," Becca offered. "You want to go along, Coach?"

Liz's eyes widened, not expecting her daughter to invite the coach. Sheridan checked her watch.

"I have some phone calls to make but I could meet you somewhere. Maybe losing by thirty-five points won't seem so bad after a cup of coffee." She seemed genuinely pleased to have been invited. "Where can I meet you?"

"Pizza Barn," Liz replied quickly, not sure why she was so anxious.

"I'll meet you in fifteen minutes." She smiled over at Liz.

"Okay," Liz muttered, completely captivated by her big brown eyes. Liz and Becca took their time crossing town to the Pizza Barn. Becca ordered a small pizza and a coke. Liz wasn't hungry. Somehow the anticipation of Coach Ross meeting them smothered her appetite. She sipped a cup of decaf and kept an eye on the door.

"God, Mom," Becca declared. "She'll be here. Relax."

"What are you talking about?" Liz frowned innocently.

"You haven't taken your eyes off the door since you sat down."

"Don't be silly."

Becca chuckled under her breath. She ate one slice of pizza before transferring her attention to some of her friends in another booth.

"Be right back," she said, sliding out of the booth.

"Take this with you," Liz said, sliding the pizza to the edge of the table. She knew Becca would be there a while.

Becca visited with her friends while Liz checked her watch, watched the door and waited. Just as she was ready to give up on the idea Sheridan would join them, the door opened and she stepped in. Liz's face instantly lit up.

"Sorry, I got delayed." Sheridan slid in across from Liz. "The Chilton Lady Stingers are front page news. Seems everyone wants to ask the coach what she thinks about losing by thirty-five points." She groaned dramatically.

"And what does the coach think of the loss?" Liz asked.

"I told the reporter I was happy about it. I said it could have been worse. We could have lost by fifty points."

"You did not." Liz leered at her.

"I explained it was a learning situation. I said we were confident we could use it to improve and eliminate some bad habits in our game. I also said I didn't plan on having a loss like that again this season."

"Did you add the other coach was bent on running up the score on us?"

"No. That isn't my problem. That is Coach Riley's decision. She's the one who has to coach as she sees fit. I feel sorry for her next year though. All five of her starting lineup will graduate and she will have a bench full of players with no game experience. She wants to repeat as conference champions but she'll be in the cellar after that."

Sheridan sipped at a cup of coffee and scanned the room.

"I've never been here before. Looks like a fun place."

91

"Becca and her friends hang out here. I think this is where the players come after practice," Liz explained.

Becca, Deb, Jen and their friends waved from the big corner booth. Sheridan waved back. The door opened and Robin strode in, scanning the restaurant. Sheridan motioned her over to the booth. Liz's delight at having Sheridan share a table with her was quickly dissolving as Robin crossed the room, grinning at Sheridan and patting her on the shoulder. Sheridan moved over and Robin slid in next to her. Liz didn't expect to be so disappointed at seeing them together, their shoulders touching as they sat next to each other in the booth. After all, Liz liked Robin. She was a dedicated and helpful assistant coach. She was also funny and amicable. She had assumed Robin was gay from her gait and demeanor but now Liz wrestled with the idea she and Sheridan were more than just friends and co-workers. It was a surprising disappointment for her.

"Hi," Robin said over the noisy crowd. "Sorry I'm late. I hope it's okay I invited myself."

"No problem," Liz replied, trying desperately to control her stare.

"Coach Ross tells me you think you played too much tonight. She said you were disappointed in your performance," Robin stated, a sympathetic kindness in her voice.

"Yes. Don't you? We played pretty poorly."

"What would you have done differently?" Robin asked.

"Everything," Liz replied with a chuckle. "First I would have played a deeper zone on defense. Maybe double up on their center."

Sheridan and Robin listened as Liz voiced her opinion. They discussed each point and gave counter suggestions and reasoning. The debate went on for over an hour. Liz, Sheridan and Robin sipped coffee and shared a pizza as they discussed the game. Liz had finally had enough rehashing the game and talking above the growing noise. Her body was tired and spent.

"Becca," she called. "I'm ready to leave. Come drive your mother home."

"In a few minutes, okay?" she replied from the corner booth

where six of her friends were in a huddle over one of the girl's boyfriend.

Liz smirked and sank down in her seat.

"I think I've had enough for one night myself," Sheridan said. She pushed her cup back and motioned for Robin to let her out. "Come on, Mom. I'll give you a ride home." She waved Liz up. "Leave the kids to their fun."

"Thanks Coach," Becca said, overhearing Sheridan's offer.

"I guess I have a ride," Liz replied, stunned at the offer.

"Later Robin," Sheridan said, dropping a tip on the table and handing a twenty-dollar bill to the cashier for their refreshments.

Sheridan popped the locks on her sleek, black Mustang and opened the passenger's side door for Liz. Liz smiled to herself as she enjoyed the gracious gesture. She had almost forgotten how it felt to have someone open a door for her. Not many of the women she knew would have considered it, even the most butch women.

"Thank you," she said as Sheridan came around and slid in.

"No problem. Which way?" Sheridan asked as she waited for the traffic to clear at the edge of the parking lot.

"That way," she pointed. "Four-fifty-two Danforth." Liz stifled a yawn and fought the fatigue that was tugging at her eyelids. They rode across town in silence, Liz blinking back the need for sleep. "There, last house on the right," she said.

"Cute house. I love the bay windows," Sheridan said as she pulled in the drive, her headlights illuminating the front.

"I'd invite you in but it is a mess and I'm exhausted."

"It's late. Another time."

"Thanks for the ride." Liz looked over at Sheridan. "And I'm really sorry about the game. I feel bad about that."

"Don't beat yourself up about it. It was a team loss. That includes me. See you at practice tomorrow. By the way," she added as Liz climbed out. "Becca was right. I may have to ream everyone a new one tomorrow."

"I'll remember that."

Chapter 10

The first overnight away game was a worrisome event for Liz. It meant leaving Becca in charge of The Sugar Bush for two days. By the time the charter bus left the gymnasium parking lot for Binghamton, New York, Becca was ready to strangle her mother from all the notes and instructions she left around the restaurant. Liz spent the first forty miles of the trip wondering if she had covered every contingency.

"Are you worried about the game?" Sheridan asked, sitting down next to her.

"No, not really." Liz took a cleansing breath and forced a smile.

"What is it then? I saw that frown all the way up front."

"This is the first time I have left Becca to do all the ordering and cashing out. She has to cover a luncheon in the banquet room for twenty-five Red Hat Ladies. I'm just a little nervous."

"Sort of like when she went off to kindergarten for the first time?" Sheridan teased.

"Oh please," Liz snickered. "She was *so* mad at me when I took her to school the first day. I cried and cried. She put her little hand on her hip and said, "Mommy, go home and get a grip.""

"She'll do fine. Cut her a little slack." Sheridan gave a reassuring smile. "How about going over some game plans to take your mind off Becca and The Sugar Bush?"

"Okay," Liz agreed, hoping it would help. Sitting next to Sheridan was definitely helping to take her mind off the restaurant. The coach's radiant skin and sensual charisma was a pleasant distraction, one she hoped would last for the entire ride to Binghamton. In fact, Liz had trouble concentrating on the game plays when Sheridan leaned over and touched her arm to make a point.

The bus pulled into the hotel parking lot and the team streamed off the bus. Liz shared a room with Deb. Sheridan had her own room, the only member of the entourage to do so. The bus driver and the Chilton College radio station announcer were the only two men in the group.

"After you get settled in your room, get into your warm-ups. We have the use of a school gym for an hour so we'll have a shoot around," Sheridan explained, handing out the room keys.

After the practice, the team returned to the hotel for dinner and a team meeting before the game at Merriam College. It was a hard-fought game, both teams using a fast-paced attack and multiple substitutions to keep fresh legs on the floor at all times. The score remained a seesaw battle until the final minute of play when Chilton was able to open up a four-point advantage. Liz was given the job of controlling the ball for the final twenty seconds, avoiding the full-court press. She kept her body low and the ball away from the tenacious hands of the opponent, preserving a Chilton victory.

"Good job, ladies," Sheridan announced, striding into the locker room. "Much better work inside. Way to take care of the ball." She went around the room, congratulating each player and exalting their individual effort with specific plays and accomplishments.

"Good ball control, Liz," she said, shaking her hand. "But we've got to get you to stop passing the ball away when you have an open shot. Take those jumpers. I don't care if you miss a few. You can't score if you don't shoot."

"Okay, Coach," Liz replied, fully expecting that censure. She knew she had been tentative about her shots tonight, blaming it on her distraction about Becca.

"And Becca is doing fine without you." Sheridan smiled then winked. "She won't burn the place down in one night."

The team dressed and returned to the hotel, tired but elated over their victory. Several of the girls brought swim suits and took a late-night dip in the indoor pool. Liz fought the urge to call Becca for an hour then gave in to it. It was a short conversation, Becca exasperated with her mother's nervous concern and Liz relieved that everything was fine.

Liz had brought her running clothes and planned an early morning run before breakfast. Since the team wasn't scheduled to leave for Ashton until ten o'clock, all the players could sleep in if they chose or they could rise early and swim. Liz was in her running shorts and out the lobby door by six in the morning. It was a beautiful late autumn morning with the leaves fluttering through the air and crunching beneath her shoes as she reached her stride. She had plotted out a route that sent her past a historic cemetery, a quaint red brick church and a residential neighborhood of small Craftsmen style bungalows before circling back past a strip mall to the hotel. The morning weather was perfect for running, cool enough to keep her body temperature down but warm enough so her face didn't chill. Liz found that the circle drive through the neighborhood was too inviting not to take a detour. She rounded the circle twice, studying the architecture of the early twentieth century houses and getting ideas for curb appeal for her own home.

Sheridan, Robin, Jasmine and the trainer had a short meeting before they went down to the lobby for breakfast. Several of the players were already eating.

"How's everyone this morning?" Sheridan asked, filling a coffee cup and deciding on a pastry.

"Great, Coach. You should have gone swimming with us last night," Deb replied.

"Next time," she said, scanning the room. "Is Liz up yet?"

"She wasn't in the room when I got up. I figured she'd already be down here."

Sheridan went to the window to see if she was in the pool. When she wasn't there she went to the front desk and had her paged.

"You didn't see her at all this morning?" Sheridan asked Deb, concern growing on her face. Deb shook her head.

"Was she there when you went to bed?"

"Yes, she was already in bed and snoring by the time I got up there. Hasn't she been down here?"

"I haven't seen her and neither has the clerk at the front desk but she just came on at seven." Sheridan wasn't sure where to look next. She checked her watch. She canvassed all the players, the driver, the coaches and even the hotel maids but no one had seen Liz since last night. Sheridan was contemplating a call to the police when Liz came trotting across the parking lot and into the lobby, her face dripping sweat. She was breathless but satisfied with her run. Sheridan strode across the lobby to her, the vein on her forehead popping out noticeably.

"Where have you been?" Sheridan asked, forcing restraint.

"Running," Liz replied, wiping her sleeve across her upper lip. "Beautiful morning." She stood, shaking one leg then the other as she cooled down. "I got about six miles in."

"You went running without telling anyone?" Sheridan's jaw rippled.

"I knew I'd be back before we had to leave. What's the big deal?" Liz scowled back at her. "I run all the time. How do you think I stay in shape?"

Sheridan could see the rest of the team watching as she stood arguing with Liz.

"Next time you go out like this, you tell someone," she explained stiffly.

"Do you want me to call you when I get up at five-thirty to tell you I'm going for a run?" Liz asked sarcastically.

"Yes," she replied, with her hands on her hips.

"What if I go out at five?" Liz asked, knowing she had the upper hand. "Or four? Are you worried I might get lost? I always know where I'm running, Coach." Liz unhooked a can of pepper spray from her waistband. "And I'm always careful."

Sheridan smirked.

"Go take a shower and get some breakfast. We're leaving shortly." She walked away.

Liz grinned and winked at the players who were watching the conversation.

Chapter 11

By the third week in November the splendid autumn color had disappeared from the trees. The days were growing shorter and the Lady Stingers had split their first six games, winning three and losing three, two of which were heartbreakers at the buzzer. Liz had learned her teammate's habits and shortcomings. She knew who was likely to succumb to defensive pressure and who was confident enough to take a shot under adverse conditions. She knew who could snag the ball one-handed and who would sacrifice themselves to dive for the ball in a crowd. She also knew who needed an occasional boost of confidence and who needed slowing down. Sheridan and Liz had short meetings after each practice and each game to discuss what needed to be changed and what was working. Liz's experience on the court made her an invaluable asset to Sheridan's game plan.

"What are we doing for Thanksgiving this year?" Becca asked, holding the large stainless steel refrigerator door while Liz loaded trays of washed vegetables.

"I hadn't thought about it. Why? Do you have something in mind?"

"I was going to invite Deb to eat with us. She isn't going home since Coach Ross scheduled practice for Saturday and Sunday."

"Sure. She's welcome to eat with us. Do you want something special for the three of us?"

"Well, duh." Becca gave her valley girl impression. "It's Thanksgiving, Mom."

Liz smiled to herself. She knew Becca loved turkey with all the trimmings almost as much as she loved pizza.

"Turkey?" Liz asked, wiping her hands on a towel.

"And stuffing and mashed potatoes and green beans," Becca added hopefully. "We'll help. I'll mash the potatoes. Mark can carve the turkey. Guys like that macho knife crap."

"Four of us?" Liz offered.

"I think Jen will be in town, too. Her mom doesn't do Thanksgiving dinner. She goes on a cruise of something. She'll probably just be alone in the dorm eating cafeteria food."

"Invite her too, honey," Liz insisted. She saw where this was going. "Is anyone else on the team going to be alone for the Thanksgiving?"

"As a matter of fact, almost all of them. Plane tickets are too expensive for just a two-day trip. Since The Sugar Bush isn't open on Thanksgiving I thought—"

"Okay, invite them all." Liz announced, reading her daughter's face. "We'll use the restaurant and feed the whole crew."

"It's okay if they bring a guest, isn't it. You know, boyfriend, girlfriend, roommate."

"Yes, Becca. That's fine too." Liz perched her hands on her hips and began making a mental shopping list.

"Coaches, too?"

"Coaches, too," she advised. The image of Sheridan Ross having dinner with them became a pleasant distraction.

"Mom, you better invite Pauline and Georgia, too. You'll need some help," Becca warned.

"I thought you and Deb were helping with this rapidly growing affair."

Becca looked at her with wide eyes.

"We can't cook for that many, Mom. We'll help but get real."

"All right, Miss Elliott. Your job is to get me a list by the end of the week. I want to know exactly how many will be coming, within one or two. And yes, you will be helping big time."

"No problem," Becca agreed, a satisfied grin on her face. "What time should I tell them to show up?"

"Two o'clock. We'll eat at three," Liz replied after calculating prep and cooking time.

She knew Pauline, Georgia and their partners would jump at the chance to join in, lending a hand in the kitchen as well. Even though they would never ask for it or expect it, she would include a little extra in their checks to cover the hours she knew they would dedicate to the meal. Liz would also invite her father to join them. He wouldn't come, but she would invite him anyway.

By Saturday morning Becca had a sheet of typing paper filled with names as well as who was bringing a guest. The coach's names were on the list, even Sheridan's.

"Coach Ross wasn't going to come," Becca said, handing the list to her mother. "Her parents are flying in for the game on Wednesday night and for Thanksgiving. I told her you expected her to be here and that you wanted her parents to come too." Becca grinned as if she had pulled off the great jewel heist.

"Becca Elliott, that is a fib. I never said anything of the kind." Liz scowled at her.

"I know. But I wanted the whole team to be here. And she is the coach," Becca argued defiantly. "And you don't mind if they come, do you?"

"Of course not, but don't lie about it," she declared.

"Well, when I told her you said that, she changed her mind. So it worked."

"What is the final count then?"

"Thirty-one," she replied proudly. "That isn't too many is it, Mom?" she asked apprehensively.

"No. That's fine." She patted Becca's face. Thirty-one was about what Liz had expected. She was experienced in judging crowd size and estimating food quantities. She hadn't always, but time had taught her the tricks of the trade.

The Wednesday night game brought out a small crowd of spectators. Only the ardent team followers braved the cold temperatures and threat of snow flurries to watch the Lady Stingers play Vermillion College from New Brunswick, New York. The Lady Lions were a scrappy team of stocky women with lightning-fast feet and accurate shots from short range. At least that was the scouting report. Liz played well but she was distracted by the plans for the Thanksgiving meal. While standing at the free throw line to attempt a foul shot, she found herself estimating how long two twenty-five-pound turkeys would take to cook. She missed the first shot and scolded herself for her lack of concentration. She took a deep breath and set her mind. She made the second shot. With just a minute to go and a tie score, Sheridan called a time-out. Liz trotted to the huddle, muttering to herself.

"What did you say?" Sheridan asked, looking at her scowl.

"I said damn turkey," she gasped, catching her breath. "We would have a one point lead if it wasn't for turkey." Liz bent over and rested her hands on her knees.

Sheridan frowned at her curious reply then turned her attention to setting the play she wanted to run. The Lady Stingers pulled out a two-point victory when Liz was fouled with six seconds left in the game and made both of her free throws.

"Nice shot from the line. Did that have anything to do with turkey?" Sheridan asked as they walked to the locker room.

"Nope," Liz replied, smiling happily. "I figured that out already. Gravy was almost a problem though."

"Oh really?" Sheridan had no idea what she was talking about.

Liz showered and rushed home. She had a million things to do. There were going to be over thirty people in her restaurant tomorrow at two o'clock but somehow she could only focus on one, Coach Sheridan Ross.

Liz arrived early at The Sugar Bush, a list of chores and a timeline for her menu taped to the wall. She lined up the tables and covered them with long banquet cloths. She set the places with attention to every detail. She meticulously arranged full silverware service down to the special bread knife across the bread plate. She brought out the best of everything for their guests—the new cloth napkins she hadn't yet put into service, polished silver serving pieces, spotless glassware and attractive centerpieces. She applied her calligraphy skills to tiny placecards for each guest. Deciding who should sit where took almost as much time as setting the table.

"It doesn't matter where you put them," Becca said, setting salt and pepper sets along the table.

"Sure it does. You have to put people next to those they get along with or can have a pleasant evening in conversation."

"Yeah, but they'll all just move the placecards and sit near who they want."

"You're right," Liz replied and stopped agonizing over where to put whom. She did put her own card at the end of the table closest to the kitchen so she could jump and run to refill serving bowls. "Is Mark going to be here?"

"Yeah, I told him he was."

"Didn't you ask him?" Liz asked.

"Heck no! He'd do that groany thing about having to get dressed up. So I just told him to be here and wear clean jeans." Becca returned to the kitchen. Liz followed. "I also told him he'd be sleeping alone for the entire Thanksgiving vacation if he didn't show up and help wash dishes." She winked at her mother.

"Shame on you, Becca." Liz smiled to herself.

"Hey Mom, he's a guy. He's been in Boston for six weeks. He's desperate for a fuck."

"BECCA!"

Becca laughed, well aware she had embarrassed her mother.

Liz didn't say anything but she remembered those years when sex seemed paramount. She had to admit to herself, sex was still important. After all, she wasn't dead yet.

Pauline and Georgia arrived early, carrying in salads, relish trays and several pies. They were dressed in their Sunday best, not the jeans and tunics they wore to work.

"Happy Thanksgiving, Liz," Pauline said, sliding the salads into the refrigerator. She gave Liz a hug then hugged Becca. "How is my little Becca?" she said, pinching her cheek. She knew Becca didn't like it but she pinched anyway. It was one of those can't-resist things.

"Stop pinching her, Pauline," Georgia scowled. "One of these days she's going to haul off and smack you. Happy Turkey Day, sweetie," she said, hugging Becca warmly.

"Where are Emily and Didi?" Liz asked, looking toward the door.

"Emily will be a little late. She had to take a cake to the nursing home," Georgia replied. Emily was her partner of fifteen years, a hardworking, big-hearted woman with only an eighth-grade education.

"Didi will be along shortly. She is making gingerbread and wanted it to cool a little before bringing it out in the cold air. She is sure it will fall." Pauline smirked, registering her disapproval. Didi and Pauline had been together for five years and spent most of their time arguing over recipes. Both were accomplished cooks but strong willed. Didi occasionally filled in at The Sugar Bush but it was common knowledge the pair couldn't work together full time without fur flying.

As the players, coaches and guests began to arrive Liz and her kitchen crew were busy coordinating the meal. Liz could point, stir, instruct, taste, take up and serve without a single wasted motion. To watch the food go from raw to finished and garnished in the serving bowls was like watching a work of art unfold.

"Is it safe to come in?" Sheridan asked, sticking her head in the swinging door.

"Hi," Liz said, tasting the gravy. "Sure, come on in, but watch out. We have been known to run in to each other."

"I just wanted to bring you this," she said, setting a paper sack on the counter. It looked suspiciously like a wine bottle and had a gold bow on the top.

Liz wiped her hands on her apron and went to look.

"Thank you, Coach," she declared, examining the bottle of imported cabernet. "This is very nice of you. But you didn't have to bring anything."

"I didn't bring enough to serve to everyone but I wanted to bring you something for asking us over. Now I don't have to burn something for dinner. When it comes to cooking, I don't impress my folks."

"I will save this for something special, like when I can score more than six points in one game." Liz laughed and slipped the bottle back in the sack.

"Liz, do you want these rolls brushed with butter before we heat them?" Pauline asked, ready to push the pans in the oven.

"I better go back to work if we want to eat on time," Liz said, touching Sheridan's arm. "Thank you for the wine. That was very sweet of you."

There was a sparkle in Sheridan's eyes as Liz touched her.

"You're welcome. I'll get out of your way."

The chaos of taking up the food, arranging the serving bowls on the table and getting everyone seated all came together at precisely three o'clock, surprising even Liz. She had served many banquets and special events before but was still amazed when things came together without a hitch. Becca was right. The girls had adjusted the seating arrangement so friends sat next to each other. By the time Liz came to take her place at the table, Sheridan's father had moved to her usual seat at the end of the table. Sheridan was on one side of him and her mother on the other. He had adjusted his place so he had plenty of room, pushing Sheridan and his wife's plates down slightly. He leaned back in his chair like a king waiting for the trivialities to be finished so he could begin his feast. Liz saw her placecard tossed on the serving cart with the extra water glasses. But Martin Ross's rude behavior wasn't going to spoil her day. She forced a smile, ignoring the urge to say something to him. She found an empty chair at the furthest corner of the table, the place that provided the longest walk to the kitchen for refills. Liz took her place between someone's roommate and the placecard with her father's name on it. She always set him a place but he rarely showed up.

Hector Elliott, or Hec as he was known, was a farmer. He harvested sap and made maple syrup, grew vegetables for his own consumption and milked thirty head of Holsteins. He had pared back his operation over the years, refusing to take on help to get the work done. He and Liz had a quiet relationship. Hec didn't like large crowds so Liz knew he probably wouldn't show up for dinner. He would, however, come knocking at the back door about five o'clock when the leftovers were still available. He was a thin man of medium height with a farmer's tan and ruddy complexion. Hec was a soft-spoken Vermonter, one who stayed at home, tended to his chores and stoically carried on after losing his wife to cancer. Liz was shaken to the core when her mother was diagnosed with ovarian cancer. Her twenty-eight months of chemotherapy, radiation, surgery and suffering seemed to fly by, leaving no time for good-byes or regrets. Hec and Liz stood next to each other at her graveside service, numb and speechless at the loss. Liz never saw her father shed a tear but she knew they were deeply in love. She had seen it in the way her parents looked at one another over the breakfast table, the way she fluffed his pillow before he sat down in his favorite chair, the way she touched his arm as he passed through the kitchen.

Liz smiled to herself and set his placecard on the plate. He would be along later and she would fix him a plate, one filled with more than he could eat.

Grace was said then the food parade began. The numerous bowls of mashed potatoes, corn pudding, stuffing, giblet gravy, sweet potato and almond casserole, homemade cranberry sauce, green beans and baby onions, as well as turkey and relishes couldn't be passed quickly enough. Baskets of rolls and corn bread muffins were added to the great mountains of food. Liz and Pauline made the first refill runs. Didi and Georgia jumped to their feet for the next refilling. The afternoon was full of good food, jokes, satisfied moans and pleasant conversations. Sheridan had to endure several jabs about the lopsided score of the first game but she was a good sport about it. She teased the players, accusing them of shooting at the wrong basket. How else could the score possibly be that bad, she joked.

Sheridan rose to her feet and held out her water goblet.

"I think it is only fitting that we first and foremost thank Liz and Becca for inviting us to join them for this wonderful Thanksgiving feast," she offered. "I have to say, for a basketball player, Liz can really cook." Everyone laughed. "But seriously, I do thank you, Liz. So do my parents and all the players, coaching staff and guests. You can cook for my team any time." She saluted Liz with her glass. Everyone stood and did the same.

Liz blushed and nodded her appreciation.

"Thank you, Coach Ross. I am so glad you all could come be with us. Becca and I consider you all part of our family." Liz picked up her goblet and held it up. "Here's to our new family, may you always find happiness in one another." She saluted the crowd then sipped.

The meal wound down with desserts soon after which a few of the girls left but most stayed and enjoyed the camaraderie. Sheridan's mother insisted on helping carry dishes to the kitchen even though Liz refused to allow it.

"You might as well let her do it," Sheridan said, leaning over to Liz. "She isn't going to listen to you."

"Amelia, you are our guest. I don't want you in the kitchen."

"I told Sheridan I wouldn't come to dinner unless I could help with the cleanup. It isn't fair to leave you with all this mess."

"I have an automatic dishwasher," Liz insisted.

"Well, you have to load it," Amelia declared, hurrying by with a stack of plates.

"Liz, we sure want to thank you for dinner," Martin said, wrapping an arm around Sheridan's shoulder. "You are a good cook. My daughter tells us you own this restaurant. That's quite an under-taking."

"I'm very glad you could come, Martin. I hope you'll stay awhile and make yourself at home." Liz shook his hand warmly.

"Thanks, I need to walk around a bit. I'm stuffed. I ate too much but it was all delicious. God knows what we would have had if we left it up to Sheridan to cook. Amelia would have had to do the cooking."

"Hey," Sheridan scowled. "I can cook, sort of."

Martin chuckled.

"Sweetheart, you are a coach, not a cook. Leave the cooking to someone else. You need to spend your time coaching and inter-viewing, not trying to be Betty Crocker."

The word interviewing brought on a nervous look from Sheridan.

"It was great, Liz." Sheridan quickly steered the conversation in another direction. "I liked the sweet potato casserole. What was in that?"

"Almonds, lemon juice, brown sugar and nutmeg. Also some Vermont secret ingredients."

"What's that?" Martin asked, his eyes narrowed with interest.

"Maple syrup," she whispered coyly.

"We've got to get some of that to take home. Amelia always takes some home when we come to visit. I tell her she can buy it at the Safeway in Springfield but she says it isn't the same. Hell, maple syrup is maple syrup. Isn't it, Liz?" he said, demanding she agree with him.

"You'd think so, wouldn't you? But it isn't the same." Liz looked around, as if she was going to divulge a secret and didn't want anyone else to hear. "We keep the good stuff in Vermont for ourselves." Liz gave Martin a serious nod.

"How can you tell the good stuff?" he asked.

Becca walked past, trying not to snicker. She knew her mother had found another gullible tourist and was about to weave the family fable.

"We keep the syrup made from the virgin maple trees. It is much sweeter and doesn't turn sour with age," she said in a covert whisper.

"Really?" he replied, buying the story hook, line and sinker.

She nodded carefully.

"It's one of those things we like to keep secret so don't let anyone know I told you, okay?" Liz reported, gripping his arm.

"Oh, no. I won't say a word."

"You make yourself at home now. I better get these leftovers in the refrigerator." Liz smiled warmly at him and looked at Sheridan, a mischievous grin on her face. Sheridan was trying not to chuckle but she knew Liz had just fed her father a line of bullshit and he swallowed it right down. He had turned and walked toward the window, looking out at the dirtied piles of snow along the sidewalk.

"Virgin maple trees?" Sheridan asked with a twinkle in her eye.

Liz couldn't help herself. She giggled then bit down on her lip.

"It's an inside joke for us Vermonters," Liz whispered then gave Sheridan a playful bump with her hip.

"Virgin maple trees," she repeated with a chuckle. "You know he's going to ask every clerk in every store in Ashton if they carry maple syrup from virgin maple trees." She smiled at Liz as if to acknowledge her successful ruse then strode off to visit with her players.

Liz went into the kitchen and began the job of packaging the leftovers. She mentally calculated what specials she could add to tomorrow's menu. Mashed potato pancakes perhaps. Turkey tetrazzini casserole for the Sunday brunch. Cornbread stuffing fritters with the stew on Saturday.

Becca and Mark manned the big dishwasher, loading the trays to be sanitized after the hand washing. Pauline, Georgia, Didi and Amelia all went to work scrubbing anything that wasn't nailed down. The project was finished in no time, a testament to cooperation in spite of Didi and Pauline's arguments over how much nutmeg went into the sweet potatoes.

"Thank you, ladies," Liz said, bringing out a box of Godiva

dark chocolates from her office. "I have a treat for you." She opened the box and shared them with the kitchen crew. They stood around the wooden-topped work island, nibbling the precious goodies and moaning how full they were.

Liz carried the two trash bags out the back down toward the dumpster in the alley. As she approached the corner of the building she could hear Martin and Sheridan standing on the sidewalk, talking. She didn't want to eavesdrop but the conversation sounded important, not one she should interrupt.

"Dad, you can't say things like that in front of the players." Sheridan sounded concerned, even angry.

"Hell, Sheridan. They know you are looking for another job, don't they? They know you'd never settle for a little podunk college like this."

"No, they don't. I don't want them to know I put in other applications. At least not until the season is over. We've got eighteen games left to play. You know how important it is for them to trust me. They have to play with confidence. They can't do that if they think I'm leaving as soon as the season is over."

"You've got a pretty soft team this year, kiddo. How the hell do they expect you to make anything out of that bunch of girls? You don't have any size inside and that point guard," he said with a snort. "How the hell old is she anyway? Liz may be a good cook but come on, Sheridan. We're talking basketball here. You need someone with quick hands and quick feet."

"Dad, that's enough. Not another word about it. Let me handle this. It's a delicate situation," Sheridan demanded.

Liz could hear their footsteps heading back to the front door of the restaurant. She stood frozen, letting what she heard sink in. If she hadn't heard it with her own ears, she wouldn't have believed it. Could it be true? Was Sheridan really moving on to a bigger college or university? Was Chilton College just a stepping-stone in her career? This was only Sheridan's second year at Chilton. Liz knew she came with glowing credentials, Becca had said so. Coach Ross's accolades and accomplishments were impeccable. Liz couldn't believe Chilton hadn't made a longer commitment to her.

Two years was barely long enough to learn the players' personalities, let alone establish a coaching record. It didn't matter to Liz since she only had one year to play. But Becca would be back as well as Deb, Jen and all the rest. They deserved a dedicated, committed and well-recommended coach. They deserved Sheridan. She had a gift for coaching, a gift for understanding the players and their potential. Robin and Jasmine were both good assistant coaches but they weren't ready to be a head coach. Robin's temper was too volatile and Jasmine was only one year out of the university herself. Something else nagged at Liz as she contemplated Sheridan's departure from Chilton but she couldn't put her finger on it. Whatever it was, it wasn't pleasant. She tossed the trash bags into the dumpster then stood in the alley for a moment to regain her festive mood. After all, she had a restaurant full of guests who were busy laughing, joking and enjoying their time together. This wasn't a time to be depressed.

Liz had no sooner washed her hands and entered the dining room than she heard a knock at the kitchen door. It opened and Hec stepped in, holding his hat in his hand. His thin gray hair was slicked back and his face looked freshly scrubbed and shaved. He was wearing a navy blue suit that had the faint aroma of moth balls. His brown lace-up boots had been brushed clean of pasture dirt. Liz greeted him with a big hug and a smile.

"Hi Dad," she said, adjusting his rumpled collar. "You look dapper this evening," she added, taking a long, proud look at him.

"Happy Thanksgiving," he replied, his eyes soft and gentle.

"Come on in and meet some of the girls on the team." Liz locked her arm through his and escorted him toward the swinging door.

"I can't stay too long," he said then pulled back. "I have chores to tend to at home."

"I'm sorry you couldn't be here earlier. Can I fix you a plate, Dad?" She knew if she forced the issue of meeting the crowd of people in the other room he might leave without his Thanksgiving meal.

Hec Elliott was raised on a farm in Vermont and had been a soldier during the Korean War. He was a simple New England country boy and fought bravely for his country. He returned in one piece but the trauma of what he had seen and done left him unable to deal with loud noises or crowds. He avoided shopping centers, airports and even sporting events, including his daughter's and granddaughter's basketball games. But Liz understood the excuses he offered were merely his self-defense. Hec was still a devoted father and doting grandfather. He hungrily watched the few televised basketball games and scheduled his day around the radio broadcast of the games on the Chilton College station.

"Sit here and tell me about your day while I fix your plate," she said fondly, pulling a stool up to the island.

"I don't want to be a bother," he offered.

"No bother, Dad. Sit down." She patted the stool and touched his arm. He seemed relieved to eat his meal in the kitchen rather than in a room full of people he didn't know. Liz took the plate she had made for him from the refrigerator and warmed it in the microwave along with a roll and a corn bread muffin. She poured him a cup of coffee in his favorite green mug that hung on the nail by the cabinet. Hec liked a particular knife, fork, spoon and plate that she kept clean and ready for his visits. It wasn't from her best dishes but it was what he liked and she respected that. His needs were simple. His love as a father was simple, too. He loved Liz and Becca unconditionally. He just had trouble expressing it. Instead of verbal expressions of love, he would leave a basket of wildflowers on her porch or a quart of fresh maple syrup in her car. She knew he kept all the clippings from the newspaper that had anything to do with Becca or with her. Twenty years ago he had subscribed to the Chilton College newspaper so he could track Liz's accomplishments. When Becca started college he renewed his subscription. Liz had sent him a poster and calendar with the team picture on it at the beginning of the season knowing he would have it hanging on the wall next to his radio.

"How have you been? Did you see the doctor about your arm?" she said, spreading a cloth napkin across his lap.

"It's fine now. I soaked it in Epsom salts." He wasted no time in digging into his dinner. He used his roll as a pusher as he gobbled down large bites.

"Be right back, Dad," she said and headed for the dining room. Within a minute she was back, Becca following her through the swinging door.

"Hi, Grandpa!" Becca gushed, hugging him around the neck and kissing his forehead. "Did you get the card I sent you?" she asked, leaning on the island and picking a bite of turkey from his plate.

He nodded, continuing to eat.

"When are you coming out to go through that box of picture frames?" he asked between bites.

"Maybe this weekend." Becca took a sip of his coffee then refilled it. "Mark can carry it down out of the attic."

"Is that the boy you brought out last summer to ride horses?" Hec asked cautiously.

"Yeah," she replied.

"Nice boy," he muttered, scooping up a chunk of sweet potato and downing it in one bite.

"Did you fix the sleigh, Grandpa?"

He nodded.

"Broken runner clip. Fixed it last week." He pushed his plate back and started on his pie.

"Good," Becca replied with a broad smile. "You can take us for a ride this weekend. Mark and I can sit in the back and you can drive us." She winked at him.

Hec lowered his eyes, trying not to show his grin. Becca held the key to her grandfather's heart and she knew it. The two of them had an inseparable relationship. She loved him in spite of his shy and reserved ways. He loved her in spite of her overbearing manner. It was a happy balance.

"Better wear a heavy coat," he warned.

"We will," she announced. "Thank you, Grandpa. Later," she chirped and returned to the gathering in the dining room.

"I better be getting back," he announced and settled his hat onto his head. He wiped his mouth and left the napkin on the stool.

"Are you sure you can't stay awhile, Dad?" Liz followed him to the back door.

"Cows won't milk themselves, daughter. You know that." He turned and looked at her. Liz knew this was his good-bye stare and if she wanted a hug from him she had better reach for it now. She did and he hugged her back, holding her tightly.

"You make a good meal, Liz. Your mother would be proud of you." They stared at one another for a moment as memories filled them.

"Thank you, Dad," she replied and kissed his cheek softly. "You come by for lunch next week. Becca will be here if I'm not. You should come every day. What are daughters for if not to take care of their fathers." She knew he would agree but seldom showed up. "You call me tomorrow, okay?"

"I will," he replied as he stepped out into the parking lot. Liz waved as he climbed into his pickup truck and pulled away.

"Take care of yourself, Dad," she whispered as his truck headed up the street.

Liz waited until his truck was out of sight then joined the others. The dining room had been transformed into a practice court. The tables had been pushed to the side and the players were arguing over who could set a better pick. Sheridan and her father were giving advice and offering tips. Mark was even trying his best to be a Lady Stinger but his footwork left much to be desired. Becca was pushing him from behind, muscling him out of the way as she demonstrated her technique.

"We missed you," Sheridan said, leaning against the counter as she watched the fun.

"My dad came by for a minute," Liz said, taking a seat.

"Oh, is he still here? I'd like to meet him."

"No, he had to run. He has to milk this evening."

"He has a farm?" Sheridan asked, sitting down next to her.

"Yes. Not a big place but it keeps him busy."

"I bet he is a nice man," she offered.

"Yes, he is," Liz replied softly.

"Coach, how about this?" one of the girls said as she showed her style.

"Spread your feet more. You're not a wide enough target." Sheridan smiled at her then returned her attention to Liz. "I really appreciate your invitation. Dad and Mom are having a great time. He loves to coach kids."

"I'm glad you could make it. I just can't imagine having Thanksgiving without a room full of people to share it with."

"Is that why your dad didn't come for dinner? I heard Becca say something about he didn't like crowds."

"He wouldn't have come anyway. Two years ago I didn't plan a big dinner. It was just going to be Becca and me so we invited him to the house. I thought he could handle that. He showed up two hours late. He came to the back door in his muddy boots and stayed just long enough to eat a turkey sandwich. But he has always been like that. It's just easier to accept it."

"And you love him dearly," Sheridan offered.

Liz smiled and nodded.

"Way more than he will let me tell him."

Chapter 12

The last week of November was rainy and cold. The days grew shorter. Coach Ross's team settled into their conference schedule, playing teams from up and down the Connecticut Valley from Maine to New York to Massachusetts.

"Robin," Sheridan called when she noticed her walk by the open office door.

Robin stuck her head in, quickly swallowing the last bite of her candy bar.

"Yep," she said.

"Did you get a look at this tape of the Hanover team?" Sheridan was studying a videotape, replaying a particular play.

"Yes." She came into the office and looked over Sheridan's shoulder.

"They run that same deep cross every single time a team shows a man defense against them."

"Did you see they've got two players who shoot with either

hand? But they are definitely better shooters with the right hand." Robin pointed to the players in question.

"They're shooting lefty just to draw fouls it looks like," Sheridan said, watching closely. "The point guard picks up her dribble a lot and she heads right into the corner. Is she a freshman?"

"No, a sophomore. But she didn't play much last year."

The tape ended and Sheridan ejected it then rummaged in a stack for another tape.

"I had another phone call from that high school coach in Harrisburg," Robin reported. "Did I tell you about her call? Anyway, she sure thinks you should take a look at the Jefferson twins. They are undecided about college but they both have excellent stats."

"Like what?" Sheridan asked, sorting through her tapes.

"Kaneesha is averaging eighteen points per game this year and fifteen per game for her high school career. Regina is averaging fifteen this year and fourteen overall."

"What kind of students are they?" Sheridan asked, showing some interest.

"Honor roll, both of them. They are taking prep courses for college so it wouldn't be a stretch for them to come to Chilton," Robin reported.

"How big are they? Six-footers?"

"No. Something like five-nine. But they can shoot the lights out from the line. She said they are real coachable with a good work ethic."

"They're seniors?"

"Yes. Might be worth a look," Robin suggested. "We lose two starters next year."

"Three," Sheridan corrected. "Liz, too."

"Oh, yeah."

"Ask the coach to send a tape I can see," Sheridan said.

"Okay, but I think she was hoping you'd come take a look in person," Robin reported.

"I might but I want to see them in action before I make a trip to, where is it again?"

"Harrisburg."

"If she'll send a tape, I'll make a decision."

Robin smiled coyly.

"What?" Sheridan asked, noticing something in Robin's expression.

"I got the idea she wanted you to come down for more than just to scout the twins." Robin raised her eyebrows.

"What are you talking about?" Sheridan asked with a frown.

"She said she knows you," Robin offered. "Bobbi O'Neil?"

Sheridan drew a short gasp of recognition.

"Oh. Yes, I know Bobbi," Sheridan couldn't stop a reflective smile from crawling across her face. "She used to coach a high school team in the same district I did. She's a good coach. A little hotheaded but she is dedicated." Sheridan leaned back in her chair and folded her hands behind her head.

"Dedicated, huh?" Robin said as she studied Sheridan's smug expression.

Sheridan let Bobbi's image crystallize in her mind. It had been eight years since they had shared a high school conference and a bed. Bobbi was a feisty, hot-tempered Irish woman with red hair, hot lips and a body that sent a shiver down Sheridan's spine every time they met.

"Why not take a weekend in Harrisburg?" Robin suggested with a wink.

"No," Sheridan replied, returning to the stack of tapes. "Some things are better left in the past."

"Oh, really?" Robin smiled at her.

"Bobbi is a good coach but she is a little too demanding for my taste."

"Ah! Velcro-girlfriend?"

"You might say that. I need a little room to breathe, if you know what I mean." Sheridan looked up, suddenly sorry she had made that admission. Robin was an efficient assistant but she didn't need to know Sheridan's personal business.

"Damn, how do you manage that? My last two relationships went from a drink at a bar to a two-room apartment with a dog faster than the speed of light." Robin smirked and shook her head.

"That can happen," Sheridan said, taking a Coke out of the small refrigerator in the corner of her office. "Coke or Sprite?"

"Nothing, thanks. I just finished one."

"Who's the lucky person this time?" Sheridan asked lightheartedly.

"No one right now. I just spent four months getting Megan and her dog's hair out of my apartment. I'm giving myself a break. What's your secret? How do you stay unattached?"

"You mean how do I keep from having dog hair in my apartment?" Sheridan teased.

"Yeah."

"There's no secret. You just have to remember what you want out of life. Your goals. Robin, don't you want to be a head coach someday?"

"Sure. But I'm talking about relationships, not careers."

"Exactly. You have to stay focused and not let a relationship get so serious you can't see your goal." Sheridan spoke as if she believed her advice completely.

"Can't you have both? Goals and a serious relationship."

"Some people can. It has never worked for me. It's a struggle out there. There are a hundred people trying to reach the same pinnacle that you want. You have to stay focused. I'm not saying you shouldn't have relationships. God knows, I'm no nun." They laughed about that remark. "But I keep things balanced. I need my mind clear so I can give one hundred percent to the team and my players. Tell me something. When the dog lady moved in with you, did you know everything about her? Or did you just jump in together?"

"Shit. She had stuff hanging in my closet before I knew she had a brother in Iraq, a father who was a cop and an ex who played pro tennis." Robin heaved a deep sigh.

"My point, exactly," Sheridan replied. "It takes a long time to get a relationship right. You can't rush it."

"So, you play the field, right?" Robin suggested.

Sheridan sat up and stared decisively at her.

"If you mean do I cheat, no. I'm as faithful as a bird dog. I just don't get all balled up in a relationship before I'm ready." Sheridan again was surprised she was so open with her personal affairs. It must be Robin's easygoing nature and her nonjudgmental attitude that told her she could trust her with her inner thoughts.

"Sounds like you are still playing the field," Robin said. "It sounds like you are playing a zone defense with your heart. You are roaming from person to person, blocking out anyone who gets too close. One of these days some cutie is going to change your mind, Coach. Just you watch."

"Is that what happened to you? Some cute thing turn your head?"

"What can I say? I'm a sucker for long hair, big brown eyes and tight jeans," Robin said with a shrug.

"You have to stay focused," Sheridan said adamantly.

"You better be careful, Coach. Don't stay so focused you let love slip through your fingers," Robin advised.

"Dean Carlton is on line two," Mary Lou said over the intercom. "I think he wants to congratulate you on the game last night."

"See you at practice," Robin said as she headed for the door.

"Later," Sheridan said as she reached for the telephone. "Hello, Dean Carlton."

"Coach Ross," he said in his low raspy voice. "Mind if I come have a look at practice today?"

"Not at all. Four o'clock," she advised. "We'll be glad to have you."

The players had spent a full two hours at practice and were well sweated by the time a gray-haired man strode into the gymnasium with his hands in his pants pockets.

"Looking good, Coach," he said, ambling over to where Sheridan was standing on the sidelines. He loosened his tie then took a letter from his inside jacket pocket.

"Hello, Dean Carlton." Sheridan watched her players intently. "Come on, Trish. Quit picking up your dribble," she yelled across the court.

"I got a phone call from a Channel Twenty-Two TV station in Springfield, Massachusetts. They want you and Liz Elliott to come down to be on that woman's afternoon show, Carol's Tea Party or something like that."

"Well, I hope you told them no." Sheridan kept her eyes on the team as she visited with him. "Why are you escorting that player down the lane, Miriam? Go after the ball or keep her from shooting," Sheridan said and shook her head.

"Her show has quite a following. It's part of the evening news."

"Send someone else, Dean. I don't have time for crap like that." Sheridan blew her whistle and reset the teams.

He waited for scrimmage to start again.

"We'll pay for your gas and dinner and whatever else you need," he said. "Consider it public relations. If Liz Elliott can put more people in the bleachers just because she's forty years old, we can certainly take advantage of it." He sounded insistent. "Your draw has been pretty dismal so far this year."

"It's getting better. A winning team will put just as many people in the bleachers as an older player. And she is only thirty-nine."

"Maybe so, but we need both. You've got a couple days between games this week. You two can run down there, do the show and be back before nine o'clock."

"I've got practice every day this week," she replied with a furrowed brow.

"That's what your assistants are for. Consider this an assignment, Coach Ross." He narrowed his eyes at her.

"Why don't you go down and be on the show. You're the PR expert," she argued.

"Wednesday. Be in Springfield by four o'clock for pre-show interviews. You'll be on at five thirty. They said they would take care of your makeup. We wouldn't want our head coach looking sickly on television," he commanded, handing her the paper.

"Dean Carlton," she said staunchly as he headed off the court.

"Have a good time, Coach," he called without turning back to her.

"What's up?" Robin asked, noticing Sheridan's smirk.

Sheridan closed her eyes, trying to suppress her frustration over the assignment.

"Some television show in Springfield wants me to bring Liz down for an interview and Dean Carlton wants us to go." She muttered something crude. "I may send you," Sheridan declared sarcastically.

"Not me," Robin said, holding up her hands. "I'm just a lowly assistant. They want a real coach." She laughed. "Thank God."

"Shit!" Sheridan scoffed and threw her whistle across the floor. "I don't have time for this."

"I guess he thinks you do. And after all, he is the dean."

Sheridan glared at her.

"Send them to the showers," she snipped as she turned on her heels and strode off toward her office. She stopped and looked back at the players. "Liz," she called.

"Yes," she said, trotting over to her.

Sheridan heaved a disgusted sigh.

"Dean Carlton accepted an invitation for you and me to be on television."

"I hope you are kidding," she scoffed.

"I wish I was. We are going to be on Carol's Tea Party," Sheridan said with a disapproving smirk. "He thinks it will be a good public relations opportunity."

"Carol's Tea Party is on Channel Twenty-Two in Springfield," Liz offered.

"I know. He has us scheduled for Wednesday."

"This Wednesday?" Liz's eyes widened. "I can't go this Wednesday. That's my big delivery day. And I have a luncheon for the chamber of commerce at one o'clock. I'm sorry but I can't possibly go."

Sheridan nodded her head.

"You have two days to find someone to fill in for you. Can't Becca take care of it? She handled things while you were on the road trips."

"But I can't ask her to do it again this week. I told her I'd be here all week."

"Better un-tell her, then," Sheridan explained. "Look, I don't like the idea either. I don't have time to be running off for a damn TV show but this comes from the top. Dean Carlton was very adamant. He thinks the publicity will increase ticket sales. I must admit, he is probably right. Not many college basketball teams have a thirty-nine-year-old on the team, much less one who is a starting point guard."

Liz walked away a few steps, running her hand through her hair.

"Sheridan, I really don't want to go. Can't you get us out of this?" Liz said, turning back to her with a desperate look in her eyes. "Please."

"Sorry. If you can find another thirty-nine-year-old on the team between now and Wednesday, let me know." Sheridan offered a small smile. "Think of it this way, the college is paying for it so you might as well consider it homework. Just sit back and enjoy it. I'll pick you up about ten Wednesday morning. We'll eat lunch and dinner on Dean Carlton."

Liz rolled her eyes and turned to leave.

"It better be a damn good dinner," she muttered, striding off the court.

"I heard that," Sheridan replied with a chuckle.

Liz spent the days before the trip to Springfield catching up on orders, paying bills, menu changes and worrying about the burden she had placed on Becca to cover for her. Becca used the time to tease her mother about being a television celebrity and reminding her she was about to be watched by thousands of her customers and friends. Liz tried to ignore her but it wasn't easy. She certainly didn't want to be a television celebrity and she didn't want to look silly either.

Begrudgingly, Liz was dressed and ready Wednesday morning. Becca frowned a bit but agreed to handle The Sugar Bush for her mother. Liz covered the morning rush, allowing Becca to come in at nine thirty.

"She's here," Becca said, sticking her head in the kitchen and grinning broadly. "Have you seen her car, Mom?"

"Yes, I have."

"It's so cool." Becca was veritably drooling at the thought.

"What is it, Becca?" Pauline asked as she stirred the pancake batter.

"Brand new black Mustang GT with tinted windows and spinner hubcaps. That is the hottest car I have ever seen." Becca waved Pauline to the swinging door and pointed out the front where Sheridan was parked by the front window.

"Looks expensive." Pauline scowled then went back to the grill.

"They may be but they sure are hot looking." Becca stayed at the door, staring.

"Becca, you'd think you had never seen a car before," Liz teased as she collected her jacket and bag. She came up behind Becca and looked over her shoulder. Liz gasped but it wasn't at the sleek black car. It was at the tall woman in sunglasses leaning against it. Sheridan was dressed in a pair of black slacks and a black leather jacket with the collar turned up, cradling her jaw. The wind swirled around her, stirring her hair. She didn't look anything like a coach. Liz couldn't take her eyes off of her.

"Isn't that the coolest thing you ever saw?" Becca asked dreamily.

"Yes, it most certainly is," Liz whispered and heaved a sigh.

"Have a good time," Becca said as Liz went out the front door.

"You too, honey," Liz said absentmindedly, still staring at Sheridan.

Becca smiled, seeming to know what had captured her mother's attention so completely.

"Hello," Sheridan said, as she opened the passenger's door for Liz. "You all set to go?"

"I think so." Liz slid in and buckled her seat belt.

"I really am sorry if this is a problem for you," Sheridan offered as she pulled out of town. "Dean Carlton was dead set on us going so I didn't have much choice."

"That's okay. Becca didn't mind. She actually seemed happy to get a chance to be in charge again. The power must have gone to her head."

"Good for her."

Liz had to admit the idea of spending the day with Sheridan had its advantages. Having lunch and dinner with a gorgeous, intelligent woman couldn't possibly be all that bad. Liz smiled out the side window as a warm glow floated over her.

The trip was a pleasant one. They chatted about basketball, classes, childhood, food and cars. They stopped for a leisurely lunch in Brattleboro, laughing and visiting across the table. Sheridan smiled easily and often, putting Liz completely at ease in her presence. The strict and demanding coach was replaced by a soft-spoken woman with a dimple in her cheek when she laughed. She held the door for Liz and listened intently to her stories as if she could listen to them all day. Liz had such a good time she was almost sorry when they pulled into the parking lot at the television station.

"I guess we're here," Sheridan said, turning off the car and looking over at Liz. She smiled softly at her.

"I guess so," Liz replied as she returned her stare.

They sat silently for a moment, neither one ready to end the gaze they shared.

"I'm glad we have the ride home tonight," Sheridan said quietly.

"Me too," Liz replied softly.

Chapter 13

"Coach Ross, how is it different having a player on your team who is almost your own age?" Carol asked.

"Actually it is easier to communicate with an older player. Their experience gives them a keener insight and a better understanding of what is expected."

"So you don't find it difficult having an older player?" she asked, heavily accenting the older reference.

"No," Sheridan answered succinctly.

Carol looked at her curiously, assuming she would elaborate. She left a gap but Sheridan didn't care to fill it.

"Liz," Carol said, shifting her attention. "What made you decide to return to Chilton College to play your last year of basketball eligibility? Was it one of those dreams you had always wanted to come true?"

"Actually, it was my daughter's idea."

"Your daughter?"

"Yes, Becca decided I should go back to college and finish my degree. She seemed pretty adamant about it. She even helps out at my restaurant, The Sugar Bush, so I can spend time in class and with the team." Liz hadn't intended on using the opportunity to advertise her business but it seemed too convenient to ignore.

"So you own a restaurant. How do you find time to do everything? What with classes, homework, practice, games and a business to run."

"Like I said, Becca helps out and I have terrific employees. They have gone above and beyond the call of duty to get things done when I can't be there. I want to thank them from the bottom of my heart. I couldn't do this without their help."

"Do you have plans to change your career once you have your bachelor's degree in hand?"

"No. I love my restaurant. It's what I always wanted to do."

"Then I have to ask," Carol stated with a bit of skepticism. "Why spend the time and money to finish if it won't make a difference for you? Was it just done on a lark?"

Sheridan shifted in her seat as if she wanted to answer the arrogant question and the condescending tone.

"Why?" Liz asked with a furrowed brow. She looked down, squinting at the floor as she controlled the urge to laugh out loud. This woman either was told what questions to ask or she didn't have a clue about why a middle-aged woman would return to college to finish out a long awaited degree. "I guess I just wanted to finish what I started twenty-one years ago. Haven't you ever wanted to finish something, Carol?"

"So it's pride that brought you back to Chilton and the Lady Stingers basketball team," Carol declared, attempting to recover from Liz's question.

"Yes. That's a good description."

"Not to mention, she's a good player," Sheridan added. "She is our point guard."

"Is she the point guard because of her age?"

"She is point guard because that is where she makes the best contribution to the team."

"Can you explain for our viewers, without going into too much detail, just what a point guard does?"

"She is the floor general. She brings the ball up the court. She reads the plays I send in and relays them to the team. She also has to read the defense and make adjustments based on our game plan," Sheridan explained. "She is also the best ball handler as well as an outstanding outside shooter."

"As an older player, just how much time does Liz play during a game?" Carol seemed bent on accenting Liz's age limitations.

"Well, let's see. The games are two twenty-minute halves. She plays forty minutes, unless we have a large enough lead so she can sit out a few minutes. So far this season she hasn't asked to be relieved because of fatigue."

"So you play the whole game?" she asked in Liz's direction. "That's amazing. A forty-year-old woman, returning to college after twenty years at her daughter's request and is able to play a full game right along with the younger players."

"Yes. And I'm thirty-nine, not forty," Liz corrected. Carol ignored her.

"Coach Ross, how will things be different next year after Liz has graduated? How will the team change?"

"College teams change every year. The chemistry and makeup of the team changes as players graduate and new players arrive. Their personalities are all different. My coaching staff has to mold the players' talents into a team we think can be successful. Sometimes it is more of a challenge than others," she said with a half smile. "Liz Elliott will be missed. She is a vital part of our offensive attack." Sheridan glanced over at Liz. "We are lucky she decided to return to Chilton when she did."

"Thank you Coach Sheridan Ross and Liz Elliott. We wish you and the Chilton College Lady Stingers success with the remainder of your season." The camera honed in on Carol as she announced the guests who would appear after the commercial then the director cut to the tape.

"Thank you, ladies," she said, standing up and heading for the makeup girl. "Check my forehead," she ordered. "I think I touched it. I may need some powder."

Sheridan and Liz were escorted off the set by an assistant. They collected their coats and headed for the parking lot as if their fifteen minutes of fame had come and gone.

"Now there is a warmhearted, understanding journalist," Sheridan scoffed sarcastically.

"I think it is called sensationalistic journalism," Liz replied. "They have to make something out of nothing."

"Dean Carlton told me to watch out for her. He was right. She asked stupid questions then doesn't listen to the answer," Sheridan said.

"Thank you for what you said. I appreciate it."

Sheridan's cell phone rang before she could reply.

"Hello, Dean," she said, raising her eyebrows at the coincidence of his call.

"Good job, Coach," he said proudly. "Tell Liz she did a good job, too."

"I will."

"I'm glad I caught you before you started back." There was urgency in his tone. "Have you heard the weather?"

"No," Sheridan replied, popping the locks on her car. "What's up?"

"It's snowing here. We've got four inches already and more predicted. It started right after you left. A front came down from Canada. The weatherman said it was stronger than they thought it would be. Nothing terrible but we will have eight to ten inches by midnight."

"Shit. It takes us every bit of four hours to get home if the roads are clear," Sheridan replied with a worried look.

"No!" he said at once. "Don't try it. Find a hotel in Springfield and stay the night." No sooner had he said that than snowflakes began to fall lightly.

"It is almost six o'clock. We might be able to make it by ten or so," she offered, looking up at the snow filling the night skies.

"Coach Ross, consider this an order from the front office. We don't want you getting stranded along the highway in a snow bank. Get a hotel. We'll pay for it. I told Coach Riccio the same thing. He's got the men's team over in Portland with an inch of ice on the roads. Call me in the morning and I'll let you know how things are then." He hung up.

Sheridan folded the phone and stuffed it in her jacket pocket.

"Where would you like to go for dinner? There's no hurry. We aren't going anywhere tonight," she announced with a disgusted smirk.

"You're kidding. Why?" Liz immediately made a mental list of things that needed her attention.

"There's four inches of snow in Ashton already with more expected this evening. Guess it snuck in on them. Dean Carlton wants us to get a hotel and stay overnight in Springfield. Ed Riccio is stranded in Portland with the men's team, too."

"No," Liz groaned heavily. "I have a test tomorrow and orders to make for the restaurant. And Becca wasn't scheduled to work tomorrow afternoon. I was." She frowned and scanned the sky. "It isn't snowing that bad. Can't we try to make it? I can help drive if you need me to."

Sheridan shook her head.

"Orders from the boss. He said no." Sheridan smirked as well.

"Damn," Liz muttered as she climbed in the car.

"Maybe we should find a hotel then have dinner. Do you know anything about Springfield?"

"Not much. I know Boston Road. It runs east-west. Riverdale Road runs north-south."

"The Basketball Hall of Fame is downtown along the river but I don't remember if there was anything close to it or how to get there." Sheridan searched both ways before pulling out onto Chicopee Avenue. "Let's head back north toward Holyoke. It's just a few miles up the road and there should be some hotels right off the highway."

"There's always Northampton," Liz offered.

"How far is that?"

"Fifteen miles or so. Straight north from Holyoke."

Sheridan chuckled.

"What?" Liz asked, studying her face.

"Nothing," she replied as another snicker crept out.

"What is so funny?" Liz insisted.

"From what I've heard, it just seems the words straight and Northampton shouldn't be used in the same sentence." Sheridan raised her eyebrows.

"Oh," Liz replied with a small smile. "Probably not."

"Come on, let's try for Northampton. What do you say?"

"That's fine with me," Liz said. "We'll be closer to Vermont in the morning."

They headed north on the interstate, the snow falling faster and heavier as they moved north. By the time they turned off on the Northampton exit the pavement was covered with white and the air was thick with large flakes. Sheridan's rear wheel drive and big horsepowered car made steering a chore. The Mustang slid and fishtailed as she rounded the corner onto Bridge Street and headed into town. A few pedestrians bundled in heavy coats and scarves strolled along the sidewalks. Several pairs of women walked the business district arm in arm, window shopping and enjoying each other's company in the winter wonderland.

"Any ideas where a hotel might be?" Sheridan asked as she stopped for a red light. They both looked up and down the side streets.

"I have no idea. There has to be one someplace. There are two colleges here."

As two women stepped off the curb to cross the street in front of them, Sheridan put her window down and leaned out.

"Hi," she said in their direction. "Do you know where we can find a hotel?" Sheridan pulled her head back in the car and looked over at Liz. "God, I sound like I'm trying to pick them up."

The two women walked over to the car and looked in.

"Three Gables Motel is about five blocks up then take a right and go about half a mile," the taller woman said, huddling inside her parka.

"Don't send them there," the other one argued. "It's a flea bag." She looked in at Liz and smiled as if apologizing for the suggestion. "Go back to the light, take a left. Go about a mile. There's a nice place on the corner right before the mall. It's newer."

"Thanks," Sheridan replied.

"Any good places to eat around here?" Liz asked, leaning over Sheridan to see out the window.

"Murphy's," they both said instantly. "You'll pass it on the way to the hotel. It's on the right. Don't let the outside fool you. Great food."

"Thanks," Liz replied.

"See you around," they said and strolled off holding hands.

Sheridan followed the directions and pulled into the hotel parking lot, her car skidding the last fifty feet on its own.

"I sure hope they have a couple rooms. I doubt we could make it much farther. It is getting slick." Sheridan climbed out. Liz stepped out as well and immediately slipped. She caught herself on the side of the car.

"You okay?" Sheridan asked, hurrying to help her up.

"I'm fine. Remind me not to wear leather sole shoes when it's going to snow."

"If I knew it was going to do this, I would have told Dean Carlton to forget it."

They leaned on one another as they slipped and slid their way across the snow-covered parking lot to the front door.

"Hello, ladies," the woman behind the counter announced cheerfully as she hung up the telephone. "Is it getting deep out there?"

"Well, it isn't deep yet but it is slick," Liz replied, brushing the snow from her pant legs.

"Do you have two rooms?" Sheridan asked as she stomped her feet on the snow mats.

"If you had come in five minutes ago, I would have said no, we are all full up. But I just had a cancellation. Seems things are getting bad all the way up through New York state. You're in luck. We have one room left. It's a nice big room with a king bed." She placed a registration card on the counter for Sheridan to sign.

"Just one?" Liz asked.

"Yes." The woman had a curious look on her face as if she was surprised at Liz's question. "Sorry but that's it. Do you want it? I'm sure we'll have calls for rooms all night. Every hotel in Northampton is full."

Sheridan and Liz looked at each other. They both knew they had no choice. The weather was too bad to roam the area for a different hotel and the chances of finding something with two rooms seemed pretty slim.

"We'll take it." Sheridan placed her credit card on the counter. "What about that restaurant down the street, Murphy's? Is it worth the walk?"

"Absolutely," the woman replied as she made their entry in her computer. "Great little place. Don't let the outside fool you."

"We know," Liz said with a smile. "How's the food?"

"Real good. They have homemade soups and I think tonight is beef stew, if they have any left." She licked her lips dreamily.

"Sounds like my kind of place," Sheridan said. "By the way, do you have a couple of those complimentary toiletry kits? We didn't expect to be stranded here for the night."

"Sure." The woman dug two small zipper bags out of the drawer behind the counter. "Where are you from?"

"Ashton, Vermont."

"I recognize you two. You are the ones on Carol's Tea Party this evening," the woman said, her face suddenly bright at the revelation. "I love her show. She asks the stupidest questions." She laughed.

"Why do you love it if she asks stupid questions?" Liz asked curiously.

"Because her nephew is gay and she won't even acknowledge him. She acts like he doesn't exist. He is a sweetheart, too. He lives in Holyoke. I love to see her make a fool of herself." They all laughed. "Here are your room cards. Room three-sixteen. The elevator is around the corner. Breakfast is from six thirty to ten. The pool is at the end of the hall and the fitness room is across from it. Have a nice evening, ladies."

"With no luggage, using the pool or fitness room will be difficult," Sheridan replied.

"Oh yeah," the woman replied with a giggle.

They rode the elevator to the third floor in silence, both of them considering the possibilities of what to sleep in since they had only the clothes on their backs and one bed to share. Liz told herself it should be no big deal. They were both adults. She had shared a hotel room before. Two years ago she spent a weekend in Boston for a food service convention and shared a room with Belinda Haggerty, owner of the local Dairy Queen. They treated it like a slumber party. They watched the late movie, ate potato chips in bed and laughed about the terrible food at the convention. Liz reminded herself Sheridan had seen her naked. After all, she was the coach and had been in the locker room when the team was showering. But spending the night in a hotel room with Sheridan Ross *the woman* seemed different. As much as she wanted to ignore it, she had growing feelings for Sheridan and she didn't want them to make the evening difficult. Sheridan was a beautiful, confident woman. She was intelligent and funny. As a coach, she had invested herself totally in her work. She also was probably going to be gone by the summer, off to a fresh, new coaching position in a big city with a big name university. Getting too excited about spending the night in a hotel room with her on a romantic snowy night was exactly the wrong thing to do. Liz had to put those feelings out of her head or she was just going to get hurt. At that moment, Liz would trade her four-point grade average for a pair of flannel pajamas.

Sheridan slid the card in the door lock and pushed it open for Liz.

"Not bad," she said, following her inside and snapping on the light.

The king size bed had a bright yellow-and-orange floral bedspread, one that seemed to flash its presence like a neon light. The rest of the room was accented with greens and soft yellow. A small microwave and coffee machine were on the dresser along with a television and video game machine. Sheridan turned on the television and searched for the news of the weather. A forecaster was in the midst of showing the snowstorm's path and expected accumulations. With inches approaching a foot in some areas, they both felt a sinking feeling in the pits of their stomachs.

"Do you think we'll get home tomorrow," Liz asked quietly.

"I don't know. I guess it depends on when it stops and how fast the road crews get out."

"This is New England. They are already out plowing, I'm sure." Liz looked out the window into the blinding white of the night.

"Are you up to walking back to Murphy's? It seems to be the place to try." Sheridan hadn't taken off her jacket and stood by the door.

"Sure," Liz replied. "We have to eat."

"Now remember—" Sheridan advised as she opened the door and held it for Liz.

"Don't be fooled by the outside," they said in unison as they headed for the elevator. They stood in the lobby, buttoning up their jackets and pulling on gloves before heading out into the storm. Like giant marshmallows, the shrubs around the building were covered with snow. The streetlights illuminated the snow-filled skies with a soft amber hue. Sheridan and Liz stepped out into the snow, their shoes making a scrunching sound with each step. There was a silence in the air that suggested talk should be done in a whisper.

"Listen," Liz whispered. "It's so still. Isn't winter a beautiful time of year?"

"Yes, it is. I'm usually inside during the winter since it is basketball season. But you are right, it is beautiful." Sheridan looked up. A snowflake lit on her eyelash, another on the tip of her nose.

They started up the street toward Murphy's, speculating on what it looked like and what they were supposed to forgive.

"There it is," Sheridan announced as they rounded a bend.

"It can't be," Liz replied, staring at the sheets of plywood covering the windows.

"That's what it says." Sheridan pointed to the sign hanging over the door. Only half of the letters were illuminated, making it look like *urpy's*. "Remember what they said."

"I know, but—" Liz said, trying to see in the small window on the front door. Suddenly it burst open. The smell of coffee and garlic floated out to greet them.

"Excuse me," a woman said with a wide grin. She had a take-home box in her hand and a tall red-haired girl on her arm. "Better go on in. Food's great."

"Yeah. We heard." Sheridan held the door and waited for Liz to venture inside. In spite of the deepening snow, the inside was packed with customers. Tiny tables with mismatched chairs were clustered in the center and booths lined the walls. A vintage juke-box stood guard just inside the door with several women crowded around it selecting tunes. The narrow aisles between the tables were busy with waitresses scurrying back and forth from the kitchen, nearly running into one another as they came through the single swinging door. The walls were decorated with vintage movie posters from the forties and fifties. A few black-and-white framed photographs of famous actresses hung strategically on each wall. Most of them sported an autograph. The menu was hand-written on an old home movie screen suspended from the rafters and gently waving in the breeze as the front door opened and closed. All the waitresses were dressed in jeans and a red turtleneck with a screen print of a movie reel on the back.

"Do you see a place to sit?" Sheridan asked as she dodged a waitress carrying a tray of food.

"Back there, in the corner." Liz led the way, snaking through the tables to the booth under the picture of Katherine Hepburn. "Is this okay?" she asked.

"Sure," Sheridan said as she removed her jacket then slid into the booth across from Liz. "Classy woman," she said nodding her head toward the photograph.

"Can I help you?" asked the waitress, wiping the table with a rag and replacing the salt, pepper and ketchup in their rightful places.

"Coffee?" Sheridan asked in Liz's direction.

"Yes. Decaf." She rubbed her hands together to warm up.

"Two decaf, please," Sheridan said.

"Do you have any beef stew left?" Liz asked, studying the menu.

"Yep, should have. She made extra today. Snow brings out the stew eaters," the waitress said as she produced napkins and silverware from her apron pocket.

"Stew for me," Liz said.

"Me too," Sheridan offered.

"Corn bread or biscuits?" the waitress asked.

"Both?" Liz suggested hopefully.

"Sure." She disappeared into the kitchen and returned carrying their drinks with paper coasters in the shape of movie reels and a small box of movie theater popcorn.

"Cute place," Liz said, taking in all the details.

"Murphy must like to go to the movies," Sheridan said.

"It's Helen Murphy," the waitress offered. "She was a movie actress. You know, *Gentlemen's Mistress*, nineteen forty seven. *Boston Fair*, nineteen fifty."

"Oh, really," Liz replied, trying to act like she knew who she was talking about.

"She died about ten years ago. Her daughter runs it now. Be right back with your stew," she added and returned to the kitchen.

Sheridan leaned forward and whispered across to Liz. "Have you ever heard of Helen Murphy?"

Liz shook her head.

"Me either."

"By the way, in case you don't remember Helen," the waitress said as she placed their bowls on the table. She leaned down and spoke discreetly. "She was a porn star during the Second World War." She winked at them.

"Oh," Liz replied with a giggle.

"No wonder I've never heard of her," Sheridan muttered.

"How's your stew?" Liz asked as she crumbled some corn bread on the top of her bowl.

"Good. But I'm so hungry and cold anything hot would be good. How's yours?"

"Okay." Liz seemed distracted.

"Don't you like it?"

"Oh yeah, it's great. I was just trying to remember if I put enough vegetables on the order so we can serve stew this week. I have to call Becca this evening when we get back to the room."

"You can call her now if you want," Sheridan offered, pulling her cell phone from her jacket pocket.

"Thank you, but I have a cell phone, too. It's just she won't answer until after class. She is taking an evening class. Marketing strategies for the independent businesswoman."

"Wow, now that sounds like a heavy class."

"You'd think so. I looked over her textbook. It sounds like one of those television infomercials for growing your small business."

"You're an independent businesswoman. Do you have any marketing strategies?" Sheridan asked jovially.

"I have one for Murphy's," she said, watching the waitresses. "They need two doors into the kitchen. I wonder how often they collide and spill trays."

"You have two doors, right?"

"Yes. The Sugar Bush didn't used to. It was just an open space between the dining room and the kitchen. It meant the customers could see and hear all the noise and mess in the kitchen. So I had a pair of swinging doors installed. It actually helped with the traffic flow in and out. Plus it makes it a little more pleasant for the diners. I hate to see a trash barrel full of wilted lettuce while I'm eating. It's the little things you do for the customer to make them feel special that keeps them coming back."

"Like what?" Sheridan asked, showing genuine interest.

"Like I use sugar bowls instead of packets. And I use cotton napkins that match the table cloths. It is a homey touch. I also use cups with saucers. Coffee mugs are okay in their place, but that isn't the ambiance I am working for."

"You sound like you have a pretty clear picture of what you want for your restaurant." Sheridan finished her stew and pushed the bowl aside. She rested her arms across the table and studied Liz's face. "Have you always been like this?"

"Been like what?" Liz asked, eating her last bite.

"Determined, focused."

Liz laughed out loud.

"No," she replied, shaking her head. "Did you win the very first game you coached?"

"As a matter of fact, yes. Twenty-one to sixteen. It was a junior high game. I had exactly five players and so did the Pearson Wildcats. We played two ten-minute halves." She chuckled at the thought. "I lost only two games that year. Both of those were when Kristi Wallace was in the hospital with the measles."

"Well, it took me a lot longer to find my stride as a restaurant owner."

"How did you come to own The Sugar Bush?"

Liz wiped her mouth and sipped her coffee as she formulated her reply. Some of the history Sheridan didn't need to know.

"After Becca came along, I needed a job so I went to work for the Sanders, Tia and Clive. They owned the café and needed someone to help run it. They didn't have any children and wanted to hire someone who could take over while they took a week off now and then. I don't think they ever took a vacation before I went to work for them. After Clive passed away, Tia tried to run it alone but she couldn't handle it all. She made me the offer to buy her out with payments to come from the restaurant's profits for ten years. It was tough for a while but I made it. Becca was fourteen when it officially became mine. She pretty much grew up in the restaurant business. Poor kid spent many a Saturday in the kitchen folding napkins and filling water glasses."

"She's a good kid," Sheridan said with a smile. "A little head-strong but you should be proud of her."

"I am. And yes, she's stubborn at times but she is a sweetie. And she's a nice looking woman, if I do say so myself."

"Yes, she is nice looking. She takes after her mother," Sheridan advised softly as she leaned in.

"Heavens, no. Becca has adorable dark sultry features," Liz said. "Fortunately she didn't inherit my blonde paleness."

"Becca is attractive but I like her mother's looks better." There was a tenderness in Sheridan's eyes as she looked over at Liz.

Liz blushed and looked away as Sheridan's words melted through her. When she looked back, Sheridan was still looking at her, her eyes capturing Liz in a warm silent moment. Liz couldn't help herself. She studied Sheridan's slow-growing smile as if it was a work of art.

"Would you like dessert, ladies?" the waitress asked as she filled their coffee cups.

"No, not for me," Sheridan said, still staring at Liz.

Liz shook her head, still captured by Sheridan's gaze and her compliment.

The waitress smiled coyly and left the ticket on the table.

"Tell me something," Sheridan started. "How did you decide to have Becca? I mean, how did you . . ."

"You mean how did I become pregnant with Becca since I don't date men?" she asked softly.

"Yeah," Sheridan replied, seemingly relieved she didn't have to ask the question herself.

"Artificial insemination." Liz looked down and fiddled with the button on her jacket. She diverted her eyes from Sheridan's inquis-itive stare. "I just knew I wanted a baby. And yes, timing wasn't wonderful but hey, you have to do what you have to do."

"Were you in a relationship at the time?"

"Yes. But it ended before Becca came along."

"She didn't want the baby?" Sheridan asked carefully, as if test-ing how much Liz wanted to share with her.

"Actually she didn't know I was pregnant."

"Does she know now, about Becca, I mean?"

"Yes," Liz replied then scanned the room as if looking for something else for them to talk about. She caught sight of a couple in a booth across the room. The young man looked like a geeky college student and the girl was hopelessly devoted to every word he spoke. "See the guy in the booth over there, the one with the short hair and button-down shirt," Liz said nodding her head in that direction.

"Yeah," Sheridan replied, taking a discreet look.

"He looks like Becca's boyfriend, Mark. He's a junior at Harvard, pre-law or so Becca says. He told me he wants to be a schoolteacher."

"Harvard," she said with a nod. "Good for him."

"He's a National Merit Scholar. Earned a full scholarship." Liz sounded like a proud parent. "He is a nice boy. Becca has known him since they were both in diapers. His father is the president of the bank in Ashton."

"How does Becca feel about your lifestyle?"

"You mean being a lesbian? I don't think she gives it much thought. It has always just been who I am. Like my blonde hair, it's just me."

Sheridan looked pleased with the answer.

"How about you?" Liz asked.

"Me?" Sheridan chuckled.

"Come on, I have told you all about me. Let's hear something about Coach Ross." Liz downed the last of her coffee and set the cup aside.

"I coach basketball." Sheridan leaned back in the booth and placed her hands in her lap. "That pretty much covers it. I've been coaching since I graduated from the Indiana University. I wanted to play some pro ball but I've got a bad knee. So I coach. You know the old saying, those who can, do. Those who can't, teach."

"That isn't all to the Sheridan Ross story. Come on. Tell me something good, something juicy. I want to hear Sheridan's secrets." Liz wiggled in her seat as if she was getting ready for some deep dark mystery to be revealed.

Sheridan studied the rim of her cup.

"Sorry to disappoint you but there isn't anything sinister in my past. No deep dark secrets to divulge, no juicy tidbits. Like I said, I coach basketball. That's all. I started at a small high school, moved up to a five-A school then to a junior college. Now I'm here." Sheridan picked up the check and put on her jacket. "Shall we head back? I bet the snow is getting pretty deep out there."

Liz studied her for a moment. She thought she saw something in Sheridan's eyes, something that made her look vulnerable. Sheridan led the way to the register, retracing the path between the tables. They stepped out into the crisp night air still filled with huge snowflakes. Several more inches had blanketed the deserted streets. The night was still and peaceful as the snow gently filled the darkness.

"I love to walk in the snow," Liz said, snuggling her jacket around her. "It's one of the things I love about New England. The winters are incredible."

"Let's walk in the street. I don't think any cars are coming." Sheridan led the way to the middle of the street. It was untouched with virgin snow. They strolled along, enjoying the quiet solitude, the snow ankle deep.

"How many relationships have you had?" Liz asked cautiously, determined to take up where she left off with her interrogation.

Sheridan shoved her hands in her jacket pockets and thought.

"Let's see," she started. "Relationships. How are we categorizing these? Live with or just dating?"

"Live with," Liz clarified.

"That's the tough one."

"That many?" Liz teased.

"No. Just the opposite."

"If it's a small number it should be easy to remember then."

Sheridan ambled along, shuffling her feet and kicking at the tufts of snow.

"Come on, Coach. Let's have it. How many? Five? Ten?" Liz

bumped her playfully.

"How about none?" Sheridan offered.

"Oh, come on. I won't tell anyone."

Sheridan stopped and looked over at her.

"None," she repeated confidently.

Liz saw a vulnerability in her she hadn't seen before, one hidden behind the stoic exterior.

"None?" she replied. "You mean you've never lived with anyone? You've never shared an apartment?"

"No," Sheridan answered and started up the street again. "And no partners, no companions, no spouses, no significant others," she added.

"How about the other category? How many have you dated?" Liz asked gently.

"Now that number is bigger," Sheridan joked. "Way bigger. Maybe twenty or twenty-five."

"Let me guess. Lunch, dinner, coffee, movie. That sort of thing."

"Yes. And ballgames, weekends at the lake, ski trips, conventions, the normal getaway stuff."

"But no one good enough to live with," Liz suggested.

"It was more like no one lasted long enough to live with," Sheridan corrected. "It was just as well. Between coaching, teaching and moving around, I'm too busy. I don't have time for a serious relationship. They are a lot of work. Dating is easier. Keeps things fresh and simple."

"You don't have to give someone a hundred percent of your time. If you love them, a hundred percent of your heart is enough."

"How about you? How many live-ins have you had?" Sheridan asked.

"Just one," Liz replied. "And before you ask, I've had maybe ten of the other kind."

"Is there a current person you are dating?" Sheridan asked curiously.

"There isn't one right now," she admitted. "How about you?

Who is Coach Sheridan Ross being seen in public with at the moment?"

Sheridan looked at Liz and smiled.

"Liz Elliott," she replied matter-of-factly.

"No, I meant who are you seeing right now?"

"Liz Elliott," she repeated with a chuckle.

"No, silly. I didn't mean right this minute. I meant who will you be asking out to dinner next weekend?"

Sheridan looked down and kicked a ball of snow.

"Liz Elliott," she replied softly, then looked over at Liz.

Her words warmed Liz more completely than a roaring fire. She was so surprised at Sheridan's remark and her tone, she couldn't reply.

"And what would Liz Elliott say if I ask her to dinner on Saturday night?" Sheridan asked, still staring at the ground.

"Liz would say yes, she'd love to go to dinner with Coach Ross."

"It isn't Coach Ross who is asking," Sheridan added gently. "It's Sheridan who is asking."

"She'd say yes to Sheridan, too." Liz looked over at her, their eyes meeting.

Sheridan stopped walking and reached out, taking Liz's arm. She gently pulled Liz to her and kissed her. It was a brief kiss, but one that sent Liz's heart to her throat and started it pounding furiously. Sheridan looked down at her and seemed as surprised as Liz at her action.

"I'm sorry," Sheridan said and started up the street with long strides.

"Hey!" Liz called. She perched her hands on her hips and stared, still standing on the spot where they kissed. "Why are you sorry?" she asked.

"That was a mistake. A big mistake. Please, just forget I ever did that." She kept walking.

"That's like telling someone not to think about elephants. It's too late. I'm already thinking about them."

"Rule number one. Coaches don't kiss players," Sheridan

144

scowled.

"But the coach didn't kiss me. Sheridan did." There was tenderness in Liz's reply that floated up and gripped Sheridan, making her stop in her tracks. She turned around and stared at Liz. Suddenly the roar of a truck and the scraping of metal on pavement rounded the corner behind Liz, catching them in its headlights. The snowplow rumbled down the street like a huge mechanical monster, gobbling up the snow and spitting out rolls of dirtied ice.

"Look out," Sheridan yelled frantically, running toward her. Liz screamed and jumped for the curb just as Sheridan grabbed her collar and pulled her on top of her. They landed in a pile of snow just inches from the metal blade as it sliced past them.

"Are you all right?" Sheridan asked, fear painting her face. "Are you hurt?"

Liz lay in the snow next to Sheridan, blinking and sputtering away the snow that covered her face.

"I'm okay," she replied. "How about you?"

"I'm fine," Sheridan insisted as she brushed the snow from her own face. "Covered with snow, but fine."

"See what you did?" Liz declared, trying to look angry. "You kissed me and then threw me in a snowbank. Shame on you. How am I supposed to know what to think? Kissed one minute, snow-covered the next."

Sheridan scowled at her.

"I was way out of line. You are one of my players. It is highly unethical for me to be doing that."

"Says who?" Liz plucked a clump of snow from Sheridan's hair.

"Says me. I have to keep a clear head. I have to remember who I am and who you are." Sheridan declared, pulling herself to her knees and brushing off the snow.

"You make it sound like I'm not good enough to kiss. Like I'm just a lowly player," Liz argued. "I'm not sure I appreciate that."

"I didn't say that and you know it. I just know from experience, coaches and players need to keep a safe distance."

"Safe distance," Liz replied as she scrambled to her knees, facing Sheridan. "What is a safe distance?"

"You know what I mean. I have to remain in a position of—" She didn't know how to finish.

"Power?" Liz asked, her eyebrow cocked.

"Authority," Sheridan corrected. "How can I be an effective coach if I let my emotions get in the way of my decisions?"

Liz grabbed Sheridan by the lapels of her jacket and gave her a full-mouthed kiss, parting her lips and allowing her tongue to explore the inside of Sheridan's mouth. Sheridan seemed to be wrestling with her dilemma. Should she responsd to Liz's soft lips or remain unyielding? When she didn't fold her arms around Liz and kiss her back, Liz leaned back and looked into her eyes.

"What are you doing?" Sheridan asked in a whisper.

"I'm taking the coach's advice. If you don't make a move, you'll never score." Liz kissed her again, this time pulling her body tightly against Sheridan. The force of her action tipped them over in the snow, Liz on top of Sheridan. This time she responded. Sheridan laced her hands through Liz's hair and orchestrated a long meaningful kiss, one full of passion and curiosity as their mouths devoured each other. Liz pulled herself against Sheridan, her leg slipping between Sheridan's legs. Sheridan wrapped her arms around Liz and rolled them over, pressing her body against Liz's lean frame. Even through their jackets, they could feel the other's breasts and hips pressing ever harder and insistently against each other. Sheridan rolled off of Liz and looked down at her, touching her face tenderly. They didn't speak for a long moment, their eyes communicating feelings beyond words.

"I hate to be a spoilsport, but I have snow in my shirt and my pants. And it is cold," Liz stated, her whole body beginning to shiver.

Sheridan climbed to her feet then pulled Liz up.

"Let's get you out of those wet clothes and into a hot bath before you get frostbite," she said.

Chapter 14

They hurried along the freshly plowed street toward the hotel. Sheridan wrapped her arm around Liz and held her against her side as they walked, rubbing Liz's side to warm her. Just as they entered the lobby, Liz's cell phone rang. It was Becca.

"I almost forgot I was going to call her," she whispered as she answered the call. "Hi, hon," she said.

"Mom, where are you? It is snowing like crazy here." Becca sounded out of breath and concerned.

"Are you all right, Becca? What's wrong?"

"I had to walk home from work. I couldn't get my car out of the parking lot, so I left it behind The Sugar Bush."

"We're in Northampton. We got stranded too. How much snow do you have in Ashton, honey?"

"About a foot. Well, maybe ten inches."

"Is everything okay at The Sugar Bush? All locked up?"

"Yes, Mom," Becca replied, then heaved an exasperated sigh. "I do know how to lock up, you know."

"I'm sorry. I know you do. There is a phone number in my address book at home under the name Pella Jones Snow Removal. Call them and remind them about plowing the parking lot tomorrow. I signed a contract with Pella so don't let her say they can't work you in. I paid extra to be on first-day call."

"But Mom, we don't need to be open tomorrow morning. No one can get to town." Becca seemed adamant that the request was ludicrous.

"Don't kid yourself, Becca. Pauline and Georgia will be there. And you will have customers, believe me. Maybe more than usual since some folks will be off work. Have plenty of coffee and cinnamon rolls ready. I'm sure Pauline will make a double batch. She knows all about snowstorm customers. They love to walk downtown in the fresh snow and they will be in to warm up in droves. Bell River will be plowed, I'm sure."

"You mean I have to walk back down there in the morning? In the snow?"

Liz chuckled and smiled to herself.

"Yes, dear, you have to walk back down there in the morning in the snow. If you call Brad down the street, maybe he will give you a ride to the restaurant since he drives one of the city plows."

Becca didn't reply but Liz could hear her exasperated gasps.

"Becca, are you there?"

"Yes, I'm here."

"I'm sorry honey, but I'm depending on you to handle things. I wish I was there to take over but I'm not. You can do it, Becca. I know you can."

"It isn't that, Mom," Becca started then hesitated as if something else was troubling her.

Liz and Sheridan had ridden the elevator to the third floor and were about to enter their room.

"What is it?" Liz asked, sensing something in her daughter's voice.

Sheridan read the concern on Liz's face.

"Is she all right?" Sheridan mouthed to Liz.

Liz nodded then shrugged.

"Becca? What is it, sweetheart?"

"There was a phone call tonight," she started.

"From who?"

"Sara," Becca said cynically.

Liz drew a short breath then froze.

"She called looking for you," Becca continued. "She said she saw you on TV today."

"What did she want?" Liz asked warily.

"She didn't say. She just wanted to talk to you."

"Did she say where she was?"

"No. And she didn't leave a number."

"If Sara calls again tell her—" Liz started but didn't have anything to add. Whatever Sara wanted, Liz wasn't interested. Even the thought of talking to her sent a shudder down Liz's spine. Sara talking to Becca was even worse.

"What do you want me to tell her if she calls again?" Becca asked.

"Nothing, Becca. Don't talk to her. Just hang up. Do you hear me?" she added harshly. "Just hang up."

"God, Mom," Becca replied tersely. "Don't have a fit about it. I didn't say anything to her. What's the big deal?"

Liz sat down on the edge of the bed and tried to regain her composure.

"I'm sorry, sweetheart. I know you can handle things. I'm sorry."

"She won't call again. I told her you were out of town."

"I wish you hadn't done that." Liz's mothering instinct engaged.

"Why?"

"No reason," Liz muttered, wishing she was home more than ever.

"I have to go, Mom," Becca interrupted. "Mark is going to call."

"I'll call you tomorrow. You take care of yourself, sweetheart." Liz hung up, a worried look on her face.

"Everything okay?" Sheridan asked, noticing Liz's concern.

149

"Yes," she said then went to the window and stared out at the snow-filled skies.

"Who is Sara?"

Liz crossed her arms and rubbed them as a cold chill shot up her body.

"Sara Ruddick," she said, her voice caustic and bitter. "She's the one."

"The one you lived with?"

Liz nodded.

"She called Becca?"

Liz nodded again. Sheridan stood next to her and joined in watching the snow.

"What happened with you and Sara?"

"We were teammates at Chilton. We moved in together our sophomore year and lived together for about a year and a half." Liz's voice trailed off as if she was in another time, another place.

"Then Becca came along?"

"Actually our relationship went sour before that. I moved out the summer after our junior year. That's when I went to work for the Sanders. Sara started her senior year but dropped out after a month. She moved away. New York City, I think. I heard she was a bouncer at a gay bar in Brooklyn. She was probably very good at that."

"You haven't seen her since she moved away?" Sheridan asked.

"Once. She showed up in Ashton when Becca was about five. She was between jobs and having a tough time. She asked for some money. I gave her fifty dollars and she disappeared again."

"Sounds like your relationship ended on difficult terms."

"Yes." Liz didn't offer any more. She shivered again, her wet clothes chilling her to the bone.

"Come on," Sheridan insisted. "Get out of those wet clothes and take a hot bath. You'll catch pneumonia if you wear those things any longer." She wrapped her arm around Liz and led her to the bathroom door.

"Yes, Coach," Liz replied with a half smile, relieved someone was there and concerned about her.

"Take all the time you want. I'll be out here if you need anything."

Liz wanted to say she needed a hug, a warm embrace to protect her and comfort her, but she knew that would require more explanation. She ran her bath and undressed, Sara's call still preying on her mind and her soul.

Sheridan had no sooner found a basketball game on television and gotten comfortable on the bed than the bathroom door burst open and Liz came rushing out, a towel wrapped around her dripping body.

"Where is my cell phone?" she asked frantically. "I've got to call Becca." She rifled through her jacket pockets looking for her telephone.

Sheridan leaped to her feet and assisted in the search.

"What's wrong? Did you forget to tell her about the order for vegetables?"

"I have to tell her not to answer the phone. I don't want her talking to Sara. There's nothing she needs from that woman." Liz's eyes flashed and her nostrils flared as she rummaged frantically through the room.

"Liz," Sheridan interrupted, taking her by the arm. "Relax. Don't get yourself all worked up about it. Becca can answer the phone without tragedy striking her."

"You don't understand," Liz replied and pulled away, returning to her search. "There it is," she declared, grabbing it from the bedside table. She fumbled with the buttons, bringing up Becca's number on her menu.

"Liz," Sheridan said calmly, closing the telephone before she could send the connection. "Give me that." She took the cell phone from her and wrapped an arm around Liz. "Whatever your problems were with Sara, don't include Becca in them. Don't call her and scare her with something from your past that she doesn't need to know tonight. I don't know what happened between you and Sara Ruddick but I do know that was twenty years ago. I also know you are a good mother. You raised Becca well and she is old enough to answer the phone or open the restaurant or anything

151

else that comes along." She looked deep into Liz's eyes. "You just have to trust her, Liz."

Liz didn't say anything. She just stared at Sheridan like a frightened child.

"She doesn't know about Sara," Liz whispered. "Becca is so young." A tear welled up in Liz's eye, ready to spill out.

"She is a woman," Sheridan replied softly. "She is old enough for you to trust her."

"It isn't about trusting her. It's about protecting her," Liz replied.

The tear spilled out and ran down Liz's face as her chin began to quiver. Sheridan gathered her in her arms and held her close. Liz wrapped her arms around her and buried her face in Sheridan's shoulder. The fear and worry about Becca and Sara diminished as she lost herself in Sheridan's strong arms.

"You have to put Sara out of your mind," Sheridan said in a soothing voice. "You can't do anything about it right now. Tonight you are just Liz Elliott, the woman. Not Liz Elliott, the mother. If the past is ugly, leave it there where it belongs—in the past."

Liz tightened her grip on Sheridan and pressed against her, blocking out the demons that threatened to consume her. Another tear ran down her face. Sheridan wiped the tears from her cheeks and smiled tenderly at her.

Liz wanted Sheridan to touch her, to caress her. She wanted to feel Sheridan's body against hers. She wanted Sheridan to make love to her, possess her. It was more than want, it was a need. Liz looked longingly into Sheridan's eyes. She didn't have to say another word. Sheridan understood Liz's need as well as her own. She held Liz's face in her hands and kissed her. Sheridan then picked her up and carried her to the bed. She reached up and turned off the light then stretched out next to her.

"For tonight, forget the past. Forget anything that hurt you. I am here with you to protect you. No one can hurt you," Sheridan whispered, stroking Liz's face. "I'm here for you, Liz." With gentle kisses and kind hands, Sheridan removed Liz's towel and pulled her body close. Liz closed her eyes and surrendered to Sheridan's reassuring touch. Liz turned her lips to Sheridan's and kissed her.

Sheridan traced tender kisses down Liz's body as her hands caressed her firm round breasts. Liz's nipples quickly hardened as Sheridan's tongue flicked and licked at them. Liz moaned softly as Sheridan's hand slid down her abdomen, her fingers parting Liz's patch of light hair. Liz arched her back and strained for more of Sheridan's touch. When she could wait no longer, she reached down and pressed Sheridan's hand firmly against her pubic bone, groaning as a shiver shot up her body. Sheridan slipped two fingers down her valley and massaged the growing nub. Sheridan's other hand held her breast, her thumb and index finger gently stroking Liz's nipple.

"Sheridan," she gasped. "I need you to touch me."

Sheridan allowed her hand to curl around Liz's moist valley and enter her. With careful strokes, she moved in and out, feeling Liz's tightening chamber. Liz bit down on her lip as her body heaved upward toward Sheridan's touch. Liz felt Sheridan's breath warm against her neck, her tender touch reminding her how special intimacy could be. As if they had known each other for years, Sheridan seemed to know all the right things to say and do to bring Liz to her peak in persistent and growing waves. Liz's breath grew rapid. She threw her head back as she climaxed, the ecstasy of it like a thousand explosions of light and thunder crashing through her body. She shuddered and fell back exhausted, her skin glistening with sweat. Sheridan looked down at her then gathered her in her arms. They lay together in the darkness, feeling each other's hearts beat and silently watching the snow fall outside the window.

Sheridan pulled the covers over Liz and kissed her then went to take a shower. Liz watched her as she slipped out of her slacks and sweater and hung them across the chair. She drew a long breath and smiled over at Liz.

"What is it, Sheridan?" Liz asked softly. "Is something wrong?"

"No," she replied. "There's nothing wrong." She went into the bathroom. Liz could hear the shower running. She went to the bathroom door and listened for a minute then slipped inside. She pulled back the shower curtain and stepped in with Sheridan, her body covered with soap and shampoo.

"Are you sure you're all right?" Liz asked, her hands touching Sheridan's back.

"I didn't hear you come in," Sheridan gasped, fighting the urge to cover herself.

"Turn around. I'll wash your back," Liz said softly.

Sheridan hesitated for a minute then turned around. Liz soaped and massaged Sheridan's back with slow, soothing strokes. Her hands moved over Sheridan's back and down her bottom while she stepped closer and kissed the back of Sheridan's neck. Sheridan stiffened at first, her muscles flexed under Liz's wandering touch.

"Relax," Liz whispered, her hands flowing around to the front, wrapping Sheridan in her arms. "Relax and enjoy it," she added, her mouth slithering down Sheridan's back, her tongue tracing a line down her spine.

Sheridan closed her eyes and breathed deeply, her body already tingling at Liz's touch. The warm water flowed over them as Liz slowly and methodically washed Sheridan's body, caressing and stroking her lean legs and long arms. She turned Sheridan around and carefully washed her neck, her chest and her abdomen. She moved over her small but perfectly shaped breasts applying soap in gentle circles. Sheridan's dark nipples began to harden as Liz caressed each one with painstaking detail to every inch of her glistening skin. She applied soap to Sheridan's stomach and her patch of dark, curly hair then carefully pulled herself against her, using her own body to massage Sheridan, wrapping her arms around her. Liz kissed her passionately. Sheridan pulled Liz close, devouring her mouth and tongue hungrily. Whatever reservations she had about Liz touching her or making love to her rapidly disappeared like the soap flowing down the drain. It no longer mattered that Liz was a player and she was the coach. Sheridan pulled Liz under the water with her and continued kissing her as they both rinsed. She cupped her hands over Liz's bottom and pulled her tightly to her, feeling her pubic bone rub against her own. Liz's nails skated down Sheridan's thighs then back up again. She reached around and turned off the water.

"Let me touch you," Liz whispered. She gently parted Sheridan's legs, propping one of her feet on the side of the tub. Sheridan leaned back against the tile, her eyes closed as Liz's fingers found her clit. Liz then traced her tongue down to the top of her moistening valley. Sheridan moaned and grabbed the shower head as Liz took her clit in her mouth. Liz cupped her hands around Sheridan's hips, her nails digging into her bottom as she aroused Sheridan with soft flicks and daring jabs.

"Don't stop," Sheridan gasped, guiding Liz's head with her hand. "Yes, right there. Don't stop, baby."

Liz increased the pace of her rhythmic strokes as Sheridan stiffened. Liz could sense her peak nearing as Sheridan's breaths shortened. With forceful sucks and rapid flicks, Liz guided Sheridan to the pinnacle of pleasure. Sheridan gasped as her body shook, her muscles straining. Liz could feel the swollen nub pulsing against her tongue. She continued her pace as the orgasm intensified. Sheridan grabbed the shower head with both hands as her body gave a great shudder.

"Oh, my God!" she groaned.

Liz held her throbbing spur in her mouth, feeling its hot palpitations. Sheridan slowly relaxed her taut muscles as the climax subsided. They dried off and slipped into bed, warm and comfortable in each other's arms. Neither one had slept in someone's embrace in a long time. A very long time. Liz had found the tender, caring woman of her dreams. She could no longer deny her feelings for Sheridan, even if she was her coach. They both slept serenely in their winter wonderland, if only for the night.

Chapter 15

Liz slept soundly, something she hadn't done in months. Her own natural alarm clock didn't wake her just after five o'clock like it had been doing since Becca was a baby and demanded two feedings a night. The warmth of Sheridan's body next to hers had been a security blanket against the nightmares she had been fighting for years. She stretched and yawned then pulled the blanket around her shoulders. The bedside clock radio read seven forty. She hadn't slept this late since she had the flu two years ago. The drapes were open enough to see the sun trying to shine through the snow-covered window.

"I wonder how much snow we got," she said softly. When no one answered, she turned over, expecting to see Sheridan sleeping next to her. But she wasn't there. Liz instantly sat up. "Sheridan?" she called. Again no one answered. Her clothes were gone and so was her jacket. Liz rushed to the bathroom, hoping to find her combing her hair. "Where are you?" she muttered. Could

Sheridan have been so traumatized by Liz's insistence they make love that she left? Was she walking the halls, so disillusioned with Liz's request and her bathroom antics she couldn't face her? Liz's mind was doing gymnastics over the possibilities.

She went to the window and peeked out. The world seemed colorless. Everything was white except the spikes of black where the light poles stood in the parking lot. She stood naked, watching a hawk circle overhead. Suddenly the door opened and Sheridan stepped in carrying two cups. She closed the door with her foot and smiled broadly.

"Coffee?" she asked, holding them up. "I thought I could get back before you woke up."

"That was sweet of you. Thank you. I could use some hot coffee," Liz replied. A feeling of relief flowed over her at Sheridan's smiling face. She climbed back into bed and pulled the covers up under her armpits.

"I don't know how hot it is," Sheridan said as she handed Liz one, then sat next to her on the bed. They sipped, then both grimaced at the strong tasting stuff.

"Wow," Liz declared. "They need to clean the filter basket in the coffee machine."

"They need to change the oil too. Yuk!"

"Professional coffeemakers have screens that need to be cleaned or they get really nasty. We clean ours every day."

"This tastes like it hasn't been cleaned in a year," Sheridan announced, holding up her cup.

"How much snow did we get? Any idea?"

"Officially nine inches here. But there are some drifts reported as high as eight feet. I haven't heard how much Ashton got."

"It looks pretty nasty out there," Liz said, pointing to the window.

"Actually it isn't too bad. We might get out of here in a couple hours. The highways are plowed and open. As soon as they finish the side streets from here to the interstate we can leave. I saw the plows working down the street. I borrowed a broom from housekeeping and cleaned off the car while you were sleeping." Sheridan took another sip then set the cup aside. "How did you sleep?"

"Wonderful." Liz sat up and wrapped her arms around her knees, snuggling against the blanket. "How about you?"

"I slept well," she replied, smiling softly.

"Good." Liz placed her chin on her knees and smiled back.

"Would you like to come down to breakfast with me?" Sheridan asked, seemingly uncomfortable with Liz's stare.

"Yes, I'm famished," Liz declared and threw back the covers. "Give me five minutes."

"You only need five minutes to get dressed and washed? Wow!" Sheridan teased.

"I'm a basketball player. We girls know how to dress in a hurry. Locker rooms get pretty hectic." She patted Sheridan's arm then grabbed her clothes and headed for the bathroom.

When she was out of sight, Sheridan reached down and turned Liz's cell phone back on. If only for a few hours, she wanted Liz to have a peaceful night's sleep. She knew Becca could reach her through the hotel operator if it was an emergency.

True to her word, Liz was washed, dressed and fresh in five minutes flat. They went down to the lobby and joined the crowd of hotel guests eating breakfast, all anxious to know how long they would be stranded and how much snow they would have to fight through as they continued their journey. Since no one could get out of the parking lot, everyone lingered over the strong coffee and chewy bagels. The hotel opened the pool and the fitness rooms so guests had something to do while they waited. Sheridan and Liz joined two older women in a game of gin rummy, one that they both lost lopsidedly. They walked around the building, their nerves growing thin as the hours ticked away. They sat together on the sofa in the lobby and read the newspapers from three cities as well as several out-of-date magazines.

"Look at this," Liz said, showing Sheridan a magazine ad.

Sheridan chuckled to herself. It was a Victoria's Secret ad for push-up bras.

"Nice color," she announced.

"Not that, silly," Liz smirked. "The little ad in the corner. Victoria's Secret is now offering sports bras through their Web site."

"Oh," Sheridan replied and went back to her newspaper. "I like the red one with spaghetti straps better," she muttered.

"Can you see me wearing something like that under my jersey? I'd set a pick and a strap would pop." Liz giggled. "Maybe that would be a good thing. It would distract the other team long enough for me to get in the open for a three-pointer." Liz made a pretend shot. "Whatever it takes to win, right Coach?"

"I don't think so," Sheridan declared without looking up.

The sound of cheering rose from the front door where several of the guests were watching a snowplow finish the last swipe across the parking lot and out into the street.

"The street is open, finally," a woman said as she turned on her heels and hurried down the hall to her room.

"Thank goodness," Liz agreed, tossing the magazine on the table and heading for the parking lot.

They had already checked out and were ready for a quick departure. The hotel management had provided a snack in the breakfast room but it sat untouched as the hotel guests wasted no time in leaving. Sheridan followed the stream of traffic that snaked its way to I-91. The highway had been plowed down to bare pavement, leaving huge banks of snow along the sides of the road. The closer they got to Vermont the deeper the snowfall. Ashton had enough accumulation to reduce traffic through town to a few four-wheel drives and some trucks. The city plows were busy clearing the main streets and roads before moving on the side streets. As Liz had predicted, her street had been cleared and was nearly dry. Brad must have done it twice. There was a deep ridge of snow piled in front of her driveway that needed to be shoveled. Sheridan waited while Liz changed her clothes then gave her a ride to The Sugar Bush.

"Thanks for the ride," Liz said, looking in the open passenger's door.

"Call me later when you and Becca need a ride home," Sheridan suggested. "I'll have my cell phone on."

159

"That's okay. We'll manage."

"Don't be silly. It's cold outside and slick. I don't want my point guard twisting an ankle or catching cold. Call me," she demanded. She took a pen from the door pocket and wrote her number on a paper napkin then handed it to Liz.

"Thank you." Liz smiled to herself as Sheridan pulled away. It had been a long time since anyone took such an interest in her well-being, even if it was for team reasons.

Becca had opened the restaurant on time and had handled the walk-ins like a pro. The parking lot was plowed, the vegetables were washed and in the refrigerator and the waitresses were hustling orders to the tables as they neared the three o'clock closing time.

"Hi, honey," Liz said, hugging Becca and waving to the kitchen help. "It looks like you did a super job, sweetheart. Thank you."

"You were right," Becca declared as she carried a tray of glasses to the dishwasher. "We've been swamped all day. We've sold six dozen cinnamon rolls and nine dozen biscuits. We used four crates of eggs before ten o'clock. Can you believe it, four crates?" Becca sounded excited and exhausted at the same time. Liz watched her and grinned, pleasantly surprised at how energized she seemed with her work. "And Mom, do you know how many hot chocolates we served?"

"How many, sweetheart?" she asked with a grin.

"Well, I don't know exactly but I bet it was at least fifty. Everybody wanted to sit in the window booths, watch the snow and drink hot chocolate." She smirked and shook her head. "People need to get a life," she muttered.

"Hey, I remember someone sitting in a window booth sipping hot chocolate just last week." Liz pinched Becca's cheek. "And it wasn't even snowing."

"That was different," Becca argued. "I was doing homework."

"Oh, I see." Liz laughed and checked the invoices. "Becca?"

"Yeah," she replied, changing the rack in the dishwasher.

"Did Sara call again?" Liz hated to ask but she had to know how serious Sara was in getting in touch with her.

"Nope, no one called. Except Mark," Becca replied then grinned.

"Good. How's Mark?" she asked, relieved at the news.

"He's fine. He got an A on his psych test. I helped him study for it."

"That's great sweetheart. Tell him I'm proud of him." Liz lost herself in work. Long after the last customer left and the doors were locked she continued to pore over her computer, entering invoices and receipts, placing orders and paying bills. Becca and the rest of the after-hours crew finished the cleanup. It had been a long day for the nineteen-year-old but she seemed proud of her accomplishment. It was the first time she had opened and closed The Sugar Bush on her own, even if mom was sitting in her office a few feet away.

"Becca," Liz called from her desk.

"Yeah," she replied, stacking the last empty milk crate outside the kitchen door. She walked into Liz's office, wiping her hands on the towel draped over her shoulder.

Liz stood up and gave Becca a big hug.

"I am very proud of you, sweetheart. I didn't interfere this afternoon. I let you finish up on your own. And you did a wonderful job. I'm not sure I could have done better."

"I told you I could do it," she replied, leaning on the doorjamb.

"You look tired, baby." Liz pulled a lock of hair from Becca's face and nestled it behind her ear. "Can I fix you something special to eat? Or would you like me to take you out for pizza? Whatever you want."

"Actually, if you can lock up, I was going to leave in a few minutes. Deb and Mellyn and I are going over to Trish's. We're going to shoot some pool and cram for a lit quiz tomorrow. Shakespeare is way overrated. We'll probably just crash in her basement. She's got two sets of bunk beds down there. We may go out for pizza later."

"Aren't you tired?"

"Naw. I'm okay. Deb is coming to pick me up in a few minutes. She has her dad's Jeep. My car's in the alley. Can you take it home for me? Trish said her street hasn't been plowed yet." She handed Liz her keys.

"Have a good time. And be careful. It's slick in spots," Liz warned in her usual mothering tone.

Liz finished her work just after sunset and headed home in Becca's car, an older sedan with poor suspension, one mismatched door with a window that didn't go down and in desperate need of a paint job. It wasn't fancy but it got her where she wanted to go, at least around town. Becca didn't seem embarrassed by it. To the contrary she considered it a statement, a symbol of her individuality and a triumph of mechanical determination.

Liz pulled up in front of her house, glad to finally be home. It had been a long thirty-six hours, both emotionally and physically. She spent thirty minutes working on the driveway then climbed into a hot bath to ease her stiff muscles. She would finish shoveling tomorrow. She closed her eyes and sank back in the tub, the thought of Sheridan's naked body standing in the shower a pleasing memory as she soaked. She slept well, hugging her pillow as sweet dreams of Sheridan washed over her. She woke the next morning refreshed. She went for an early run. It was as much to linger in the pleasant memories of their night together as it was for the exercise.

Liz was in the middle of pouring cake batter into a huge rectangular pan when the swinging door opened and a bouquet of flowers came through it, Becca's hands holding it up in front of her face.

"Flowers for Liz Elliott," Becca announced then peeked around from behind the large crystal vase. She grinned broadly at her mother and set them on the counter.

"For me? You're kidding," Liz said, trying to keep from spilling the cake batter as she stared wide-eyed at the huge bouquet of gold mums and white daisies.

"Here's the card," Becca said, plucking it from the midst of the blooms and handing it to Liz.

"I have no idea who is sending me flowers," she said, furrowing her brow.

"Maybe they're from Ernie for that bad batch of tomatoes he delivered," Pauline joked.

"They were addressed to the house but Wilma Gentry said she knew you wouldn't be home so she delivered them here," Becca reported.

"Open the card," Liz said, her hands to busy to do it herself.

Becca opened the tiny envelope and read the card. A coy smile lit her face as she turned it around for Liz to read.

"Yes, it was a lovely snow. From Sheridan," Liz read then blushed as everyone in the kitchen looked on, smiling at her fondly.

"Nice," Pauline said with a giggle then went back to the grill.

Liz took the card and reread it, smiling at each word.

"Where do you want me to put them?" Becca asked, filling the vase with water. "There's no room in here."

"I don't know. How about on the pastry counter in the dining room? Wait."

Liz took a long, lingering whiff from one of the huge mums. Becca winked at her mother as she carried them back into the dining room. Liz finished pouring the cake batter, slipped it into the oven and washed her hands. She then went into the dining room to admire the flowers and reread the card for the third time. She grinned happily as she turned the vase to get the best view then adjusted the stems a bit. She fawned over them for several minutes, humming to herself at Sheridan's generosity and her sentiment. Sheridan had put a broad smile on her face that she knew would be there all day. The employees winked at each other and snickered at Liz's cheerful mood and the twinkle in her eyes. It was obvious to even the newest employee that Liz was smitten with Sheridan. She wouldn't admit it but she never looked happier. Twice she slipped away to her office to call Sheridan to thank her for the flowers but both times she was called back to handle restaurant business before reaching her.

Just after four o'clock, the last of her employees left the restaurant and she locked the door behind them. She went into her office and dialed Sheridan's number.

163

"Coach Ross here," Sheridan said brightly.

"Hello, flower lady," Liz replied.

Sheridan chuckled. "So you got them."

"Yes, thank you. They are gorgeous. I've never seen mums so big. It was very nice of you."

"Are you home already?" Sheridan asked.

"No, I'm here at The Sugar Bush. The lady from the flower shop brought them here."

"Oops! Was that a problem? I told her your home address."

"No problem. Wilma knows me. She delivers flowers here all the time when the Chamber of Commerce or Rotarians are having luncheons."

"I didn't want to create a situation for you at work," Sheridan said.

"It wouldn't take very long for the news of a flower delivery to reach downtown anyway. That just goes along with small-town living. But I don't care. I love the flowers and I wanted to show them off. I have them proudly displayed on the pastry counter."

"I'm glad you like them. I wanted you to know how much I enjoyed our trip to Northampton." There was a velvety softness in Sheridan's voice. "Did you have a good time, in spite of the snow-storm?"

"I had a wonderful time—*because* of the snowstorm," Liz replied.

"I wish I didn't have a faculty meeting tonight."

"Lucky faculty," Liz replied, leaning her head into the receiver and closing her eyes, remembering the way Sheridan had touched her skin and kissed her lips.

"Lucky me," Sheridan added. "I get to see you tomorrow at four o'clock."

"That's basketball practice, silly." Liz snickered.

"I know, but it will be brighter with you there," Sheridan replied.

"I've don't think I've ever gotten flowers from my coach before."

"You still haven't. Coach Ross didn't send them," she said in a sultry voice.

There was a silence neither one filled.

"I have to go, Liz. I'll see you at practice."

"Tomorrow," Liz replied and hung up, a contented smile on her face. She couldn't help it. As much as she knew Sheridan was her coach, she felt them crossing to the other side of a relationship and there was nothing she could do about it. It was a warm, comfortable place she hadn't experienced in years and she wanted to protect it.

Chapter 16

"Anyone who wants to sign Coach Ross's birthday card come see me after practice," Robin said as she crossed the locker room.

"When is her birthday?" Liz asked.

"Today."

"I didn't know that. Why didn't she say something?" Liz frowned at the thought Sheridan's birthday might have gone by unnoticed.

"She didn't even tell me. I found out about it accidentally." Robin replied. "I saw the birthday card her mother sent."

"Forty-two, right?" Liz suggested.

"Forty-three," she whispered. "Come on, ladies. Let's hit the floor. We've got a lot to cover today." Robin held the door as the players filed out.

The practice was long and grueling with extra work on the plays that had failed them in last week's game. Sheridan squatted on the sidelines, watching intently as the players executed their moves and countermoves. She heaved a disgusted gasp and blew her whistle after Deb missed an easy shot.

"There are three things I can't accept. Missed layups are number one," she yelled and walked onto the floor. "Number two is giving the opponent a second-chance shot. Number three is turning the ball over when the game is on the line. And you, ladies, have done all three today. Congratulations." She stood at mid-court and scowled. "Let's try to think out there. Our season is in trouble. It's practically on a respirator. We need to do a little triage here. You all know what triage is, I assume. It's all over television. That's when you decide what needs to be done first to save the patient. And ladies, this team needs some saving. We're going to run two plays, one right after the other. Liz, run blue cross and come right back with gold cross. I want to keep running them until I tell you to stop." She clapped her hands and stepped off the court then blew her whistle to start the action. For twenty minutes they ran the plays, switching players occasionally so the defense and offense could both practice. Sheridan and Robin moved up and down the court with the players, pointing and challenging them to execute better. Liz remained point guard, yelling at her teammates and directing their breaks. Sheridan signaled her to change the play to see if everyone was paying attention. When Jen didn't react to the new play, Liz pointed at her and repeated her hand sign. By the end of practice they were proficient in at least two plays or at least they hoped they were.

"You've got two days to get yourselves mentally ready for our game against Amherst. The gym will be closed tomorrow for some work on the floor. I want to see you in the weight room for at least an hour tomorrow." Sheridan collected her papers and clipboard. "We'll leave for Amherst at ten thirty. That's a.m., ladies. Be on time and be ready." Sheridan looked over at Liz. "I just heard their point guard sprained her ankle. They moved one of their six-foot seniors into that spot. She'll be trying to shoot the lights out on you so be ready. And Deb, remember Amherst has a six-ten center and she weighs about two-fifty. She's not going to just stand there

167

and let you take that turnaround jumper. You'll have to lean on her." Sheridan finished her list of notes then released the players to take a shower.

"Is it true, Coach?" Jen asked. "Is it your birthday?"

"Yeah, Coach," Deb added. "Is it?"

Sheridan frowned at Robin.

"Rumor. Just a nasty rumor," she replied and went back to her clipboard.

"Come on, Coach," Liz teased. "You can admit it to us. We're your best buddies." She laughed devilishly.

"Yeah," the other players added, goading Sheridan into an admission.

"Okay," she agreed finally. "I admit it. Now can we forget it and move on?"

Liz cleared her throat loudly.

"Happy birthday to you," she began to sing.

"Happy birthday to you," the others joined in boisterously.

"Happy birthday Coach Ross, happy birthday to you." Everyone held the last note long, loud and off-key.

"Thank you," Sheridan said through a broad grin, her face bright red. "It's a good thing we don't have to sing against our opponents."

Everyone laughed and hooted.

"All right, catch a shower, ladies. Practice is over."

Deb, Jen, Miriam and several others went into a huddle, whispering something sinister then meandered toward the locker room. Liz, Robin and Jasmine followed. Sheridan brought up the rear, jotting something on her clipboard. When Sheridan entered the locker room she was ambushed by a group of players.

"Hey, what's going on here," she scowled as they descended upon her and swept her off her feet, one on each arm and leg and two supporting her middle.

"We decided you need a birthday shower, Coach," Deb declared.

"Put me down right now," Sheridan yelled, struggling to free herself. One of the girls ran ahead and turned on all the shower heads, pointing them toward the center of the common shower. Robin laughed and applauded as Sheridan was carried through the doorway. She grabbed onto the doorjamb with both hands, struggling to prevent the dousing.

"Wait a minute," Liz called and rushed to Sheridan's side. "You can't do that," she said sternly, then smiled at the coach. She removed Sheridan's watch and stepped back. "Okay, now go." She cheered and applauded as Sheridan was dragged through the door, her tall stature and firm grip no match for the players' strength of conviction.

"Put me down, you goons," Sheridan scoffed, realizing she didn't stand much of a chance. "This is insubordination. It's mutiny."

All the players and coaches crowded into the shower room and cheered as she was placed in the shower. Two of the players sacrificed themselves to hold her under the water until she was completely drenched, her hair matted to her head and her clothes soaked. She came out from under the shower heads spitting a slow arching fountain of water. She shook her hair like a wet dog, sprinkling everyone in the room.

"Next practice, look out. You'll be running wind sprints for two hours," she grumbled, trying to act mad.

"No hard feelings, Coach?" Deb said, grinning and offering a handshake.

"No hard feelings," she said, accepting her hand then pulling her under the shower as well. This brought on a fresh round of cheers and laughter.

Liz tossed Sheridan a towel, staying back out of her reach.

"Happy birthday," she teased.

"I'm trading you for a draft choice to be named later and a junior high school reject." Sheridan wiped her face and fluffed her hair.

Liz laughed at her. The other players went about showering and dressing, occasionally teasing Sheridan about her age, wet clothes and being no match for their strength. Liz showered and pulled on her slacks and sweater.

"Do you have something dry to wear home?" she asked.

"I think there are some old warm-up pants and shirts in the store room," Sheridan replied, blow drying her hair.

"It serves you right for not telling me your birthday was coming up." Liz flopped her towel at her then tossed it in the bin.

"Birthdays are no big deal. They're just like a cold. I get one every year." Sheridan pulled her wet and clinging clothes away from her body then headed for her office. She took two more towels from the rack on her way out. Liz followed her out of the locker room.

"Don't you have a birthday dinner or party or something planned?"

"NO!" she frowned. "The less said about it, the better."

"Sheridan Ross, you big phony. Everyone enjoys celebrating their birthday, even if it's just a candle in a cupcake."

"I have work to do," she grumbled, trying to ignore her.

Liz laughed at her and stuck out her tongue then headed for the parking lot. As she reached for the door handle she suddenly remembered Sheridan's watch. She tossed her bag in the car and trotted back in the gymnasium. By the time she got into the locker room it was empty. She unlocked her locker and retrieved the watch from the top shelf. She knocked on Sheridan's door then stuck her head inside. Sheridan was just hanging up the telephone and waved her in.

"That was Middlebury Junior College. I just traded you. I'll teach you to assist in a mutiny." Sheridan frowned, then smiled a cockeyed grin.

"Oh stop," Liz said, closing the door. "You know you'd never trade me. How else would you get all this attention if you didn't have an over-the-hill woman on your team?"

"I'd much rather get attention for a winning season." Sheridan shivered deeply, her wet clothes chilling her.

"You need to change out of those wet clothes."

"I sent Robin to check the storeroom and see if there is anything I could use," Sheridan said as her telephone rang. "One second," she added then answered it. "Coach Ross here," she said in a business tone.

Liz stood next to her desk, diverting her eyes as Sheridan discussed hotel reservations for an upcoming road trip. As her eyes wandered across the room and down to the desk, she caught sight of a typed letter with a University of Kansas logo on the letterhead. She didn't want to be nosy but the words interview and coaching veritably jumped off the page. Could what she overheard Sheridan and her father talking about in the parking lot be true? Could she really be actively searching for another coaching position? The University of Kansas was a Division I school. It was a huge step up from Chilton College, both in size and in distance. Liz told herself Sheridan deserved it, after all she was definitely good enough to coach a Division I school, or at least she had the potential to be that good if she had a Big Twelve team to coach.

"Sorry," Sheridan said, hanging up. "Comfort Inn in Buffalo only had six rooms. I had to change our reservations."

"I could always share a room with you," Liz said then winked.

"Oh, no, you couldn't and you know why too." Sheridan stood up and went to the file cabinet. "I don't need the kind of trouble that would cause."

"What's the matter, Coach? Are you afraid of rumors?" Liz continued teasing her. "What's that? Do I see a blush?" Liz pointed and snickered at her.

"Don't you have a restaurant to run or a kid to potty train?" Sheridan replied, trying to hide her blush.

"Actually, I came back to return your watch," Liz said, handing it to her.

"I guess I should be thankful you at least rescued that."

"What are your plans for tonight? How about letting me cook you a birthday dinner?" Liz asked, leaning against the desk with her arms crossed.

"I don't need a candle in a cupcake, thank you."

"If I promise not to put a candle in a cupcake, can I make you dinner? I hate to see anyone spend their birthday alone."

Sheridan leaned back in her chair and looked up at Liz.

"No candle?" she asked sternly.

"Scout's honor," Liz replied, crossing her heart and holding up her hand as a pledge.

"Can you give me an hour to finish up here? I have some e-mails to send and a couple of calls to make."

Liz checked her watch.

"Let's say eight-thirty. Is that okay with you?" Liz asked, making a mental list of what she needed for the dinner.

"Where?"

"Sugar Bush," Liz said. "I don't cook much at home. The pantry at the restaurant is much better stocked than mine."

"Eight thirty at The Sugar Bush," Sheridan declared, reaching for the telephone as it rang again.

"Come to the back door off the parking lot," Liz said as she turned to leave Sheridan to her business. Sheridan nodded.

Liz hurried to her car and took a pad from the glove box to make a list. Within a minute she had created a menu, shopping list and food preparation schedule for a full three-course dinner. It had been a long time since she had cooked an elaborate meal for just two. Becca never had time to sit long enough for a big dinner. The idea of cooking for Sheridan brought a smile to her face as she pulled out of the parking lot and headed for the grocery store. There were no wasted steps as she sailed down the aisles and selected the perfect ingredients for the birthday dinner. As she hurried up to the checkout, she passed the bakery counter. A tray of chocolate frosted cupcakes caught her eye. She knew she had promised she wouldn't but she couldn't resist. She bought two cupcakes and one small yellow candle.

"Would you like sprinkles and if so, what color?" the woman behind the counter asked.

"Do you have gold? You know, for the Chilton Stingers."

"Yes. It's one of our most popular colors." The woman made tiny gold stripes of sprinkles across the chocolate frosting.

Liz checked out and sped across town to The Sugar Bush to set her dinner in motion. Spinach and walnut salad, filet mignon with mushrooms and grilled vegetables, rice pilaf with orzo and fresh parsley and cupcakes for dessert. Twice she had to remind herself she was cooking for just two, not forty. She didn't need the three-gallon bowl to mix the salad. And she didn't need to make a quart of her special blue cheese and dill salad dressing. She set the bottle of wine Sheridan had given her for Thanksgiving out on the counter to come to drinking temperature. She set the table in one of the secluded corner booths. She placed a candle on the table and dimmed the lights to a soft glow. When she saw the lights from Sheridan's car pull into the parking lot she started the rice and spread the vegetables on the grill.

"Hi," Liz said, opening the back door for her. "I see you found some dry clothes." She looked Sheridan up and down.

"I'll have you know I had to ride home in my wet clothes. Robin couldn't find anything for me to wear. You had your chance to save me, but *nooooooo*."

"Come on in and hush. You know you enjoyed it. The girls had a good time and so did you."

Sheridan looked around at the mess in the kitchen.

"I didn't mean for you to go to so much trouble," she said, frowning at the sink full of dishes.

"No trouble. This kitchen is very efficient and easy to use. It cleans up well, too." She turned the vegetables on the grill. With a spatula here and a spoon there, Liz looked like an orchestra director creating something magical.

"Can I help?" Sheridan asked, not sure what she should do.

"Yes. Could you stir the rice a minute?" She pointed to the pan and handed her the wooden spoon. "Gently but scrape the bottom."

"I didn't know there was a special technique for stirring rice," she said as she did her job.

"I hope you like rice pilaf."

"I eat about anything. When you don't cook you have to adapt."

"What do you mean you don't cook?" Liz looked at her accusingly.

"I don't eat ravioli out of a can, if that's what you think. But I'm so busy I seldom have time to do all this at my apartment. Don't laugh, but I eat out a lot. It is just easier."

"I'm not laughing," Liz replied. "I live off people who eat out. I understand busy. Believe me, I understand. Sometimes all I have time for is to grab a bite as I fly through here. Pauline and Georgia are the real cooks."

"Well, at least it smells good, whatever it is."

"So you live in an apartment?"

"Duplex over on McDougal. It is great. All the comforts of a house and none of the yard work. Duplexes are great. Easy in, easy out." Sheridan studied the rice. "I think this might be done."

"You can turn it off and set the lid on it."

"Anything else?" Sheridan asked, watching as Liz turned the steaks.

"How about opening the wine," she suggested, pointing to the bottle on the counter.

"Opener?"

Liz pointed to the utensil rack hanging on the wall as she carried the salads into the dining room and lit the candle on the table. Sheridan worked the obstinate cork out of the bottle as Liz prepared the plates and took them to the table. Liz wiped her hands on her apron then removed it and tossed it on the counter.

"Dinner is served, birthday girl." Liz took Sheridan by the hand and led her through the swinging doors to the dining room.

"Wow, you certainly went to a lot of work." Sheridan smiled broadly at the cozy table for two. She slid into the booth and poured the wine as Liz took her place across from her. "This looks wonderful. Thank you," Sheridan said, holding up her glass. "Here's to The Sugar Bush and its owner." She smiled fondly at Liz.

"Here's to Coach Sheridan Ross. She may be forty-three but she looks only twenty-three." Liz smiled back and clinked her glass against Sheridan's. They sipped the wine, their eyes swimming together. They ate slowly, enjoying every bite and every moment together. Just after nine, a gentle snow began to fall, turning the street into a frosted fairyland.

"Isn't that beautiful?" Liz said, noticing the lacy flakes covering the pavement.

"Almost as beautiful out there as it is in here," Sheridan said softly, her eyes never leaving Liz.

"Thank you," she whispered.

Sheridan refilled their wineglasses but kept her eyes on Liz. If she was flirting with her, she was doing a wonderful job of it, Liz thought.

"You sit. I'll be right back." Liz jumped up and carried their plates to the kitchen. She took the cupcakes out of the pastry box and placed them on plates with doilies for decorations. She lit the birthday candle and carried the plates into the dining room singing Happy Birthday. Sheridan threw her head back and laughed robustly at the cupcakes, pointing at Liz with a sly grin.

"You promised," she chuckled.

"I know, but I couldn't resist." Liz placed them on the table and slid in. "Make a wish, Coach."

Sheridan closed her eyes then opened them and blew out the candle.

"By the way, I'm not a coach tonight," she whispered, wiping her finger across the frosting then licking it.

Liz stared deep into her eyes, a serenity flowing over her. Before she could reply, her mind's eye remembered the letter she had seen on Sheridan's desk. Her curiosity was too strong to ignore.

"Sheridan, I have to ask you something. I hope you don't think I am prying into your business or snooping but I noticed something on your desk."

"What was that?" she asked, leaning in with a smile.

"It looked like a letter from the University of Kansas."

Sheridan's face seemed to melt a little, the twinkle disappearing from her eyes.

"Oh, that," she said dispassionately. "It's nothing."

"I just wondered if you were interviewing for a coaching job out there." Liz hated the way that sounded. She knew she was stepping out of bounds by asking.

Sheridan took a sip of wine as she considered her response.

"For a coach, interviews are just part of the job. Whether you are high school, college or pro, there are always job offers out there. Someone always wants to replace a coach. It's like getting junk mail. I receive stuff all the time." She offered a small reassuring smile. "Some of them sound pretty interesting though."

"I'm sorry for asking. It was none of my business." Liz nibbled at her cupcake.

"That's okay." Sheridan went to work on her cupcake, peeling back the paper and devouring it in three bites.

"Lean over here," Liz teased, wiping the dot of frosting from Sheridan's chin then licking it from her finger. "See! You survived a birthday party," Liz advised fondly.

"Barely," Sheridan quipped, taking a deep satisfying breath. "I must say, I am full as a tick. You are a good cook."

"Will you let me cook for you again sometime?" Liz said over the rim of her wineglass.

Sheridan leaned forward and pulled Liz's hand to her. She gave a sultry look then sipped from Liz's glass.

"Anytime you feel the need to cook for someone, let it be me." Sheridan's words were full of innuendo.

"Should I get a new cookbook or was this all right with you?" Liz said suggestively.

Sheridan took the wineglass from her hand and set it down then kissed Liz's palm.

"You don't need a new cookbook. Experimentation is the best teacher." Sheridan had formed her knees around one of Liz's and was holding her in her grasp. Nothing she was doing was going unnoticed. Liz was spellbound by this woman's voice and eyes. At that moment they were neither coach nor player. They were simply two women lost in the romantic winter night's spell, gazing across the table at one another and incapable of moving. Sheridan slowly slid out of her side of the booth and into Liz's side, their eyes still locked. She moved closer. With a soft smile and a tender touch, she stroked Liz's cheek.

"Eighteen," Sheridan whispered, touching a lock of hair over Liz's forehead.

"Eighteen what?" Liz replied, leaning into Sheridan's touch.

"In this light you look like you are eighteen. You are so lovely, Liz. Like a little girl without a care in the world."

"Sometimes I wish I was eighteen again."

"I wish I had known you then. I bet you were something when you were eighteen." She gave a small chuckle. "I bet you were a little hellion."

"Not really. I was just naive." Liz placed a hand on Sheridan's thigh.

"And now?"

Liz stroked her thigh tenderly, the warmth of Sheridan's touch soothing her apprehensions.

"I'm thirty-nine. I've weathered many a campaign since then. I know what I want and what I don't want." Her lips were just inches away from Sheridan's.

"And what is it you want?" Sheridan asked in a whisper.

Liz leaned in to her and pressed her lips against Sheridan's, parting them slightly. Sheridan pulled Liz to her, her arms holding her tightly. Liz fell into Sheridan's embrace completely, allowing her to orchestrate a long and sensual kiss. When Sheridan released her, it was slowly and almost regrettably. Liz placed a hand on Sheridan's face, her fingertips tracing her lips. Just as she was about to kiss Sheridan again, she noticed the indiscernible shadow of someone across the street, staring at them through the parted curtains. Liz quickly sat up and pushed Sheridan back.

"No," she stated, nodding toward the window. "We have an audience."

Sheridan stood up and collected the last of the dishes and headed to the kitchen. Liz followed, turning out the lights in the dining room.

"I'm sorry about that," Sheridan said.

"No problem," Liz replied, touching her arm. "I just didn't want to make a big scene." She smiled coyly. "It is Vermont but you never know who is watching the dyke in the window."

Sheridan put the dishes in the big sink and turned on the water to start washing them. She pushed up the sleeves on her sweater but before she could begin Liz reached over and turned off the water. Without words she turned off the light then took Sheridan's face in her hands and kissed her. Sheridan gathered her into her arms and devoured her mouth. Her hands slid under Liz's sweater and stroked her back. With one quick flick, she released Liz's bra.

Liz moaned quietly as Sheridan's hand formed around her breast, holding it firmly. Liz cupped her hands over Sheridan's ass, pulling at her tight muscles. Sheridan maneuvered Liz back against the wooden island, her mouth still persistent and unyielding against Liz's. Sheridan unzipped Liz's slacks and plunged her hand inside, pushing aside her panties. Liz could feel herself opening to Sheridan's fingers and touch. She dug her nails into Sheridan's back as her fingers parted her folds and slid along the moistening valley. Sheridan pushed Liz's slacks and panties down over her hips then lifted her, setting her on to the island.

"Is this what you want, sweetheart?" Sheridan asked as she painted kisses down her neck.

Liz held Sheridan's head in her arms, her eyes closed as she imagined the ecstasy of Sheridan's touch.

"Yes," she muttered. "This is exactly what I want. You are exactly what I want."

Sheridan pulled Liz's sweater over her head and pulled away the bra, taking one of her breasts in her mouth. Liz closed her eyes and bit down on her lip as she flicked and aroused both nipples to full erection. Slowly Sheridan moved down, her hands stroking Liz's thighs as her lips moved closer to her valley. She pulled Liz to the edge of the island and knelt in front of her. With careful, methodical strokes, her tongue moved down her tender skin, taking her fully into her mouth. She entered her, tasting and tantalizing Liz's waiting need. Liz braced herself on the island as her body stiffened, eager for more of Sheridan's exploration.

"Oh, sweetheart, yes." Liz could barely speak, her breath tightening as her body shivered and shuddered at the growing rapture. She stiffened then felt her body jerk as she reached her peak, one that rolled through her in increasing waves and explosions. She placed a hand on Sheridan's head and held her against her as she continued to throb. Sheridan obliged, plunging even deeper as Liz rode the waves to completion. Finally Liz fell back, resting her glistening skin against the cool wooden surface, her breath fast and hard. Sheridan pulled her into her arms and held her while she rested. Liz snuggled against her, warm in her arms. This was exactly what Liz wanted, a warm passionate woman with gentle ways and soft eyes. Liz knew it would be hard to hide their growing intimacy as they moved through the rest of the season, but they would try.

Chapter 17

Liz struggled with the chaotically busy holiday season, heavy practice and game schedule and class finals. She didn't have as much time as she hoped to spend with Sheridan. They both had to settle for telephone conversations, long looks before and after practice and an occasional meal together at The Sugar Bush.

"What are you doing for Christmas?" Liz asked, refilling Sheridan's coffee cup and setting a piece of pie in front of her. She set her empty plate on the service cart.

"I'll be here for a couple days after classes let out for the holidays. I have meetings. Then I'm flying to Illinois to my folks' place for Christmas. Mom always does the big family thing. My brother and his wife and two kids will be there. And my grandmother and aunt and a couple cousins with their families."

"That sounds like fun. I love family Christmases. Snow-covered lanes and home cooking, sleigh rides and gingerbread cookies, crackling fireplaces and twinkling lights. It is a wonderful time of year." Liz closed her eyes and sighed dreamily.

Sheridan smiled at Liz's fantasy.

"I'd love a Christmas like that, too. But Christmas at the Ross's is loud and obnoxious. There will be about ten kids ripping into presents, wrapping paper everywhere, toys so deep on the floor you can't walk through the living room. Then they run off to play video games and never touch that stuff again. And when it comes time to eat, my God, Liz. I've never seen people go through so much food. You'd think it was a contest to see who can stuff the most turkey, ham and pie in their face."

Liz laughed loudly.

"It isn't funny, woman. I always get stuck next to my cousin Jack. He weighs about three hundred pounds and never met a bowl of mashed potatoes he didn't like. He insists on talking about basketball while he's consuming a mountain of food."

"Does he coach basketball too?" Liz asked jovially.

"Hell no. He's a truck driver. He delivers potato chips to grocery stores."

"You are making this up," Liz said, still chuckling at her story.

"I am not," Sheridan replied, sitting up stiffly. "Come to Springfield with me and you'll see."

Liz looked over at her, not sure if Sheridan's remark was a genuine invitation or just a tease to make her point.

"I mean it. Come have Christmas with me in Springfield," Sheridan repeated.

"Thank you for the invitation, babe. But I can't. I am very busy during the holidays. I have lots of luncheons and private parties right up through New Year's Eve. And I wouldn't leave my dad during the holidays. He doesn't have anyone else. Becca and I go out and decorate a tree for him a few days before Christmas. He cuts a little pine tree from his farm and calls when he has it anchored in the bucket, ready to go. We also fix him a Christmas dinner. That's about the only time he allows me to cook in his kitchen. He still insists on making meals for us all by himself. Usually we go for a sleigh ride New Year's Eve. It's kind of a tradition."

"Sounds like a lovely tradition."

"If you get back from Illinois, perhaps you'd like to come on the sleigh ride with us," Liz said, leaning in to make a genuine offer.

"If I get back in time, I'd love to." Sheridan looked into Liz's eyes, enjoying the softness in her gaze. "I guess I better go back to work. Robin and Jasmine will be pacing the floor. I told them to meet me fifteen minutes ago to go over some game tapes." Sheridan checked her watch.

"Have fun," Liz said, taking the check from Sheridan's table and wadding it up.

"Hey, give me that," Sheridan ordered.

"I don't think so, Coach." Liz walked away, a saucy grin on her face.

"Liz Elliott," she scowled. "I won't come in here if I can't pay for my lunch."

Liz stopped in her tracks then went back to her table.

"Yes you will and you know it." Liz winked at her then walked away. "Besides, I can afford a BLT on wheat. It won't break me. You can leave Rene a tip, if you want."

"Thank you," Sheridan said, dropping a generous tip on the table. "See you at practice."

Liz waved over her shoulder then looked back and smiled.

Chilton played two more games before the Christmas break, winning both by slim margins. Liz took her finals and passed her classes with A's. One of the campus sororities had its annual Christmas luncheon at The Sugar Bush the day after her last final, a stress she didn't need. A three-inch snow created havoc on the roads the week before Christmas but Becca and Liz made the pilgrimage out to Hec's farm, carefully maneuvering the deep ruts and snow-covered dirt road that wound for two miles from the highway to his back door.

Hector Elliott's farm was picturesquely situated on a rolling hill with a two-story white farm house, a quaint red barn, a chicken coop and a maple sugaring shed. During the spring and summer, he had a neatly planted and weeded vegetable garden. Liz and Becca spent the night at his house Christmas Eve, sipping hot chocolate by the wood burning kitchen fireplace, stringing popcorn and cranberries. Hec made extra strings of popcorn to hang in the trees outside his kitchen window to attract the birds. Liz's mother was a bird lover and he kept up her tradition of feeding them year round. Liz loved to watch her father wander through the yard, breaking up bits of stale bread and broadcasting seed as he whistled to call the birds to dinner. He was usually in bed by eight o'clock and was up by five thirty, out milking his cows. It was a simple life that he loved. Liz had respected his decision not to come live with her after her mother died. She knew he wanted to be near where they had lived. She wondered how often he strolled through the woods, talking with her about his day and telling her how much he missed her. Hec kept an old shirt box under his bed with her favorite nightgown, hair brush, a pair of combs she wore in her hair and a cotton handkerchief that she carried in the pocket of her apron. Liz suspected the handkerchief still smelled of her perfume and the peppermints she carried in her apron pocket for her indigestion.

Christmas morning Liz rose early and met him as he came in from milking.

"Merry Christmas, Dad," she said, hugging him and giving him a kiss.

"Merry Christmas," he muttered, as he went to the sink to wash his hands. "Is Becca up yet?"

"No. It's only seven fifteen. She won't be up for an hour at least."

"Do you want some oatmeal?" he asked, pulling a pan to the front burner of the stove. He kept the pan he used for everything from his morning oatmeal to pork and beans sitting on the back of the stove. The skillet he used for frying was on the other back burner, waiting to be called into service. He saw no need to put them in the cupboard after he washed them if he was going to use them again.

"Let me fix it, Dad," Liz said, taking the can of oatmeal from the cupboard.

"Nope, you are my guest," he insisted. "I'll make it."

"I'm no guest, Hec Elliott," she said, standing next to him and wrapping an arm around his waist. "I'm your brat daughter." She kissed his cheek.

He tried to refrain from smiling, blushing instead.

"You can get the bowls and pour some orange juice," he said. "Do you want maple syrup on your oatmeal?"

"Of course," she replied. She knew where he kept the jug of it in the pantry.

Hec spooned the oatmeal into the bowls and brought them to the table where Liz had set their places. She placed the wooden sugar bowl on the table, the one her grandfather had carved from a piece of burled maple. It had a perfectly fitting lid and tiny wooden scoop. Liz remembered dipping out spoons of sugar when she was a child, sprinkling it over a piece of buttered bread.

"You ready to take that damn thing home with you," he asked, pointing to the sugar bowl. "It's yours, when you want it."

"I know. But I like to use it here," she replied, smiling up at him. "Someday I'll take it. Not now." She patted his hand as he sat down, groaning a bit as he lowered himself into the chair.

"I'm glad I let you make the oatmeal, Dad. It is so good. Mine isn't this creamy." Liz enjoyed her breakfast, the warmth of a winter in the country all around her.

"How's school?" he asked, keeping his eyes on the job of syruping his cereal just right.

"I passed my classes," she replied, pleasantly surprised he asked.

"You get A's?" he asked, running a ribbon of cream around the edge of the bowl.

"Yes." She smiled to herself at his query.

"Good. You sign up for the second semester?"

"Yes, I did it online. Can you believe you can sign up for all your classes without ever going on the campus?"

"Becca told me. She sign up too?"

"Yes. She's taking a pretty heavy load this semester. Fifteen hours."

"She can do it. She's a smart one that Becca is." He nodded as if agreeing with himself. "She's smart like her mother." He looked up carefully, and smiled a small smile.

"Thank you, Dad."

"You coming out for New Year's Eve this year?"

"I think so." She got up to refill their coffee cups.

"You bringing anyone?" he asked after a hesitation.

"How did you know?" Liz said, sitting back down.

"Becca said you might be bringing that coach."

"Is that okay?" Liz looked at him seriously.

"Can she drive Judy?" he asked.

"You mean pulling the sleigh? I have no idea."

"It gets too damn cold out there at midnight for an old man like me. If I hook up the sleigh maybe you two can drive it yourself," he suggested, scraping the last bite from his bowl.

"I imagine we can."

"Good. I can't be catching cold." He took his dishes to the sink and washed them.

Liz watched him for a minute.

"Dad, I want you to come with us. I'm sure Sheridan would want you to come, too."

"Naw," he grunted.

"Please," she said, bringing her dishes to the sink. "It's tradition."

"We'll see," he said, washing her dishes and stacking them in the drainer.

"I want you to show us the trail you take over the hill and down to the river. I'd never be able to find it by myself."

He looked up at her with a frown.

"They haven't moved the river, daughter. It's still there where it always was."

Liz smiled coyly at him.

"Come on, Dad. You can drive the sleigh and we can sit in the back, just like you do for Becca and Mark."

Liz could see a smile creeping out the corner of his mouth.

"All right," he said finally.

"Good. Come on, Pops. Let's get Becca up and open presents." She rushed upstairs to roust Becca out of bed.

The gift exchange between the three of them had always been modest but filled with sincerity. Becca usually reaped the largest booty. This year Liz gave her a laptop computer and a pair of sneakers she had been drooling over in the shoe store. Becca gave her mother a new cell phone, one that sent and received live pictures, an item Liz had always thought was a luxury. Liz gave her father a new pair of leather work boots that included waterproofing and a zipper up the front instead of laces, something he had increasing trouble with as arthritis cramped his fingers. He also received a pair of pajamas with snaps up the shirt instead of buttons. Becca gave her grandfather a quart of clover honey, a treasure by his standards, and a bright red flannel shirt. Hec blushed as he opened his gifts, his excitement over the ceremony too much for him to hide. He waited until all the other gifts were opened before handing Becca and Liz theirs. Becca grinned at the wrapping paper, the Sunday comic section of the newspaper, tied with a length of red yarn.

"What is it Grandpa?" she asked, carefully untying the yarn and painstakingly opening the paper.

"It ain't much." He frowned, his hand rubbing the flannel of his new shirt as he watched her open it.

She opened the box to find another smaller box inside. It too was tied with yarn. She pulled it off and peeked inside, her mouth dropping at the sight.

"Oh Grandpa!" Becca squealed then scrambled up off the floor and rushed over to hug him. "I love them."

"What is it, honey," Liz asked happily although she already knew what it was. He had asked Liz if she thought it would be a good gift for her. Liz had reassured him Becca would love to wear a pair of her grandmother's earrings.

"Grandpa gave me the silver earrings I have always admired, see." She showed them to Liz then ran to the mirror to put them on.

"Thank you, thank you," she gushed.

"You're welcome," he replied, watching her reaction with reserved delight.

Liz smiled over at him as if to say he had made her very happy.

He went to the table where the Christmas tree sat and lifted the green felt skirt that draped to the floor. He pulled out the large red box he had hidden underneath and handed it to Liz.

"What's this, Dad?" Liz asked, as she held the box on her lap.

"I don't use it. You might as well have it," he replied then sat back in his chair and returned to stroking his new flannel shirt.

Liz released the tape that held the lid and opened the tissue paper. The gift was a complete surprise. She drew in a long gasp as she carefully pulled out her grandmother's teapot. It was still in pristine condition. It was white porcelain with tiny rosebuds and a gold rim. She remembered as a child she was never allowed to touch it. It was the most guarded treasure in her parent's home, sitting on top of the china hutch between the two matching teacups and saucers. The set had come across with her great grandparents from Scotland and had miraculously survived storms, floods, dozens of children's inquisitive hands and several moves.

"Oh Dad, are you sure about this?" she asked as she admired the teapot.

"I taped the lid on so it wouldn't fall off," he replied, pointing to the top.

"Thank you," she said, a tear welling up in her eye.

"Look in the box," he insisted.

"What else is in here?" she asked, placing the teapot on the table then searching deeper. "You gave me the cups and saucers, too?" she beamed, pulling them from the wadded up newspaper in the bottom of the box.

"Got to keep them together," he declared gruffly but his eyes were soft.

"Oh, Dad, they are just as lovely as I remember them. I just assumed you had gotten rid of them or broken them years ago when I stopped seeing them on the china hutch." She held them up and admired them.

"I wrapped them up to protect them. I figured you'd be wanting them one of these days. The time had to be right." He looked over at Liz proudly. "This was the year for it," he added.

Liz's eyes met his warmly.

"Thank you," she whispered, a lump rising in her throat.

"They are gorgeous, Grandpa," Becca added, coming to see them. "Are they bone china?"

"Yep, made in London, England. My Grandmother Elliott got them for a wedding present the year before they came to America. She was afraid someone on the ship would steal them so she covered them with mud and coal dust so they looked old and worthless. She wrapped them up in an old nightdress and carried them in a basket with a hank of garlic lying on top of them." He grinned at the story, one he never grew tired of telling.

"Will I get them someday?" Becca asked tenderly.

"Someday?" Liz replied. "But don't be in a hurry, daughter." They laughed.

"There's a gallon of syrup under the tree for each of you. I figured Becca needed her own this year since she has her own apartment."

"Thank you," they each said, knowing theirs was the best of his crop, taken from the best the sugaring barn had to offer.

After the presents were admired and the wrapping paper was cleared away, the three of them dressed warmly and went for a walk down the lane. The air was crisp but the bright sun warmed their faces as they circled the farm and crossed the pasture. Becca played with the young calves and the baby goats in the barnyard. Liz locked her arm in her father's and walked along, visiting and reminiscing about past Christmases. They ate dinner punctually at four o'clock as Hec had always done.

"It'll be dark pretty soon," he said, pushing back his plate and rubbing his full stomach. "You better get packed up."

"We'll do the dishes for you, Grandpa," Becca said, carrying the dishes to the sink.

"Nope, I'll do the dishes," he snorted. "I ain't got nothing else to do this evening."

"Let us help, Dad," Liz added.

Hec shook his head adamantly.

"I want to know you got home all right. That road is hard to drive after dark."

In his gruff way, Liz knew he was just trying to protect them.

"All right, if you are sure," Liz replied.

"Hell, yes. Don't you think a fellow can wash his own dishes?"

"Thank you for the earrings, Grandpa," Becca said, pulling back her long hair so he could see them. "I love them." She hugged him and patted his face.

"Look good," he offered. "You've got your mother's ears."

They loaded up Liz's car with the gifts and their clothes.

"If anything doesn't fit, I kept the receipts so we can exchange them," Liz said, as she climbed in and started the engine.

"They'll fit." He came down the steps and stood next to her car. Liz rolled down the window and waved him over. "What you want?" he asked.

"A Christmas kiss from my daddy," Liz replied with a smile.

He smirked but leaned down and gave her a kiss.

"Get on home now, you hear?" he said, waving up the road.

"I'll call you when we get home," Liz declared as she pulled away.

He stood at the bottom of the steps until they were out of sight, occasionally waving as they maneuvered the ruts and potholes.

Chapter 18

The week between Christmas and New Year's was busy for Liz. There were lots of downtown shoppers anxious to spend their Christmas gift certificates and eat lunch while they were out. The holidays also brought skiers to Vermont ready to enjoy the season's ample snowfall. Becca had been invited to go with Mark and his family to their vacation house in Myrtle Beach for the week. She offered to stay home to help with the holiday rush at The Sugar Bush but Liz reassured her she could handle it and it was all right for her to go. Liz still clung to the hope that Sheridan would be back before New Year's Eve and they could go for the sleigh ride even though she hadn't heard a word from her.

"What do you have planned for tonight to ring in the New Year?" Pauline asked, cleaning out the sink and putting the last of the washed utensils away.

"A hot bath and a cup of cocoa, I think," Liz replied, turning out the light in her office and locking the door.

"Would you like to come over and play scrabble with us? Georgia, Emily, Didi and I are going to fix nachos, drink cheap champagne and play board games until we fall asleep on the living room floor," she said with a chuckle. "You're more than welcome."

"Thanks but no. But hey, nachos and cheap champagne is fun anytime." Liz laughed. "Tell everyone happy new year for me."

Pauline gave her a warm hug.

"Happy new year to you too, honey. And I hope you hear from her."

"From who?" Liz asked seriously.

"Don't tell me you aren't waiting for Coach Ross to call you. I heard you talking about going on a sleigh ride with her." Pauline gave a coy smile.

"Oh, that. I haven't heard another word from her." Liz pulled on her coat and stood at the back door waiting for Pauline to collect her jacket and bag. "I bet she has forgotten all about it."

"Uh-huh," Pauline teased, raising her eyebrows.

Liz stopped at the convenience store to gas her car then headed home, a gentle snow filling the air. She checked her answering machine but it was empty.

"Hi, Dad," she said, calling him to wish him a happy new year.

"Do I need to hitch up the sleigh or not?" he asked.

"I haven't heard from Sheridan so I guess she won't be here. Would you like to take your daughter for a ride? It would just be the two of us, if that's okay." Liz said, regret nagging at her over Sheridan not being there.

"What time?" he asked.

"How about eight thirty? Is that too late?"

"I'll be ready. Wear a warm coat," he advised.

"See you then," she said then went upstairs to take a bath. Just as she was ready to step into the tub the doorbell rang. Liz pulled on her robe and hurried to the front door, peeking out to see who it was. Sheridan was standing on the front porch.

"Hello," Liz said, opening the door with a broad grin. "Come in."

191

"Happy new year," Sheridan said, beaming brightly. "Sorry I didn't call but I just got into town this afternoon. My flight was delayed out of Chicago. Am I too late for the sleigh ride?"

"I thought you changed your mind about it since I didn't hear from you."

"My cell phone was dead. The battery won't take a charge. I have to get a new one." Sheridan took off her coat and hung it over the back of the couch.

"I'm going out to Dad's about eight. You are just in time." Liz kissed her on the cheek.

"Hey, that isn't a kiss for someone who has been gone for a week. Come here," Sheridan said, gathering Liz in her arms and kissing her completely. "How was your Christmas?"

"It was lovely. We had a great time. How about yours?" Liz said, clinging to Sheridan's side and playing with a lock of her hair.

"Noisy. Crowded. Chaotic." Sheridan frowned as if she had gone through torture.

"It couldn't be that bad," Liz scowled at her. "You enjoyed yourself and you know it. You big phony."

"I had to play basketball with my nephews."

"Did you win?" Liz asked.

"Barely. They cheat. One is twelve and the other one is ten. You can't guard a ten-year-old. They are like greased pigs."

"Maybe you should be recruiting from the fourth grade," Liz joked, taking Sheridan by the hand and leading her up the stairs. "Come sit on the bed and tell me all about your trip to Illinois. I was just about to step into the tub."

"I like this idea," Sheridan grinned devilishly, following her up the stairs.

"Calm down, Coach. It's just a bath."

"Need someone to wash your back?" Sheridan asked, pinching her ass.

"Yes, I might, if you behave," Liz replied playfully.

Just as she sat down in the tub, the telephone rang.

"Would you answer that? It's probably Becca from Myrtle Beach," Liz called.

"Hello," Sheridan said, picking up the bedside telephone. "Hello."

"Who is it?"

"No one there," she replied and hung it up. "Becca must think you are entertaining," Sheridan said, coming into the bathroom and leaning against the counter.

"She knew I had invited you to go out to dad's tonight. She thought it was a good idea."

"So she knows about us?"

"Sure. She is a little snoop and would have found out anyway. Besides, she likes you, Coach." Liz smiled up at her as she soaped her arms and rinsed them. She soaped the sponge and held it out for Sheridan to do her back. "Come make yourself useful."

"My kind of assignment," Sheridan said eagerly, kneeling next to the tub and lathering her back with soft gentle strokes. "Did you miss me?"

"Yes, I did. I was busy but I still found time to miss you." Liz looked up at her affectionately. "But it was only all the time," she added, her eyes soft and caring.

"I missed you, too," Sheridan said, and leaned down to kiss her. As she did, her hand stroked Liz's breast then wandered down between her legs. Her fingertips had just begun to part Liz's tender folds when the telephone rang again.

"I guess I should go answer that, huh?" Sheridan said in a whisper.

"Okay," Liz replied, stroking her face.

"Hello," Sheridan said, answering it on the third ring.

"Who is this?" a woman asked in a husky voice.

"Who did you want?" Sheridan replied, assuming it was a wrong number.

"Is this Liz Elliott's number?" the woman asked, after a hesitation.

"Yes, it is. Can I take a message?"

The line went dead.

"Hello," Sheridan said in a puzzled tone.

"Who is it?" Liz said from the bathroom.

"Whoever it was, they hung up. They asked if it was your number but I guess they didn't want to leave a message."

"Was it Becca?"

"No, it was a woman with a deep, raspy voice."

Liz made a short gasp and stared up at her.

"Do you know someone who sounds like that?"

"No," Liz said, seemingly distracted. She climbed out of the tub and dried.

"Are you all right?" Sheridan asked as Liz went into the bedroom to dress.

"Yes, I'm fine. I told dad I'd be there at eight so I better get dressed. He doesn't do well when I'm late."

By the time they got to Hec's, he was waiting on the front steps wearing his plaid wool coat and a cap with ear flaps pulled down and tied under his chin.

"Happy new year, Dad. This is Sheridan Ross, my coach," Liz said, introducing her. "Sheridan, this is my father, Hector Elliott. But he won't answer unless you call him Hec, right Dad?"

Sheridan extended her hand to him.

"Nice to meet you, Hec," she said, shaking his hand firmly.

"You got my girl playing ball again," he said. "I like that."

"Me too," Sheridan replied.

"Come on, I'll show you how to drive the sleigh." He led the way to the barn.

"I thought you were going with us, Dad," Liz said, carrying a blanket over her arm.

He shook his head. "My rheumatism is acting up. You can handle it." He swung the barn door back out of the way and propped a piece of wood against it.

"I've never driven a horse-drawn sleigh before," Sheridan said in Liz's direction.

"No trick to it," Hec said. "Easy does it on the turns. Judy knows which way to go." He led the brilliant black mare out of the barn. She was hitched to a quaint New England sleigh that looked like it came right off of a Currier and Ives postcard. He held the horse's head while Liz and Sheridan got situated and wrapped the blanket over their laps. He handed Sheridan a pair of heavy work gloves to protect her hands. Judy shook her head and pawed at the ground, jingling the bells on her harness. She seemed to know what was in store and was anxious to get under way.

"Wrap the reigns around your hand once. You won't drop them that way." Hec helped Sheridan get her hands accustomed to the feel of the leather reigns. "If you turn loose of the reigns, Judy will just stop."

"I hope you know what you are doing letting me drive your sleigh," Sheridan said, a worried look on her face.

"I'll start some hot cocoa when you get back," he advised. "When you're done just lead Judy into the barn and close the door. I'll tend to her later."

"Wouldn't you like to come with us, Hec?" Sheridan asked warmly. "We'd love to have you."

"Nope, I'm going to bed in a while. You two have fun and watch for low branches." He stepped back and swatted Judy on the rump.

"I'm sorry he didn't come with us," Sheridan said, her eyes big as she struggled with the pull of the reigns.

"I'm not," Liz replied with a wink.

"I didn't want to take his place."

"He's glad you did. He wasn't kidding about the rheumatism. He has trouble being out in the cold for very long." Liz snuggled against Sheridan's side. "I'm glad you came back in time to come with me. Maybe we can start our own tradition."

Sheridan sat stiffly, her hands clutching the leather straps as Judy trotted along the snow covered path, her bells ringing through the still night air.

"You're taking this way too seriously, Coach. Relax. Loosen up your hands," Liz said, noticing her face pinched with concentration.

"I don't want the horse to run off with us."

Liz laughed loudly, her voice echoing through the trees.

"Judy is almost as old as I am. There's no running off left in her. Dad failed to tell you she could probably make this ride without anyone holding the reigns at all. Becca told me she tied the straps to the seat and Judy just walked along the path until they got all the way back to the barn."

Sheridan frowned at her.

"So why am I holding these?"

"So I can sit next to you and enjoy your company."

Sheridan raised her arm and encircled Liz with it, still holding tight to the reigns.

"I think I could get used to this," Sheridan said, relaxing a bit.

"I hope so," Liz whispered.

"I can see why you love the winters in New England," Sheridan said, looking deep into Liz's eyes. "Do you know how beautiful you are in the moonlight?"

"I know how happy I am with you in the moonlight."

Sheridan held Liz against her side as they rode along, a peaceful stillness in the air. Their breath curled up between them.

"Stop when you get to the clearing," Liz said, pointing to the edge of the woods. Sheridan pulled back on the straps. Judy stopped immediately, shaking her head and snorting. "Look down there," Liz pointed. "Isn't it beautiful? I never get tired of seeing it." Liz took a long pleasing sigh.

"Yes, it is very breathtaking." Sheridan scanned the valley, a surprising sense of peace and contentment falling over her face.

Even in the darkness, the bright snow and moonlight illuminated the valley that ran along the river. The white hillside and dark patches of woods seemed placed there just for them. Sheridan looped the straps over the edge of the sleigh then drew Liz into a warm embrace.

"I love you, Liz," Sheridan said, bringing her lips to Liz's.

Liz folded her arms around Sheridan's neck and returned her kiss. Their bodies were dark silhouettes against the winter's mantle as they clung to each other, their kisses passionate and long.

"I love you with all my heart and soul and body, Sheridan. I never thought I could love anyone as much, but I do." Liz eyes were full of love. "Let's go home. I want to hold you tonight. I want you to make love to me. I want to be in your arms when the new year arrives."

Sheridan didn't say anything. She smiled and took the reigns in one hand, urging Judy onward, her other arm securely around Liz.

While Sheridan returned the horse to the barn, Liz slipped inside and left a note for her father. She turned off the television and pulled an afghan over Hec as he snored in his chair. She kissed his forehead then tiptoed outside.

Sheridan drove them back to Liz's house and led her upstairs. They undressed then slipped into bed, snuggling together under the comforter, their bodies molded around each other. As the grandfather clock downstairs struck midnight, their night had just begun, a night full of passion and romance.

What they hadn't noticed was the car parked across the street from Liz's house. The driver sat in the darkness, watching Liz's upstairs bedroom window until the lights went out. The car then slowly pulled away, its headlights out as it moved down the street and around the corner.

Chapter 19

Liz noticed Sheridan's signal from the bench, the one that meant hang on to the ball and run out the clock. With a hard-fought, eight-point lead, Liz was ready to protect the last remaining minute of the game. She brought the ball over the half-court line and stalled, dribbling in a large arc just outside the three-point line. The crowd applauded and shouted out a countdown of the remaining twenty seconds. When the horn sounded most of the players were already walking toward their benches with exhausted expressions and sweat-drenched uniforms. Sheridan shouted encouragement as her team passed on their way to the locker room.

"Nice game, ladies. Way to work the ball. That's using your heads." She met the opposing coach in front of the scorer's table and shook hands, congratulating her for a good, clean game. She remained in the gymnasium visiting with well-wishers and representatives of the local press.

Liz picked up her water bottle from beneath the chair and grabbed a towel to wipe the sweat dripping down her chin before following the other players to the locker room.

"Liz," called a woman with a pair of twin daughters. They leaned over the railing handing her their programs and a pen. "Would you sign my program?" one of the girls asked hopefully.

"Sure," Liz replied kindly after wiping her face and hands with the towel. She took the pen and signed under her picture. Several of the fans stopped at the railing to offer support and congratulations on the six-game winning streak. The players slowly made their way to the locker room, pausing to accept words of encouragement along the way. Liz was surrounded with fans. She was polite to each and every one, smiling and thanking them for their kind words. She was tired, sweaty and wanted a shower but she was patient and considerate with anyone who wanted to congratulate her.

"Hey, Liz," called another woman standing at the railing. "Up here."

Normally Liz waved to the crowd and smiled to anyone who wanted her to notice them. But this voice caught her attention and sent a shiver down her body. She looked up at the woman who was resting both arms over the railing and staring down at her. Her eyes were dark pools, piercing and expressive like Becca's. Liz's jaw dropped and she took in a desperate gasp.

"I heard you were playing again," the woman declared, her stare sending a cold chill down Liz's sweaty back. "Not bad either," she added.

"What are you doing in Ashton?" Liz asked caustically.

The woman shrugged and descended the stairs to where Liz was standing.

"I thought I'd see if it was true. I was sure it had to be just a rumor. I said to myself, why would Liz Elliott be playing basketball at Chilton College after all these years. She's forty, for God's sake. She's got a kid. So here I am and what do you know? Liz *is* playing again. What happened baby? You miss the good old days?" Her

199

eyes moved down Liz's figure and back up again. "You miss the young bodies?" She laughed quietly then ran her finger down Liz's sweaty neck.

"Stop that, Sara," Liz hissed and brushed her hand away, then tried to push past her but Sara blocked her escape.

"You look pretty damn good for forty, pussycat." Sara's eyes were like hot needles as they scanned Liz's body again.

"I'm not forty and it's called staying in shape."

"I bet you still have the tightest ass on campus," Sara whispered as she leaned in to her.

"Stop it," Liz ordered, noticing they were attracting attention from the last of the spectators who were making their way toward the exit. Liz pushed by, feeling Sara's hand stroking her butt as she passed. She hurried into the locker room, her face red with anger. She opened her locker and threw the water bottle inside. Seeing Sara was not only a shock, it was an unpleasant reminder of a time she preferred to leave behind. Liz had grown adept at blocking out the painful memories of Sara but with her telephone call to Becca and now showing up in person, it was hard to ignore her larger-than-life presence. When she saw Sara at the railing staring down at her, Liz's brain had taken a quantum leap backward and it was eating her alive.

Liz slammed her locker door with a vengeance. She reopened it and slammed it again then gave it a kick for good measure. When she looked up, Sheridan was standing in the doorway, staring across the locker room at her with a worried look. Liz took a deep breath, hoping her anger would dissolve.

"Are you all right?" Deb asked, digging in her locker for her shampoo. "We won, you know. You had twenty-four points. It would have been twenty-six if I hadn't been called for goaltending on that one shot."

"Yes, I'm fine," Liz muttered as she began rummaging through her locker. "Just fine," she added through gritted teeth.

"We all are going to the Pizza Barn this evening. You're coming, aren't you?" Deb asked.

Liz thought a moment. Normally she declined the invitation to join the girls after the game but she wanted to be with people. The idea of going home to an empty house and the thought of Sara's return to Ashton were more than she wanted to accept tonight. Liz wished Sheridan didn't have a meeting after the game. She wanted to spend the evening with her, laughing and enjoying each other's company. Liz couldn't think of a better way to block out Sara's memory than by looking into Sheridan's smiling face. The two women couldn't be any different, Liz thought. Sheridan was warm, caring and tender. Sara was demanding, caustic, abusive, a borderline psychotic.

"Okay," Liz said finally. "I'd love to join you." She smiled at Deb. "Thanks for inviting me."

"Are you sure you are all right? You look a little funny," Deb replied, narrowing her eyes at Liz.

Liz peeled off her jersey and stepped out of her shorts. She stood in her sports bra and biker shorts holding her bottle of shampoo in one hand and conditioner in the other.

"I'm fine, hon. Smelly, but fine. Thank you for asking." She patted Deb's back then went to shower.

By the time Liz drove across town to the Pizza Barn, the place was crowded with players, fans, parents and locals celebrating the victory. Liz was cheered as she entered. She waved and blushed. The man behind the counter whistled at her and performed an air ball shot, imitating Liz's free throw style. She did the same and grinned back at him.

"Back here, Liz," Jen called from a long table in the back. The entire team was already there, drinking pop and ordering pizza. Robin was at one end and Jasmine was at the other, laughing and cracking jokes at the other team's expense. Liz found a chair and was poured a glass of soda from the pitcher on the table.

"Where's Becca?" Deb called. "I figured she would come, too."

"She has a big geometry test in the morning. She said she was going to get an A if it killed her," Liz teased. "She is on a mission."

"Geometry was a fucking nightmare," Miriam sneered. "I barely passed."

"Becca is obsessed with getting A's," Deb declared.

201

"What is wrong with getting A's?" Liz asked jokingly.

"Nothing, if you can't find something better to do with your time," Jen answered, bringing on a round of laughter.

Liz ate pizza and joked with her teammates, laughing and teasing each other about everything from points scored to homework to clothes. She was genuinely having a good time. She couldn't have been more pleased to have accepted the invitation until her eyes scanned the room and did a doubletake of a woman sitting at a table across from them. The woman's eyes were riveted on Liz. It was Sara. She sat at the table nursing a draft beer, her expression menacing. She had turned her chair so she was squarely facing Liz. When she realized Liz had seen her, she gave a small salute. Liz froze in her seat. Sara's dark hair and muscular physique was a bold and imposing presence.

"Isn't that right, Liz?" Jen asked, assuming Liz had been paying attention to their conversation. "Liz?"

"I'm sorry," Liz said, diverting her eyes and trying to regain her composure. "What did you say?"

"I said—" Jen began, but Liz suddenly stood up.

"I'm sorry girls but I have to go. I forgot I have some homework to finish tonight. It was fun." She pulled some money from her pocket and dropped it on the table to cover her pizza and drink. "I'll see you all tomorrow at practice." She hurried out the door and sprinted to her car. In one motion she slammed the door, started the car and pulled out, slinging gravel as she sped down the road. Liz looked in her rearview mirror. Sara was standing in the parking lot with her arms folded, her eyes following Liz's escape.

Chapter 20

Liz kept busy with the restaurant, classes, homework and a string of away games. Sheridan and Liz found time in their hectic schedules for an occasional quiet dinner or a stroll hand-in-hand. Liz didn't dwell on Sara's return to Ashton. She assumed Sara was just passing through and would soon be gone once and for all.

After dropping two games in a row while on the road, the Lady Stingers were anxious for a win and so were the fans. The home game was a chance for redemption. Liz played the entire first half, scoring eight points. As the second half started, Sheridan kept her on the bench.

"Number eight is sagging off of you and helping with double coverage on Deb," Sheridan advised. "If she's going to give you that much room, take the shot. Maybe you can drop a couple deep three-pointers before she comes out to cover you."

Sheridan's tone was totally professional. She instructed Liz as she would any of her players. But her eyes were soft and kind as she looked over at Liz. There was a sensuous quality in the way she leaned into Liz, explaining the plays she wanted her to run. No one else could see it but Liz saw it and felt it.

"Are you okay?" Sheridan asked in a concerned tone. "Do you need to rest?"

"No, I'm fine," Liz replied. She wanted to wink at her but she refrained.

Liz was almost sorry when Sheridan called for a time-out and sent her in the game. She much preferred to sit next to her, enjoying the sound of her voice and the twinkle in her eye. Liz played with determination, wanting to win this game for her team and for Sheridan. The Chilton Stingers won the game by three points, giving the home crowd an exciting overtime victory.

"Coach Ross," a woman called as she pushed her way through the crowd. She had a camera around her neck and a notepad in her hand. "Coach Ross, is it true you interviewed for a coaching position at the University of Kansas. Sources tell us you spent three days in Lawrence, Kansas over Christmas break touring the campus and meeting with the athletic placement committee. I understand KU is preparing a press conference at the end of the season to announce your appointment."

Liz's head snapped around. Sheridan looked over at her, the color draining from her face. The reporter moved closer, refusing to be ignored.

"Is it true, Coach?" she repeated persistently.

Liz stared at Sheridan, stunned at the news. She searched Sheridan's eyes, hoping to see denial but there was none. Liz turned and strode off toward the locker room.

"Liz," Sheridan called over the crowd. "Wait a minute."

Liz didn't look back. She hurried through her shower and dressed quickly then slipped out before Sheridan finished with the reporter and well-wishers. Liz threw her tote bag into the back seat and roared out of the parking lot. It was a cold evening but she rolled down the window anyway, allowing the wind to cool her disappointment and anger at Sheridan's deception. How could she do something like that behind her back? How could she lie to her all the time they were building a relationship? Sheridan had explained away the interviews as standard procedure for coaches and Liz had believed her.

Liz drove through town and out on the highway. She was too mad and too disillusioned to go home. She drove the winding road to Lookout Point and pulled off the road. She got out of the car and slammed the door. How could she do that to her? How could Sheridan make her fall in love with her all the while she was planning to leave? Liz stood at the rock wall and looked out over the lights in the valley. The winter wind whistled through the pine trees and pinked her cheeks. She slid her hands in her pockets and stared into the cold February darkness, an aching emptiness filling her soul.

Liz spent the evening driving the back roads of Addison County trying to numb her mind and justify Sheridan's actions. It was after midnight when she unlocked her front door and entered the darkened living room. Her answering machine was flashing but she didn't want to hear it. She knew her cell phone probably had messages on it as well but she tossed it on the table with her keys. She made a cup of herbal tea and carried it to the stairs. She sat down on the first step and leaned against the wall to sip her tea. She wasn't ready to face an empty bed, one without Sheridan in it.

Liz woke just before dawn. She had slept on the couch, wrapped in a comforter and her own self-pity.

"Damn you," she muttered as she tossed the comforter over the back of the couch and sat up. "If that's the way you want to play it, fine. I can play it loose and free." She went upstairs to shower. She was a survivor and Coach Sheridan Ross was not going to ruin her day, not if she could help it. After her shower Liz finally checked her messages. There were several from Sheridan. They ranged from *we need to talk* to *please let me explain* and finally *you aren't being reasonable about this*.

"I'll show you reasonable, Coach." Liz deleted them all.

After her ten o'clock class Liz went to The Sugar Bush to take over for Becca. She was relieved there was no practice that afternoon which meant she could drown her anger in work. It also meant she could avoid Sheridan.

"Mom, Coach Ross called me." Becca handed Liz the message she had scribbled down. "She wants to talk to you. She said it was important. She said you weren't answering your phone."

"Did Ernie bring the romaine lettuce this morning?" Liz asked, ignoring the message.

"Yes." Becca replied, studying her mother's face. "Mom, did you hear me? Coach Ross."

"I heard you," Liz interrupted abruptly.

"Wooooo. Dissension in the ranks," Becca announced. "Or is it trouble in paradise?" she asked in a whisper.

"Becca, I have work to do," Liz snapped.

"Sorry," Becca replied with a frown.

Liz heaved a cleansing sigh.

"I'm sorry, honey. I didn't mean to snap at you. Thank you for taking the message."

"Did I tell you? Grandpa came to town yesterday. He had lunch with me. He stayed almost a half hour," Becca offered, trying to brighten Liz's mood.

"Great, sweetie. I'm glad he did." She patted Becca's arm. "I have to get back to work. You'll be late for class if you don't get going."

"Is there something I should know, Mom?" she asked gently.

"No, everything is fine. You run along." Liz went back to work, glad to have something to take her mind off Sheridan. It was after four when she locked the front door and turned out the dining room lights. She printed the menu specials for the next day and entered a stack of invoices into the computer before locking the back door and heading home. Her telephone was ringing when she opened the front door. She contemplated picking it up but went upstairs to change into her running clothes instead. It rang again as she sat on the edge of the bed tying her shoes. She hesitated then picked it up.

"Hello," she said dryly.

"You are hard to catch," Sheridan said jokingly.

"I've been busy."

"Are you going to hide from me?" she asked.

Liz didn't reply.

"We need to talk about this, Liz. You have to let me explain."

"There's nothing to explain. I understand completely. Congratulations, by the way. KU, that's a Big Twelve school. Division I."

"Can I come over and talk with you, please," Sheridan pleaded.

"I was on my way out the door."

"Liz, please don't shut me out like this. Let me talk to you."

"I'm not shutting you out. You took care of that without any help from me. What was it you said? Interviews are just part of the job. They don't mean anything. But don't worry about it, Coach. You can go to Kansas with a clear conscious. You are still uncommitted. You don't owe me a thing."

Liz hung up and ran down the stairs. She was out the door and halfway down the street before she unclenched her teeth. Sheridan left two more messages on her machine but Liz deleted them both. By Wednesday she had simmered down and regained her jovial disposition. She arrived at practice just in time to step onto the court as Sheridan blew the whistle to start. She gave Liz a hard stare then turned her attention to the team.

"We've got three games left. One away, two at home. And I want three victories. Tomorrow night we go to Manchester. The Southern New Hampshire Wildcats will be hungry for a win. I want to work on some screens and moving the ball deep on them."

While Sheridan explained her game plan, Liz studied the floor. She couldn't bring herself to look at the coach. She tried to put their personal issues out of her mind but it was impossible not to remember Sheridan's soft touch and tender body.

"Did you hear me, Liz? Are you with us?" Sheridan called, bringing Liz back from a fog.

Liz realized she had been daydreaming and hadn't heard what Sheridan said.

"Yes. Working the ball in deep," Liz offered. That was the last thing she heard.

"You're about three minutes behind, Liz. Is there a problem?"

Liz took a deep breath and smiled.

"No. I'm sorry. Brain surge, I guess."

The players giggled. Sheridan gave her a harsh look.

"Let's get busy, ladies. We've got a lot to cover this afternoon."

Sheridan worked the team hard, running and rerunning plays until the players groaned and grumbled at the repetition. Liz was under the gun to read the defense and move the ball more efficiently. She felt Sheridan's eyes on her constantly but she narrowed her focus and played like a woman possessed, snapping passes, setting strong picks and dropping three-point shots at every opportunity.

"That's it ladies. Good job. Catch a shower," Sheridan called as she stood at center court with a basketball under her arm. "Liz, can I see you a minute?" she said innocuously as the players headed for the locker room.

Liz knew she would have to talk with her. After all, she was the coach.

"Yes?" she said, walking to center court and wiping the sweat from her forehead with her sleeve.

Sheridan waited until the other players and coaches had left the floor. She then looked deep into Liz's eyes.

"Talk to me, baby. Tell me why you are giving me the silent treatment. I love you, Liz. You have to believe that," she whispered.

"I know. That seems to be your style. Fall in love then move on." Liz's voice was cutting. "It's my own fault. You told me in Northampton you never have serious relationships. You just had friends, lovers, girls on the side. But I didn't listen." Liz straightened her posture. "I fell for you anyway." One tear threatened to spill out of Liz's eye and roll down her cheek. "You romanced me and it worked. I'm one of your victories, Coach. Put me in the win column. Damn you."

"Liz, I didn't mean to hurt you. I honestly didn't."

"If you dare say we just had some laughs, so help me I'm going to slap you, Sheridan," Liz said stiffly.

"I would never say that. It was far more than that. We had something very special. I've never had someone fill my heart like you did."

"I have to shower. Is there anything else, Coach?"

"Can we at least get through the rest of the season?"

"Sure," Liz replied stoically. "I'm a Chilton Stinger. I'm here for my team."

"I'll see you tomorrow." Sheridan's eyes followed Liz as she walked away, a hint of desperation in them.

True to her word, Liz arrived on time and had her game face on. She spent the three-hour ride reading and looking out the window of the charter bus. She eagerly took to the floor to warm up. Her shots were deadly, dropping from every corner. Sheridan watched the team from the sidelines, her arms folded across her chest. She was quieter than usual, leaving the pep calls and clapping to Robin and Jasmine as the team finished their warm-up. The Stingers scored first and often, sending the teams to the locker room at halftime with a ten-point lead. Sheridan was reserved, handing out advice and instructions to individual players rather than lecturing the entire team. With two minutes to play and an eighteen-point lead, Sheridan called a time-out and sent in her bench players. As the starting lineup filed off the floor, she gave each one a slap on the fanny and congratulated their efforts. The players counted down the last ten seconds and applauded the victory, hugging each other before going to shake hands with the opponents. Liz scored sixteen points, closing in on the career scoring record.

"Nice job, Liz," Sheridan called. She nodded at her respectfully.

"Thank you, Coach." Liz replied. It hadn't been too hard. She had survived the game and Sheridan's look. She heaved a deep sigh and went to shower. It was after one in the morning when the bus pulled into the parking lot in front of the gymnasium with its exhausted players. All Liz wanted to do was go home.

"Liz," Sheridan called as she was about to open her car door. She strode up to her and held the door. "Will you have coffee with me tomorrow?" Sheridan's eyes were full of emotion. "Please," she added, placing her hand on Liz's arm.

"It's late and I'm tired, Coach," Liz replied.

"All I'm asking for is a cup of coffee and a chance to explain."

"I don't think so," Liz replied, diverting her eyes. She knew if she looked into Sheridan's face she would crumble like a stale cookie.

"Don't you think we owe each other that much?"

"I would have thought you owed me an explanation before you took a job fifteen hundred miles away. But we don't always get what we want, do we Coach?" Liz looked up and fixed her with a hard stare. "I have to go. I'm tired and I have a restaurant to run in five hours." Liz stepped into the car and pulled at the door. Sheridan held it from closing for a moment then shut it.

Liz drove out of the parking lot without looking in the rearview mirror. She knew if she did she would turn around and go back.

The gymnasium was dark and deserted as Sheridan let herself in and walked the long hall to her office. She unlocked the door and snapped on the light then sat down in her chair. She was tired. The game had been long and exhausting both physically and emotionally. It was almost two o'clock in the morning and she should be on her way home. In a few hours she would be busy with practice, schedules, meetings and the business of coaching. She told herself that stewing over Liz's reaction to her job offer was only making a bad situation worse. But it did matter. It mattered very much to her, what Liz thought. She didn't think it would but there it was, smacking her in the face. Sheridan leaned back in her chair, closed her eyes and heaved a heavy sigh.

"Did you send in the applications, Sheridan?" her father said, wagging an angry finger at her with one hand and bouncing a basketball with the other. "I told you to send them in. You have to get out of that small school. No one will notice you if you don't send in the applications, Sheridan. Don't ignore me, Sheridan." Martin frowned at her as he con-

tinued to bounce the ball but there was no sound as it hit the floor. *"Division I is the only place to coach, Sheridan. Division I."*

Sheridan's eyes popped open, her head resting on the back of the chair. She had been dreaming and the memory of it haunted her. She checked her watch. It was five after six. She stood up, her body stiff. She went to the ladies room and washed her face, trying to wake up. The image in the bathroom mirror stared back at her as she leaned on the sink. Whoever it was, she didn't like the looks of her. That was not the Sheridan Ross she wanted to be. Success was hers for the taking. All she had to do was explain to Liz how important it was to her career. But how? Sheridan went back to her office and closed the door. She stood in front of the bookshelf that held her trophies. She picked up the one she received for winning the junior college championship. She held it in her hands, reading the inscriptions, something she hadn't done in years. She knew she could bring one home at a Division I school, one with big-ticket recruits and funding for scholarships to lure star athletes. It would be so easy to drown herself in a huge school like KU. The fans alone who attended a big university game would fill the Chilton College gymnasium many times over.

"Fuck," she yelled. She turned and threw the trophy across the room, smashing it against the door. "You are so stupid. You had it all and gave it away for a Big Twelve school." She turned to her desk, her eyes flashing with anger. She raked her arm across the desk, sending papers, mail and videotapes sailing through the air. She reached for her cell phone and punched in Liz's number.

"Hello," Liz said curiously.

"I need to talk to you, please." Sheridan pleaded.

"Sheridan," Liz started.

"Liz, I think you could manage a half hour for me. This is important."

"I'm in the middle of opening my restaurant. I also have two tests today. I don't have time for this right now," Liz replied with exasperation.

"Tonight," Sheridan insisted.

Liz didn't reply.

"Seven thirty," Sheridan added.

Liz still didn't say anything. Sheridan could hear her breathing.

"Please, babe. Thirty minutes isn't too much to ask, is it?"

"All right," Liz said finally.

"I'll pick you up at seven thirty."

"I have to go." Liz hung up.

Sheridan sat down at her desk, a small smile brightening her face.

"That's a start at least," she muttered.

Chapter 21

"Wow," Becca declared then gave a wolf whistle as she looked in her mother's bedroom. "You're looking hot, Mom."

Liz smiled to herself. She had made a special effort not to look like an over-the-hill college athlete or a restaurant cook tonight. She was pleased Becca was impressed but in spite of everything, it was Sheridan she hoped would notice.

"There are leftovers in the refrigerator. Pauline sent home some of that ambrosia salad you like," Liz said as she gave her hair the final touches in front of the mirror.

She was wearing black pants and a black satin blouse that shimmered in the light. Both fit her figure perfectly. A silver chain nestled in her cleavage.

"What's the occasion?" Becca asked, adjusting her mother's collar so it stood up at the back of her neck slightly, giving her a sophisticated look.

"No occasion. Why does it have to be just a special occasion to dress up?"

"Where is she taking you?" Becca smiled coyly.

"Who?"

"Coach Ross, silly. I'm not blind, you know."

"What makes you think I'm going out with Coach Ross tonight?"

Becca picked up two cologne bottles from Liz's dresser and gave each a test sniff.

"I'm psychic." She sniffed again and handed Liz her choice. "Where are you going? Dinner? Or straight up to make-out point?" She winked fiendishly.

"Becca!" Liz said, leering at her daughter. "We are just going for coffee to discuss some new play signals she wants to try out."

"Oh yeah? Play signals? I've never heard it called that before." Becca batted her eyelashes. She had always enjoyed tormenting her mother with risqué humor and suggestive inferences.

"Go to your room," Liz teased and pointed out the door.

"I am. I'm going to call Mark and find out when he'll be home so we can practice play signals." She turned to leave with a flourish. Liz swatted her on the rear. "By the way, I almost forgot." Becca took a yellow sticky note from her pocket. "Looks like a change in plans with Coach Ross tonight." She looked at the note and handed it to Liz.

"What's this?"

"Don't ask me. I just deliver the message."

"Gymnasium. Seven o'clock. S.R.," Liz read curiously. There was a smiley face drawn at the bottom. "Did Sheridan give you this to give to me?"

"No. It was stuck on the driver's side window of your car. She must have figured you'd see it before you left. I found it when I pulled in the drive just now."

"I bet she had a meeting or something. She probably tried to call when I was in the shower." Liz checked her watch.

"You can still make it by seven if you hurry," Becca offered. "It sure wouldn't do to keep her waiting."

Liz gave her a hug then rushed down the stairs, grabbing her jacket and keys on the fly.

"Have fun," Becca called from the stairs.

Liz looked back and smiled then hurried out to her car. It was the fastest trip she had ever made across town, past the brick pillars that guarded the campus entrance and into the parking lot behind Locklee Gymnasium. She spent the entire ride reminding herself Sheridan was leaving, moving to Kansas. It didn't dispel her enthusiasm for meeting her but she did try. There were no other cars in the parking lot. Even the janitor's pickup truck was long gone. An eerie silence cut into the chilly night air but Liz's excitement over meeting Sheridan put a cheerful confidence in her stride. The lobby lights were off but one of the doors to the gym was open and Liz could see the lights were on inside. A basketball court wasn't the most romantic and intimate place to meet and talk but it certainly fit Sheridan's agenda. Liz entered the gymnasium with long strides, her eyes searching for the coach. Instead Liz saw a basketball waiting at midcourt. She walked over to it and noticed a long-stemmed red rose next to the ball. She picked up the flower and held it to her nose. Sheridan was still doing it, still romancing her and Liz had to admit it was working. Sheridan must have remembered she said red roses were her favorite. She closed her eyes and drew in the heavenly scent.

"You remembered," she said aloud, her words echoing through the rafters. "How long are you going to make me wait down here?" she chided, perching a hand on her hip playfully.

"Not too long." Sara's voice pierced the silence like a dagger.

Suddenly the lights in gym went out leaving Liz standing in complete darkness. She screamed, dropped the rose and clutched her hands to her chest.

"Sara," Liz called through a terrified gasp.

There was only silence then the sound of footsteps descending the bleachers.

"Sara," Liz repeated, turning her head to the sound and straining to see into the inky blackness. "What are you doing here?"

"Meeting you," she replied coldly. "Gymnasium. Seven o'clock. S.R." She chuckled.

"Oh my God. S.R. was you."

215

"Who else? I must say I didn't think you'd show up." The footsteps began to slowly circle the perimeter of the floor. "And yes, I remembered you like red roses. I gave you two dozen red roses on our first anniversary. Remember?"

"Yes, I remember," Liz replied gruffly.

"You never gave me roses, Liz. Why not? Why didn't you ever buy me red roses?"

"Because I couldn't afford them. And neither could you. You used part of our rent money on those roses." Liz slowly turned at center court, trying to keep the sound of the footsteps in front of her.

Sara chuckled and kept walking, her street shoes tapping out a deliberate pace around the wooden floor.

"Why did you turn out the lights?" Liz asked nervously.

"I thought we could talk better in the dark. We don't seem to be able to talk face-to-face without you getting all upset. Besides, I can see in the dark. I have always been able to see things in the dark."

"What do you want?" Liz asked, determined not to let Sara rattle her.

"What do I want?" Sara scoffed. "What do you want, Liz? You came here tonight to meet me. You must want something."

"To tell the truth, I thought the note was from someone else. I didn't know it was from you."

Sara laughed wickedly.

"I was right. It's you and that coach, Sheridan Ross, isn't it?"

Liz didn't know how to answer and the methodical count of the footsteps was clouding her ability to think clearly.

"ISN'T IT?" Sara yelled.

Liz flinched and wrapped her arms around herself like a security blanket.

"Sara," she began.

"Have you fucked her?" Sara asked angrily.

"No," Liz said, feeling a lie was the best answer. Sara sounded mad enough already and it wasn't any of her business anyway.

"You don't lie very well, pussycat," Sara said in a low hideous voice.

"It isn't a lie. We are friends. Just friends. She is the coach and I'm on the team. That's all," Liz insisted.

Sara kept circling.

"Why did you want me to meet you? What do you want, Sara?"

"Oh, let's see. What do I want? Hmmm. How about my brother back? Yeah, that would be on the list. I want my BROTHER BACK," she bellowed. "And I want my girlfriend back. I want the life we once had back. But I guess I can't have any of those. My brother's dead. My girlfriend walked out on me. And my life has gone down the goddamned toilet. And guess what. It's all YOUR FAULT," she yelled, her words echoing through the darkness.

"I didn't—" Liz started but Sara cut her off.

"You have a new girlfriend. And you have a daughter and a life. That doesn't sound fair, now does it pussycat? You took everything away from me. You left me with nothing and you end up with all the goodies."

"I'm not responsible for your life, Sara. You are the one who made the choices."

"SHUT UP!" Sara's tone had hardened to an oppressive and demanding pitch.

"Okay," Liz replied in a calm voice, realizing Sara was working herself up into one of her wild rages and nothing would stop her until she was finished.

"You little slut. You bounce from woman to woman. You even throw in a man now and then. You can't even be a faithful lesbian."

"I never cheated on you, Sara. NEVER!" Liz yelled back defensively.

Sara stopped her circling. The gym fell silent.

"You fucked my brother," she said, veritably spitting the words out in anger.

Liz took a deep breath, trying to decide how much she wanted to say. She didn't want to torment Sara's violent temper any more than she had to. She knew full well what Sara was like when she was blinded with rage.

"You admit it," Sara chided when Liz didn't reply.

"Alan raped me and you know it." Liz spoke softly and carefully.

"You're a slut. A common, garden-variety ho. He didn't rape you. You asked for it. He was drunk. He'd still be here if you hadn't lied to the police."

"He raped me. And he raped that foreign exchange student behind the library, Sasha Lunick. She was walking home from work late at night and he attacked her."

"Lies. She lied too. You put her up to it."

"I never met her before in my life, Sara."

"Alan came to apologize to you and you spit on him. He was drunk, that's all, just drunk. You wouldn't even talk to him."

"Alan was an angry, troubled young man," Liz tried to explain.

"He was my brother. I loved him."

"I know you did," Liz offered.

"He was my family, my only family. Just like Becca is your family." There was a silence that cut through Liz. "Becca," Sara said in a whisper. There was a long silence.

"Sara?"

"She's Alan's kid, isn't she?" Sara started to laugh, slowly and quietly at first then louder until her voice was rattling through the rafters.

Liz didn't know what to say. She had always kept the rape and the fact that Becca was Alan's baby a secret from her daughter. It wasn't something Becca needed to know. The bitter anger and violence of the past was better left secure in Liz's memory. Nothing good could possibly come from Becca knowing her father was a rapist. All Becca needed to know was that she was loved and had always been the light of Liz's eyes.

"No, she is *not* Alan's baby. She's not." Liz instantly knew she sounded as transparent as the anger in Sara's voice.

"She doesn't know, does she?" Sara had a sinister lilt in her voice.

"No," Liz whispered.

"What?"

"No, she doesn't know. She doesn't know anything about it." Liz wished she hadn't admitted that, at least not to Sara. "She doesn't need to know, either."

There was an awkward silence then the footsteps began again.

"Sara, she doesn't need to know. That's ancient history," Liz continued.

"My brother is not ancient history."

"It would serve no purpose for her to know who her father was or—" Liz stopped short of saying rape, knowing it would only incense Sara further.

"Maybe. Maybe not."

"Sara. No."

There was a devilish chuckle floating toward her through the darkness.

"I wonder what Becca would think of good old mom if she knew the truth, if she knew you killed her father," Sara said.

"Sara," Liz declared. "Don't you dare!"

"Oh, pussycat. You know better than to dare me."

"What do you want? Money? I'll give you a hundred dollars if you'll promise to stay away from Becca. Five hundred."

"Wow. Five hundred bucks. A few years ago you could hardly spare a lousy fifty for an old friend. Now you are offering five hundred. It's amazing how your priorities have changed."

"Becca will only be hurt if she finds out about her father."

"Who does she think her father is? Or did you tell her you had so many affairs you aren't sure who it was," Sara said vindictively.

"I told her I was artificially inseminated. I told her I wanted a baby so bad I couldn't wait to adopt one."

Sara laughed again.

"I have never dated a man, Sara. You know that. Deep down in your heart you know that. I was never unfaithful to you. Never."

Sara kept circling, her footsteps still measured and constant.

"You asked me what I wanted," Sara began. "I'll tell you what I want. I want you to quit the team. Right now. If you don't want

Becca to know you lied to her about her father then you have to quit the team. You can't play another game. Not even one. There'll be no record-setting career for Liz Elliott."

"I can't do that. I'm point guard. We only have two games left. It won't be a terrific season but we are improving. I can't just quit. That wouldn't be fair to the rest of the team."

"It's your choice, pussycat. You quit the team now, tonight. Or I pay Becca a little visit." Sara cackled at her declaration. "After all, she's my niece. Maybe I should get to know her."

"NO!" Liz's protective nature raised an anger of her own.

"She does have my eyes, I think."

"You stay away from her. Do you hear me?" Liz yelled, her voice cracking as she spoke.

"I wonder if her long hair is soft to the touch." Liz could hear the sound of Sara's heavy breathing. "It might be fun to find out. Is Becca gay?"

"No," Liz snapped.

"Oh. What a shame. Maybe she just hasn't met the right woman yet."

"Oh my God," Liz stammered. "You stay away from her, Sara." Tears began to well up in Liz's eyes. Being threatened made her mad. But threatening Becca, her baby, her child, frightened Liz down to her soul.

"Your choice. You decide. And by the way, I will be watching you. Both of you," Sara said venomously. "Don't test me, Liz. I warn you. Don't test me," she declared gruffly.

The footsteps quickened and suddenly the door to the lobby slammed shut, leaving Liz in a silent darkness.

"Sara," Liz gasped. "SARA!" she screamed into the darkness, tears rolling down her face.

A minute later the lobby door clanged open again and the beam of a flashlight burst into the gymnasium.

"Liz?" Sheridan called frantically. She reached inside the door and snapped on the emergency lights.

"Sheridan," Liz replied through her sobs. She was crouching at midcourt like a frightened child. Sheridan ran to her and pulled her to her feet. She gathered her in her arms and held her tightly. "Are you all right?" She kissed her forehead.

"Yes," Liz replied as she held tight to Sheridan.

"Becca told me about the note. What happened?"

"It was Sara. She left the note." Liz wiped the tears from her face as she slowly regained her composure.

"Come on. Let's get out of here," Sheridan said, holding her arm around Liz as they went into the parking lot. "We'll get your car later. You are coming with me." Sheridan helped her in the passenger's side. "Are you sure you are okay?" Sheridan's eyes were inflamed, her forehead furrowed with concern.

"I'm all right. Thank you for coming when you did."

"I'm right here. I only wish I had gotten here sooner," Sheridan said regretfully. She drove Liz home and pulled into the drive. She turned to her and placed a hand on Liz's face, trying to smile through her anger.

"What did Sara want?" Sheridan asked cautiously.

Liz looked out the side window, staring at the darkness. Sheridan placed her hand on Liz's leg reassuringly. She sat quietly and waited for Liz to tell her. It was several minutes before she could find the strength and confidence to speak.

"I have something to tell you. Something"—she looked over at Sheridan, a tear glistening in her eye—"I thought I'd never have to talk about again, ever. But here it is, biting me in the ass again," she said. She looked out the window again as a lump rose in her throat.

"I'm here for you, babe. You can tell me anything. What secret is it Sara knows about you? What power does she hold over you?"

Liz looked at her, surprised at her insight and observation.

"I saw her talking to you in the gym after the Holcomb game," Sheridan added. "She has an evil look in her eyes when she looks at you."

"Evil. That's a good word for it." Liz took a deep breath. "This may be more than you want to know about me," Liz began, diverting her eyes.

"Tell me, baby. Just tell me." Sheridan placed her hand on Liz's to quiet them from their nervous fidgeting.

"I haven't talked about this to anyone in years. It is one of those things better left dead and buried." Liz slowly looked up at Sheridan, searching for understanding.

"Obviously you can't do that now. Whatever it is that has you upset and afraid has something to do with your past. I'm here to help you deal with it. Give me a chance to help."

Liz took a deep breath then began.

"It was the last week of school my junior year. It was dead week and everybody was studying for finals. Our apartment was over on Kimball, one of those little efficiencies on the second floor of an older home. It was hot in the summer and freezing in the winter. No air conditioning and a tiny little heater. But it was all we could afford. My scholarship didn't cover utilities and all the rent, just part of it. Sara was on an athletic scholarship but it didn't do much on off campus housing either. Her brother, Alan, had a habit of showing up after he'd been to the bar. He lived over in Rutland. He usually crashed on the couch then left the next morning. This one particular night he came banging on our door just after midnight. He was drunk, like always. He was carrying on about some girl at the bar who blew him off. It seems she wouldn't dance with him and refused to accept the drink he bought for her. He was calling her every name in the book. Sara was giving him sympathy and telling him he was too good for any of the girls at Chilton. She told him the girl didn't understand what a great guy he was." Liz stopped and looked away pensively. "Sara and Alan were very close. He was about a year older. Their parents died in a house fire when Alan was fifteen. The cops believed it was arson but they could never prove it."

Sheridan frowned but said nothing.

"Alan convinced Sara to go down to the bar and see this girl. I tried to tell her she should stay out of it but she was sure Alan was being mistreated. Alan was rude when he had been drinking and he was always drinking. Anyway, Sara agreed to go have a look while

Alan stayed at the apartment and drank the last beer in our refrigerator. I was trying to finish the last chapter of notes for my accounting class but he just kept on ragging on the chick at the bar. I thought it would be easier if I just ignored him but he followed me from the kitchen table to the living room. I couldn't get away from him. He wanted an audience for his anger, I guess. I finally had enough and told him to grow up. I said the girl didn't want to dance with him or have a drink with him so forget it. But I didn't stop there. I said I didn't blame her. I told him he was a drunken bum." Liz chuckled softly. "Boy, was that the wrong thing to say."

"Sounds like you had him pegged pretty well," Sheridan offered.

Liz drew a long breath as she prepared herself for what came next. As she told it, the memory crystallized in her mind as if it was happening all over again.

"What the hell do you know about it, you little shit," Alan snorted at Liz.

"Alan, why don't you go home and leave us alone?" Liz replied and folded her notes inside the textbook. She started to get up off the couch but Alan grabbed her by the throat and pushed her down.

"You think you're better than me, don't you, you little cunt?" His eyes were evil black pools glaring at her. He held her down on the couch and leaned over her, his beer breath filling her nostrils.

Liz fought back, trying to climb to her feet but his grip on her throat was too tight. Her face reddened as she tried to scream but nothing came out. She gasped for breath, clawing at his face.

"You're just like all the rest. You think you're better than me. I'll show you who's better. I'll show you," he said through gritted teeth as he raised her shirt and ripped her nylon shorts from her body.

While he held her by the throat, he unzipped his jeans and exposed his erect penis. Liz pushed her knee into his stomach, trying to force him away but he twisted her leg out of the way. She could hear a pop as her knee went numb. Alan held her leg with one hand and her throat with the other as his massive frame covered her, his member plunging deep inside her. She could feel him inside her, the head of his penis straining

223

upward, pushing her back into the sofa with each hard thrust. Liz was powerless to stop him. She could barely breathe as he held his hand over her throat and groaned ungodly sounds. She could feel his ejaculation fill her as his face strained at his climax. He fell over her, his sweaty body clammy against hers, his breathing fast and uncontrollable. He finally released his hold on her throat. Liz coughed and choked, gasping for breath. Only after she had regained her breath did the reality of the rape set in. She had survived the attack but now she had to accept it. Alan rolled off and looked down at her, a smirk on his face. He stumbled out the door, leaving Liz on the couch in shock.

"I don't know how long I laid there. I couldn't move." Liz looked down, her hand holding Sheridan's tightly.

Sheridan didn't reply at first. Her eyes were full of tears and her face was white. She stroked Liz's face, anger growing so intense within her she could barely stand it. Sheridan wanted desperately to erase the past for Liz. She would give up all she had if she could only make it disappear.

"You called the police, didn't you?" Sheridan asked, trying to control her anger for what this monster had done to Liz.

"No, not right away. I was in shock. When Sara got back, I told her what happened. She didn't believe me. She thought I made it up. She said I made it up because I didn't like Alan. She said if I had sex with him, that was bad enough but to make up a story like that was worse. She thought I wanted him. She said I was jealous of him. God knows what I could possibly be jealous of," Liz said with a small smile. "When I finally decided to go to the police, Sara had a fit. She packs quite a punch. She said if I went to the cops she would beat the crap out of me. Then I heard about a foreign exchange student who was raped behind the library two days later. She was just walking back to the dorm after the library closed and someone attacked her. I went to see her and found out it was Alan who did it. She described him perfectly. That's when I went to the police. I moved out of our apartment that same day and never looked back. Before the police could catch him, Alan drove his car off a cliff and killed himself. Sara thinks I caused it." Liz leaned against Sheridan's shoulder and breathed deeply, the secret now told.

"What was it Sara wanted tonight? What did she say to you?"

"She told me if I played the rest of the season's games she was going to tell Becca about Alan. She still thinks, in her screwed up little mind, that it was my fault he died. She thinks he wouldn't have killed himself if I hadn't provoked him."

"My God, is she crazy or something?" Sheridan scowled.

"The funny thing is, for a while I agreed with her. I thought maybe it was somehow my fault. I had no idea how but he was dead and I had a beautiful baby girl. I figured I did something wrong."

"How could you think that for even a second?" Sheridan said tenderly.

"I got over it pretty fast. I think the whole year was just a big blur for me."

"So Sara never knew you were carrying Alan's child?" Sheridan asked.

Liz immediately flashed a stare at her, one filled with disapproval.

"I was not carrying Alan's baby. I was carrying my baby. That is the whole reason I never told Sara I was pregnant. I moved out before I knew I was pregnant and I stayed away from her. She moved out of Ashton in late September so she never saw me with a fat tummy. But Becca was mine and mine alone. She was something special to me from the moment I found out I wasn't just having the stomach flu, it was morning sickness." Liz shook her head then closed her eyes with exasperation. "And boy oh boy did I ever have morning sickness. For six weeks I did nothing but throw up and sleep. I had to put off having my ACL repaired until after it subsided. And I had to have it done under a local anesthetic so it wouldn't hurt the baby."

"You tore your ACL playing basketball?" Sheridan asked sympathetically.

"Alan did it. I found out later my knee was the pop I heard

when he attacked me. I let everyone believe I did it playing basketball."

"And you never had second thoughts about having the baby?"

"NO! Never. If someone would have asked me what I thought about having babies and abortion I always thought it was a woman's right to choose. I don't approve of partial birth abortion but if a woman wants to terminate a pregnancy, it is up to her and her doctor, not politicians or ministers. But I truly wanted a baby someday. When I realized I had an opportunity to have one, I told myself it was like an answer to a prayer. It was the only way I could find something good in what happened to me. I know. I gave up playing with my teammates my senior year but it was worth it. I'd do it all over again if I had the chance. I wouldn't change a thing." Liz chuckled. "Well maybe a few things. I would never have allowed Becca to finger paint on the dining room table."

Sheridan smiled at her and wrapped an arm around her.

"What was it you wanted to talk with me about?" Liz asked, hoping to change the subject.

"It can wait. This is more important than anything I have to say," Sheridan replied understandingly. "Let's take care of one problem at a time. What do you want me to do about Sara? Should I call the police?"

"No," Liz said instantly. "I don't want to create anymore problems than I already have. What would they do anyway? There is no crime in turning out the lights in a gymnasium and talking about what happened in the past. No, all the police will do is to make matters worse. I'm going to talk to Becca myself."

"I would completely understand if you didn't want to play the last games."

Liz leered up at her, her eyes hard and fierce.

"NO! I will not give in to Sara. She is not going to influence my life any longer. I *am* going to play those last games. I have always told Becca to stay the course, no matter what. If I crawl off and hide because of something Sara said, I could never earn Becca's respect again."

"I admire that decision. Becca will too." Sheridan nodded her support.

"I have to tell Becca. If I am going to play the last two games, I don't want Sara to be the one to tell her. I want it to come from me."

"When are you going to tell her? The game is in two days."

"I'll tell her tomorrow. I can't face it tonight. I need to be calm and thinking clearly. I don't want to upset her anymore than I have to."

"Becca is an intelligent woman. Don't underestimate her ability to accept this." Sheridan patted Liz's arm. "She may surprise you."

"We'll see," Liz replied, staring out the window. "Her birthday is next week. My baby will be twenty. I hate for this to be her birthday present."

Chapter 22

Liz skipped the early morning run she had planned and went to The Sugar Bush to both start the day's activities and to plan how she would tell Becca about the rape, the lies and her worry about Sara.

"I thought you were going running this morning," Pauline said as she hung her coat in the closet.

"I changed my mind. I wanted to get an early start on the menu this morning." Liz was peeling and chopping vegetables.

"Is Becca working today?"

"Yes. She should be in by ten," Liz replied.

"I made her some potato soup last night. She said she tried it and it burnt in the pan." Pauline laughed. "That girl wants everything done in a hurry. She has no patience."

Liz hoped Becca at least had the patience to listen to her explain the secret she had been keeping from her.

The breakfast patrons came and went throughout the morning,

providing a steady stream of customers. Sheridan came in for coffee and to offer a kind smile.

"How are you doing?" she said as Liz poured her refill. "Have you talked to Becca yet?"

Liz shook her head but kept a smile on her face for the other customers.

"She gets in at ten," she offered then went to fill other cups.

Sheridan checked her watch and heaved a deep sigh.

"Do you want me to leave?" she asked, touching Liz's arm as she passed.

"No," Liz replied softly. "I think I'd like you to stay, if you don't mind."

Sheridan nodded toward the door. Becca walked in, smiling and waving to everyone.

"I'll be right here if you need me," Sheridan offered.

Liz followed Becca into the kitchen, trying to decide when was the right moment and how she would start.

"Mark called," Becca said, digging in the refrigerator for something to call breakfast. "He has invited me to go with him to Myrtle Beach on spring break. We can even cook in the kitchen. It isn't a huge kitchen but at least we can heat pizza and open a can of spaghetti." She looked over at Liz for a reaction.

"That's nice," Liz replied nonchalantly.

"Mom," Becca frowned. "What is it?"

"What makes you think something is wrong?"

"I said we would be eating pizza and spaghetti out of a can and you didn't have a fit about it. There has to be something on your mind. What is it?" She perched a hand on her hip and stared at her mother.

"As a matter of fact, I do need to talk with you for a minute," Liz said after taking a deep breath. She took Becca's hand and led her into her office then closed the door. "Sit down, honey."

"Oh, God! It's major," she joked. "You never let me sit down before you lecture me."

"Honey, this is serious." Liz sat down and patted the chair for Becca.

"What is it, Mom?" she asked, lowering herself into the chair, a frown showing her concern.

"Do you remember meeting a woman a long time ago, Sara Ruddick?"

"Yes, the tall one with dark hair. She was your girlfriend when you were in college, right? She's the one who called when you were in Northampton stuck in that blizzard."

"Uh-huh," Liz agreed. So far, so good. "She is back in town."

"Jesus, Mom. You aren't seeing her again, are you? She is creepy. She had clammy hands, I remember that. I thought you and Coach Ross were seeing each other. She is way, way better." Becca said it as if she was giving her permission.

"No. I am not seeing Sara again."

"Good!"

"What I want to tell you has to do with Sara and our relationship before you were born."

"Yeah," Becca said skeptically.

"Sara and I lived in an apartment here in Ashton during our junior year at Chilton."

"That's why you didn't live with grandpa and grandma, right? You and she were serious."

"Yes. It only lasted about a year. Then something happened. Something that changed our relationship."

"Me?" Becca asked carefully.

Liz didn't know how to answer that. She didn't want Becca to think she caused the break up.

"The fact is Sara is your aunt." Liz let that soak in a moment.

"She's my what?" Becca's eyes got big. "That means—"

"It means Sara's brother, Alan is, or rather was, your father."

"He was the donor when you were artificially inseminated?"

"Becca, I wasn't artificially inseminated. That isn't how I got pregnant." Liz leaned forward and placed her hand on Becca's. "Sweetheart, Alan was a troubled young man. He had some problems. Bad problems."

"And?"

"Alan raped me." Liz looked deep into Becca's eyes. "He was drunk and too strong. I couldn't stop him."

Becca's mouth dropped and her face drained of color.

"But you said you wanted a baby. You had always told me you didn't want to wait so you chose artificial insemination. Now you tell me I was not only an accident but the result of a rape," Becca declared, her words cold and harsh.

"Sweetheart, I did. I wanted a baby. You were so precious when you were born."

"Rape?" Becca said again, the sound of it glistening in her eyes. Becca stood up and glowered down at Liz. "Why did you lie to me all these years? Why didn't you tell me? I had a right to know."

"I didn't tell you because I wanted to protect you."

"Protect me? From what, the truth?"

"I didn't want Sara to know you were her niece."

"Why not? Are you ashamed of me? That's it. You are ashamed of me, aren't you." Becca backed up against the door, her eyes flamed with rage. "You are ashamed of me because I was the result of a rape."

"NO! Absolutely not. I am very proud of you. I have always been proud of you." Liz tried to remain calm and levelheaded so she could finish what she had to say. "I wasn't the only one Alan attacked, Becca. That's why Sara and I split up. She refused to accept that Alan could do that. I wanted to go to the police but she convinced me not to. Then he did it to someone else. A foreign exchange student. When I finally got the courage to go to the police they already knew about him. There was a warrant out for his arrest. Alan went crazy. He drove his car off the side of mountain. Sara blamed me. She always has."

Becca was still in shock, taking in the news one bitter piece at a time.

"So my father is dead," she said, her eyes lowered.

"Yes. He died before you were born. In fact I didn't know I was pregnant until after I left Sara and moved out of the apartment. I never told her you were the result of Alan's attack. I didn't want her in our lives. When she showed up in Ashton when you were five years old, I told her I had artificial insemination. I even lied to her about your birthday so she wouldn't suspect anything."

"Why are you telling me all this now?"

"Sara is the one who left the note last night. The S.R. on the note was her. I didn't know it until I got to the gymnasium. I thought I was going to meet Sheridan."

"What did Sara want?"

"She still blames me for Alan's death. She has some crazy ideas that I am the cause of all her problems in life. She can't keep a job. She has a hot temper just like Alan. Sara told me she was going to tell you about Alan, about his death. She was going to tell you I killed him. She won't admit he killed himself. The police were following him and he refused to stop. He was going over sixty miles an hour when he hit the guardrail head-on and went over the cliff. He never slowed down."

"How did she know I was her niece? I thought you lied to her, too."

"She guessed."

Liz looked away a moment then back to Becca.

"I didn't want her to be the one to tell you. I wanted it to come from me."

Becca stood staring at her mother, her mind a blur with Liz's confession.

"Would you have ever told me on your own? If Sara hadn't come to town and threatened to tell me, would you have ever done it?" she asked with a riveting stare.

Liz stood up and went to hug her daughter but Becca stepped back.

"Would you have told me?" she repeated.

"I don't know, sweetheart. I just wanted to protect you."

Becca's face melted into disappointment.

"Protect me from what? Your lies?" She stormed out of the office and into the dining room. Sheridan saw her coming and stood up, ready to offer support but Becca pushed past her and out the front door.

"Becca," Sheridan called after her but she broke into a dead-run down the sidewalk. Liz came into the dining room just in time to see Becca turn the corner and disappear. She ran her hand through her hair and gasped.

"How did it go?" Sheridan asked cautiously.

"Guess?" Liz closed her eyes and shook her head disgustedly. "I better go find her."

"No," Sheridan said, stopping Liz before she could open the door. "Give her some time. You've had twenty years to deal with it. She's only had two minutes."

"All she can see is that I lied to her. She doesn't understand why."

"I know. But give her a chance to think about it. She has to deal with it in her own way."

Sheridan wrapped her arm around Liz and walked her back into the kitchen. Pauline and Georgia couldn't help but overhear both the office conversation and Becca's inflamed exit. They tried not to stare at Liz but the silence in the kitchen was deafening.

Pauline walked over to Liz and tried to smile at her through her tears. She grabbed Liz and hugged her but didn't say anything. Georgia also came to give Liz a hug and patted her face.

"We are here for you, honey," Georgia whispered. "If you need anything, anything at all, you tell us. Okay?"

Liz nodded and smiled back at them.

"Why don't you let us handle things here today?" Pauline suggested.

"Thank you, but I'm all right." Liz went back into the dining room to check on her clientele, Sheridan following close behind.

"Liz, do you have time to sit and have a cup of coffee with me?" Sheridan asked.

"I know you want to help but I can't deal with anything else right now. I have a wedding reception for eighty people on

233

Saturday, a game tomorrow night, and my daughter thinks I'm Attila the Hun. I don't think I want to add your moving to Kansas to that list of worries right now. I'm sorry."

"I'll understand if you want to skip practice this afternoon," Sheridan offered.

Liz closed her eyes and threw her head back as she remembered that as well.

"I forgot all about practice. No, I'll be there. I haven't missed a class or a practice yet this year and I'm not starting now."

"Are you sure?"

"Yes," Liz replied, her eyes flashing her defiance.

Liz spent the day working at the restaurant and keeping a watchful eye out for Becca's return. She wrestled with how she could have broken the news to her in hopes of easing the trauma but the facts still remained the same. That she couldn't change.

Liz arrived at practice on time, barely. Becca had waited until the last possible moment to return to The Sugar Bush to take over for her mother. Becca didn't speak to anyone as she stormed into the kitchen and began helping with the clean-up and shut-down chores. Liz didn't have time to stay and talk with her and it was obvious that was what Becca had hoped. When Liz got to practice, she warmed up, taking her normal shots but it was plain that her mind was someplace else. She missed more than she made and some shots weren't even close. Sheridan gave her a kind smile and nodded her support, as if to understand what was bothering her.

Sheridan set up the scrimmage, giving special attention to some plays she thought could take advantage of the opponent's weaknesses. She substituted frequently, looking for the best combination of players to execute the sagging zone defense she planned on running. Sheridan blew her whistle and called Liz to the sidelines then restarted the scrimmage.

"Jen isn't breaking fast enough for that pass," Sheridan pointed out.

"No kidding. I've thrown it out of bounds three times." Liz gasped, regaining her breath from the fast break drill.

"Give her a half count more to get there. Don't lead her with the pass or it will be picked off."

Liz watched her teammates run the play, looking for places to improve.

Sheridan blew her whistle again.

"Catch a drink, ladies. Take five."

Liz started for the drinking fountain but Sheridan called to her then tossed her the water bottle she was carrying.

"How is Becca taking the news?" Sheridan asked carefully.

"Good question," Liz replied, wiping the sweat from her chin with her sleeve. "I have no idea. She is giving me the silent treatment."

Sheridan frowned, wishing she could help.

"I'm sorry. Can I do anything?" she offered.

"No. There's nothing to do. I just have to wait her out. I hope she decides to talk to me sometime before she graduates." Liz heaved a sigh.

"You know she loves you, Liz. She is just adjusting."

"I'm not so sure about that. She ranks me just above broccoli and below the color burnt orange."

"Wow, burnt orange. That isn't good." Sheridan winked and wrapped her arm around Liz reassuringly. "Seriously, Becca is a smart girl. She just needs a little time to work through it. Deep down she knows you were only trying to protect her."

"I wonder. I should have never lied to her. I just thought she didn't need to know the truth about her father. I thought it would only hurt her."

"Don't forget what you said last night. He was not her father. He was just a sperm donor. Nothing more." Sheridan stared at her adamantly. "You remember that. You were not protecting her from her father. You were protecting her from the vicious attack you suffered."

Liz wished they weren't at practice. She wanted to throw her arms around Sheridan and bury herself in her warm embrace. She wanted to lose herself in a long passionate kiss. But a group of ladies streamed back into the gym—and the reality of Sheridan's new job only meant there was more heartbreak ahead.

"How are *you* doing, Liz?" Sheridan asked softly.

Liz chuckled and raised her eyebrows at the question.

"Me? I'm just peachy. My daughter won't speak to me. I need roof repairs on my house and my restaurant. My business accounting professor has been calling, trying to get a date with me. He won't take no for an answer. My girlfriend took a job in Kansas. Oh, yes, I also broke a fingernail. Do you want to see which one?"

"No thanks. I think I can guess which one." Sheridan chuckled quietly. "I would completely understand if you didn't want to play the last games."

Liz leered up at her, her eyes hard and fierce.

"No! I will not give in to Sara's demand. She is not going to influence my life any longer."

"I admire that decision. Becca will too." Sheridan nodded her support.

"Send me in, Coach. I need to play." Liz turned her attention back to basketball.

"Okay, if you are sure." Sheridan blew her whistle and made substitutions then restarted the scrimmage.

After practice Liz drove by The Sugar Bush but it was closed and dark. Becca had done her job efficiently in spite of her anger toward her mother. Liz went home and made a sandwich for dinner but had little appetite. Becca wasn't home but that didn't surprise her. Liz stood at the front door, staring out into the darkness, deciding if she wanted to go for a run. She longed for the peace and solitude it would provide but she knew both Becca and Sheridan would be on her mind. She turned on her heels. She went to the telephone and dialed Hec.

"Hello, Dad," she said.

"How's my daughter and granddaughter?" Hec asked.

"We're fine." There was a hesitation in her voice.

"What's wrong?" he asked carefully.

236

"There's nothing wrong. Can't I call my father just to say hello?"

"Liz," he said sternly.

"Okay, okay. I did want to ask you something, if you don't mind," she said after a moment.

"Let's hear it."

"It's about Becca," she started.

"Yep."

"About when I had Becca," she added.

"Yep."

"I know we didn't talk much about it. That's when Mom was so sick."

"Is Becca sick?" he asked without hesitation.

"No, Dad. She's fine. Her leg is healing nicely," Liz said reassuringly.

"Good."

"Do you remember that summer, Dad?" Liz asked after a long pause.

"Yes, I remember."

"The summer I found out I was pregnant?" she added to make sure he knew what she was talking about.

"I remember," he said at last.

"Dad, do you think I should have told Becca what happened?"

He fell silent.

"Tell her what?" he said finally. "About that animal that attacked you? Hell no. That's something better left in the past. Son-of-a-bitch should have been shot. Driving over the cliff like that was too goddamned easy for the bastard." There was a venom in Hec's voice Liz hadn't heard for a long time. The last time he had carried on about Alan was the night she came to the farm and told her parents what had happened. Hec was a quiet, simple farmer. But the night Liz showed up in tears over being raped, she and her mother had to forcibly restrain him from tracking down Alan with a shotgun.

237

"I never told Becca about Alan Ruddick. I told her she was the result of artificial insemination. I thought I could protect her. I didn't want her to know the ugly truth about what happened. But something happened and I had to tell her," Liz explained.

"What happened?" he asked harshly.

"Sara, Alan's sister, is back in Ashton and she threatened to tell her."

"You aren't living with that woman again, are you?"

"No, Dad. I haven't seen her in years. She didn't even know Becca was Alan's until yesterday."

"Why did you tell her? She doesn't need to know our personal family business," he said, surprising Liz with his concern and family pride.

"She figured it out. She wants me to quit the team or she's going to tell Becca all about Alan."

"You going to quit the team, daughter?" he asked sternly.

"No, I am not. That's why I told Becca myself. I wanted her to know the truth from me," Liz explained.

"I guess you had to tell her then."

"Dad, do you think it was wrong of me to keep it from her all these years? She is so mad at me."

Hec thought a moment before answering.

"Liz, you are a good mother to that girl. Don't you ever second-guess your decisions. You always made smart choices where she was concerned."

"But she hates me. She thinks I'm ashamed of her." Liz's voice cracked.

"Don't live in the past. You can't change that." There was a quiver in his voice as if the subject was still very hard for him. "I'm very proud of you, daughter. I've always been proud of you. Your mother was too."

"Thank you, Dad," Liz whispered, her emotions tightening her throat.

"I'm proud of Becca, too. You know that, don't you? It doesn't matter that she . . ." Hec's words trailed off.

238

Liz knew what he was trying to say and it touched her deeply to hear it, even if he hadn't actually finished the thought. She always suspected her father accepted Becca without reservation but to hear it from his lips was as comforting as a hug.

"She's my granddaughter, Liz."

"She loves you too, Dad."

"She's a smart girl, that one is. You remember that. Becca's going to be someone to reckon with one of these days." Hec chuckled, as if trying to lighten the conversation.

"No doubt, Dad. No doubt."

"I have to go. Time to milk," he inserted.

"I love you, Dad," Liz said, expecting to hear Hec hang up. There was a pause.

"I love you too, daughter," he said in a low but unmistakable voice. He then hung up. One tear trailed down Liz's cheek at his words, something he hadn't said in years.

Chapter 23

"Are you sure about this?" Sheridan asked quietly as Liz sat on the bench in the locker room, double knotting her shoes.

"Yes, I'm sure. I have to play. Becca has to know I keep my word. I said I would play and I am," she replied, adjusting her shorts. "Besides, Coach. I only need six points," Liz grinned, trying to make light of the subject.

"I bet you are nervous about that," Sheridan replied.

"Actually, I'm not. I'll get them or I won't. I just plan on playing my best so we can win the game." Liz sounded confident and focused.

"I'm very proud of you, you know."

"Thank you," she said, heaving a deep sigh. "I wish Becca was. She didn't come to the game. She said she was busy."

"I'm sorry for her. She's going to miss quite a moment in Chilton history. Her mother is about to set a record that will be hard to break."

"I think worrying about Becca and how she is taking the news is what keeps me from being nervous about the game," Liz advised.

"Okay, ladies," Sheridan announced across the locker room. "Let's hit the floor and show them how it is done." She applauded encouragement as the players streamed out of the locker room and into the gymnasium.

The crowd was large and noisy. The word had spread about Liz Elliott's potentially record-setting game and that brought fans from as far away as Burlington to watch and cheer her on. The first half was slow, with the opponents setting a reserved pace. Liz scored only three points. Sheridan made some adjustments at half-time, hoping to spark the offense into a faster pace. It worked. The Stingers began to pull away, scoring ten unanswered points. Liz scored one more point from the free throw line but her outside shooting was off. Sheridan called for a time-out with less than thirty seconds left to play and Liz three points short of a record.

"Good job, ladies," she said, congratulating them as they came to the huddle. She turned to Liz with a serious expression. "Shoot a three-pointer, you hear me!" Her eyes were hard and demanding. "I know you can do it so just shoot it. Don't think about it. Just let it go." Sheridan clapped her hands and sent them back into the game.

The crowd came to their feet and cheered as Liz brought the ball over the half-court line. She dribbled across the top of the lane, looking inside for Deb or Trish to be open for a pass. She could hear Sheridan's voice from the bench calling to her to shoot a three. The fans were screaming at her to shoot as well. With four seconds on the clock, Liz stepped back over the three-point line and released a shot. It seemed like slow motion as the ball arced up in a steep angle then bounced on the rim and fell through the basket. The crowd erupted. Both Chilton and Ramsey College fans cheered wildly as the buzzer sounded. Not only did the Lady Stingers have a victory but Liz Elliott had her record-setting season. Two hundred thirteen points that no one could take away from her.

Her teammates hoisted her to their shoulders and carried her off the floor, tears streaming down from Liz's face as she waved to the crowd. Even though she knew she wasn't there, Liz scanned the crowd for Becca's face.

Sheridan waited for Liz in front of the scorer's table, applauding and whistling her achievement. She shook her hand and gave her a warm hug, the kind of hug expected of a coach, not the kind they both had exchanged in the private moments they had shared. But Liz could feel Sheridan's warm arms around her and it felt reassuring.

"Nice shot at the buzzer," Deb said, stepping into the shower.

"Thanks. You played a nice game yourself," Liz replied, rinsing the shampoo from her hair. "Did you happen to see Becca in the stands?" She didn't want to admit to Deb she probably wasn't there.

"Nope, I didn't see her. I got a text message from her on my cell phone though." Deb lathered up her hair then looked over at Liz. "It was kind of a strange message."

"What did it say?" Liz asked as she finished rinsing her body.

"She said yes, she'd meet me at Lucky's after the game. It's that new place out on the highway. She made it sound like I had suggested it. But I haven't talked to her or sent her a message since Monday. I have been busy on a term paper."

Liz frowned at her.

"Is that all the message said?" she asked with a worried gaze.

"She said she'd meet me at nine thirty at Lucky's. That's all it said."

Liz immediately wrapped a towel around herself and went to her locker. She took out her cell phone and punched in Becca's number.

"Come on, answer honey. Be there." Liz's held her breath as she waited anxiously for Becca to answer.

"Hello, pussycat," Sara said in a haunting voice.

"Oh, my God," Liz gasped as the color drained from her face.

"I told you not to play that game, Liz. You didn't listen to me. You never listen to me, pussycat."

"Where's Becca?"

"She's here with me. We are having a nice little visit about things. It's very interesting." Sara chuckled wickedly.

"It's no use, Sara. I already told her about Alan. You're too late."

"I know. You told her lies, pussycat. LIES!"

"Where are you? Are you at Lucky's?"

"I guess Deb told you about the message. Kids have no respect for their elders, you know."

"Where are you Sara? Where is my daughter?"

Sheridan had come into the locker room and overheard Liz's conversation. She stood next to her, a concerned frown on her face.

"It's hard, isn't it?" Sara said. "Not knowing where your family is. Worrying what happened to them. Never suspecting it could be tragic. Tough isn't it, pussycat?" Sara veritably hissed the words.

"Sara!" Liz screamed. "Tell me where Becca is." Her hands started to shake and her throat tightened.

Sheridan grabbed the cell phone from her.

"Sara, this is Sheridan Ross. Please, tell us where Becca is. Let us come get her and this will all be forgotten." She spoke calmly.

"Forgotten? Nothing can be forgotten, Coach. You should know that. You have my woman. How can I forget that?"

"Sara, I didn't take Liz from you."

"I have been watching the two of you. I've seen your hands on her ass. I've seen the way you look at her. Don't take me for a fool, Coach," Sara declared harshly.

"Whatever happened between you and Liz twenty years ago is history. Becca is innocent. If you want to take your anger out on someone, take it out on me, Sara. Not Becca. She had nothing to do with it. You've got the wrong person."

"SHUT UP!"

"Let us come get Becca. You don't want to hurt her," Sheridan continued.

There was an eerie silence.

"Sure, I'll let Liz have her daughter back," Sara said finally.

243

"The question is, will she want her when I'm done with her." Sara gave a witchy cackle then the phone went dead.

Without hesitation, Sheridan dialed the police. As she waited for them to answer she wrapped her arm around Liz's trembling shoulders. Deb and the other players quickly read the panic on Liz's face. They gathered around listening to the telephone call. Deb came to hug Liz, both of them pale with fear.

"The police will put out an APB for Becca and for Sara. Do you know Becca's license plate number?" Sheridan asked carefully, not wanting to worry Liz any more than necessary.

Liz looked up at her blankly, her mind too rattled to concentrate.

"I don't remember." Liz was horrified.

"That's okay. That's okay," she replied reassuringly. "They can look it up." Sheridan rubbed Liz's back, offering support and comfort. She was trying to calm her own fears while hoping to quiet Liz's growing panic. "Everyone go ahead and get dressed. The police will be here shortly. They will take care of this. Becca will be fine," Sheridan said, broadcasting a confident smile and hoping to defuse the growing alarm in the locker room. "Catch a shower and give Liz a little space here."

"I need to go look for Becca," Liz said suddenly. She went to her locker and began rummaging for her keys, unaware she was still dressed in only a towel.

"Let's wait for the police," Sheridan said, gently taking the keys from her hand. "Why don't you get dressed?" Sheridan spoke calmly, doing a good job of hiding her own concern over Sara's vicious threat. She knew Liz needed a steadying force to guide her and comfort her. Sheridan didn't even want to think what Sara might do to Becca. From what Liz had told her, anything seemed possible. Liz dressed in silence while they waited for the police to arrive. She refused to give in to tears, holding tight to her emotions.

The Addison County sheriff arrived along with three police officers and two deputies. Several campus police also offered their resources, limited as they were.

"We've already put out the description on the suspect and the victim," the sheriff offered. Liz's expression went from worry to sheer terror when he said victim.

"That's just the term they use, Liz." Sheridan scowled at the man. "Becca will be all right." She stood next to Liz and placed a gentle hand on her shoulder.

"According to the witnesses at Lucky's, they left in Becca's car," the sheriff reported.

"I don't remember the license plate," Liz offered, her voice dripping with guilt.

"We've got it, ma'am. Do you know which way they were headed?"

Liz shook her head.

"I don't know where they were when I talked to Sara."

"Did you talk to your daughter?" he asked, taking notes on a pad.

"No, Sara answered Becca's cell phone. But I assume she was with her."

"I'm sorry but I have to ask this. Did Becca have any reason to want to leave with her? Were you two having any problems? You know, mother-daughter arguments, stuff like that."

Liz hesitated then shook her head. Sheridan gave the officers a quick review of Liz's history with Sara, explaining only that they knew each other twenty years ago and that Sara's motives were jealous and vindictive. She also said that Sara's family history showed mental instabilities. When Liz mentioned Alan's name, the sheriff's brow furrowed with recognition.

"This is Alan Ruddick's sister?" he asked seriously.

"Yes," Liz replied.

"I remember her. She's the one with the temper from hell," he declared as he made a note then reached for his walkie-talkie.

"Shouldn't you be out there looking for them?" Liz declared angrily.

"Ma'am, we've got every deputy and police officer combing the county for them. State highway patrol is on the case and the New Hampshire patrol is watching out for them in case they cross the state line. So are Massachusetts, Maine, Connecticut and New York. We've even notified the Canadian border patrol in case she tries to head north. It hasn't been enough time for her to get out of state but we are taking no chances, ma'am. We'll find them." His confidence was welcome.

"I can't just stay here," Liz said to Sheridan. "I have to go look, too."

"I know," Sheridan replied, understanding Liz's need to help find her daughter.

"I've got your cell phone number," the sheriff said. "I'll call you when we hear something."

"We'll be in my car. We can be there in no time." Sheridan didn't mind admitting she had a muscle car and could put the peddle to the metal if she needed to. "Stay in touch, you hear me," she stated, fixing him with a determined stare.

"We will," he replied, reading Sheridan's inflection.

Liz wasn't sure where she wanted to start the search. She wasn't even sure why she insisted they drive by her house, The Sugar Bush, the apartment she and Sara once shared and the Pizza Barn. But she had to start somewhere.

"God, I hope Becca doesn't say anything to set her off. You know how stubborn Becca can be sometimes. She won't take crap off anyone," Liz said.

"She can handle herself," Sheridan replied, patting her hand.

"Let's head out to Lucky's," Liz suggested, her eyes darting back and forth, peering into the darkness for signs of Becca or her car.

They circled through the parking lot then Sheridan ran in to ask if anyone remembered seeing them. The police had already been there and no one had any information for them other than Becca left with a dark-haired woman shortly after she arrived.

"Where now?" Sheridan asked, sitting in the parking lot ready to take Liz to the ends of the earth if necessary.

Liz looked over at her, her chin quivering.

"I don't know where to look," Liz whispered as tears began to roll down her cheeks.

Sheridan's jaw rippled as she saw the pain in Liz's face. She wanted desperately to wipe away the tears and the fear but she felt powerless. She stroked Liz's face gently.

"I know, sweetheart. I know. I'm here for you, remember that. I'm right here." She offered a stoic smile. "They'll find her."

"I never should have played that game," Liz muttered.

"Stop that. This is not your fault. It is not." Sheridan spoke defiantly. "You are not to blame for any of this. Not the rape, not Becca's reaction, and certainly not for Sara's return to Ashton. She is responsible for what she has done. Do you hear me?" She took Liz's hands in hers. "You are a brave and wonderful person, Liz Elliott. So is Becca. Don't let Sara's irrational behavior make you think otherwise."

"I wish—" Liz started, but melted into tears. Sheridan held her in her arms and closed her eyes, fighting back her own tears. Liz's cell phone rang, making them both jump. Liz stared at it, seemingly incapable of answering. Sheridan reached over and took the cell phone from her hand.

"It's the sheriff," she said, reading the caller ID. She quickly answered the call.

"Sheriff Martin?" she said.

"Is this Sheridan Ross?" he asked with a reserved voice.

Sheridan instantly heard something bad in his words but didn't want to alarm Liz.

"Yes," she replied.

"Highway fifty-five just past Lookout Point," he reported. "We've found a break in the guardrail. I told you I'd let you know what we've found." There was a silence. "We think there is a car over the side."

Sheridan closed her eyes and swallowed hard.

"We'll be right there." Sheridan hung up and peeled out of the parking lot without saying a word. Liz seemed to know the call wasn't good news. She sat silently, staring out the window, her breaths short and shallow as she tried to safeguard her emotions. As they neared Lookout Point, Sheridan placed a hand on Liz's arm.

"The sheriff said they found a break in the guardrail," she offered. "They think a car might have gone over the edge at Lookout Point." She looked over at Liz with kind eyes. "Maybe it was someone else, sweetheart."

"No," Liz said in a whisper. "It is Becca. I can feel it." Liz's eyes scanned the dark sky as a single tear rolled down her cheek. She didn't say anything else. She couldn't. The anguish was too great. As they rounded a curve and eased past the roadblock, the flashing lights from several patrol cars, a fire truck, a rescue truck and an ambulance lit the night sky. Sheridan pulled onto the shoulder well back of the emergency vehicles. She reached for the door handle, expecting to see Liz do the same but she sat frozen in her seat.

"I can't go over there," Liz whispered. "I can't." She gazed out over the valley, diverting her eyes from the commotion at the accident site.

"You stay here," Sheridan said, patting her hand. "I'll be back." Sheridan left Liz in the car and hurried up to the group of officers looking over the edge of the cliff. The sheriff was talking with one of the rescue workers. He took a deep breath when he saw Sheridan walking over to him.

"Is Miss Elliott here?" he asked with a reserved voice.

"She's over there in the car. This is very hard for her. Is that Becca's car?" Sheridan asked.

"Yes," he stated. "It looks like they didn't even slow down. There are no skid marks." He pointed his flashlight along the pavement. "It's pretty rugged down there. We might need Liz to identify the body."

Sheridan's face dropped and her stomach immediately turned over. She felt faint at the image of Becca lying at the bottom of the ravine. She squatted down, trying to keep from passing out. She couldn't imagine how she was going to tell Liz.

"I'll do it," she said. "I'm her coach. I'll identify the body."

"We really need a family member," he replied.

"I said I'll do it," she insisted, standing up and squaring her shoulders.

"Darmen," the sheriff said to one of the rescue workers. "She'll do the ID." He pointed to Sheridan and signaled for him to help her down the hill.

Sheridan followed the rescue worker as he eased his way down the side, holding on to the ropes that had been lowered to the crash site.

"I haven't been down here yet," he said, mapping their route with his flashlight. "But I hear it's pretty bad. The car snagged on the trees then rolled over several times. One of the doors was ripped off." He seemed to think she needed to hear all the ghastly details. Sheridan kept her eyes on the trail, not wanting to see the pieces of wreckage that littered the path.

Several firefighters were prying the driver's door open. Sheridan could see someone slumped forward, their arm hooked through the steering wheel and bent back at a gruesome angle. The driver's head had struck the windshield, leaving bloodstains on the shattered glass. The passenger's door was missing, and the hood was folded back over the roof of the car. Sheridan took a deep breath and accompanied the fireman to the driver's side of the car. He looked in and grimaced then stepped back out of the way.

"Do you recognize this person?" he asked, his face pale.

Sheridan hesitated then looked in. She carefully pushed back the bloodstained locks of dark hair. Her eyes widened and her jaw muscles rippled as she looked at the shattered face. She could barely breathe as the tears streamed down her face.

"Where is the other person?" she gasped, turning away from the brutal scene.

"Over here," one of the rescue workers yelled from the darkness.

Liz had gotten out of the car and stood next to it, her arms crossed nervously. She grappled with her emotions, wanting to run to the accident but too afraid of what lie over the edge of the cliff to accept it. Suddenly she saw Sheridan's head as she climbed up the side of the hill. Sheridan brushed off her pants then looked across the road at Liz. Liz took a pained breath and started slowly toward her, her eyes riveted to Sheridan's. She stopped in the middle of the road as another head rose over the side of the cliff. It was Becca, holding a rescue blanket around her shoulders. She stood next to Sheridan, looking over at her mother. Liz couldn't speak. She screamed her daughter's name, tears flowing down her face.

"Go to your mother, Becca," Sheridan said to her. "She needs you."

Becca dropped the blanket and ran to Liz, hugging her tightly. They stood in the road, crying in each other's arms for a long time. Neither one could put into words how it felt to hold the other. Sheridan leaned against her car, watching the tender moment. She didn't want to interfere with their joy and relief at being together again. Finally Liz looked over at her and smiled warmly. She came to Sheridan and looked deep into her eyes.

"Thank you for bringing my daughter back to me."

"I didn't do anything," she replied. "I just walked her up the hill."

"But you were here for me. You don't know how important that was." Liz touched Sheridan's face. "Thank you."

Becca came over and offered Sheridan a handshake.

"I want to thank you too, for taking care of my mom for me. I know now how much she loves me. I know what she said and what she did was to protect me from that woman. It was a brave thing to do. I understand that now."

Sheridan looked at her hand but didn't shake it. Instead she hugged Becca warmly. Becca hugged her back.

"Sara said some terrible things about you and about my mom. She obviously didn't know anything about us. She was just plain crazy," Becca scoffed. "I told her I didn't need a father, not with a mother like mine."

"You are a chip off the old block, Becca Elliott." Sheridan

smiled broadly. "You are a good daughter any mother would be proud of."

"Can we go home? EMTs checked me over and said I was fine. I'm hungry and I'm cold," she said, wrapping an arm around both Liz and Sheridan.

"You're always hungry," Liz joked, laughing wildly at her. She patted her daughter's dirty face. "How you escaped that accident is a pure miracle. For that, I am truly grateful."

"When the door flew off I just rolled out."

"It's true," Sheridan agreed. "She was laying on the ground with a dazed look in her eyes. Not a scratch on her."

"And Sara?" Liz asked cautiously.

Sheridan just stared at her, her eyes revealing the dreadful answer. Liz lowered her gaze.

"She didn't deserve that," she said quietly.

"I'm glad this worked out all right for you, Miss Elliott," Sheriff Martin said, striding over to them. "Your daughter is lucky she wasn't injured."

"Do you need us for anything else?" Sheridan asked, shaking his hand.

"No, not tonight. We'll need a statement from you but we can get that tomorrow. It's pretty clear what happened here. It's a shame a woman has to die like that. She could have gotten some help, if she'd only asked for it."

"Let's go home," Becca said, wanting to put the evening behind her as much as Liz did.

Sheridan still wanted to talk with Liz about her contract but she knew this wasn't the right time. This was Becca's and Liz's time to be mother and daughter. Sheridan pulled into Liz's drive.

"My car is still at the gymnasium," Liz suddenly realized.

"I'll take you to get it first thing in the morning," Sheridan offered. "You don't need it tonight. You two have had enough excitement for one evening. Go inside and talk."

"Would you like to come in? I'm going to fix us something to eat."

"No. Thanks, though. You two have a nice evening. This is your time to be together." Sheridan seemed to understand how much they had to talk about and she respected it.

"Thank you for everything," Liz replied and kissed Sheridan's cheek. "Come on Becca. Let's feed your hollow leg." Liz followed Becca to the front steps then looked back at Sheridan and waved. Sheridan waited until they were safely inside before pulling away. She drove to the end of the street then pulled to the curb. She could hold it in no longer. She sat in her car, crying like a baby. For the first time in her life Sheridan felt her heart dictating her actions, not her work. What had she done? How could she have accepted the job at KU? She didn't even want to think about how much she would miss Liz and her daughter.

Chapter 24

The fans were on their feet counting down the last ten seconds as Liz brought the ball across the center line. The outcome of the game was already decided and neither team was anxious to run another play before the final buzzer. Liz couldn't stop the tears that welled up in her eyes, knowing this was the culmination of her dream. A sense of satisfaction settled over her as she took one more dribble then held the ball over her head triumphantly. The buzzer sounded and the crowd cheered, marking the end of the game, the season and Liz's record setting basketball career. Becca stood up, whistling and hooting from the first row of the bleachers right behind the Chilton bench. Liz pointed to her, grinning broadly, as if passing the torch to her capable hands. Sheridan stood and applauded. She knew this had been Liz's dream come true. This was her moment of fame and she deserved every bit of it. She had worked hard and set her goals high. Sheridan admired her dedication more than she could express.

Liz blushed at the fans' enthusiasm. No one was leaving. They were cheering and screaming their love and respect for her and for the team. Tears began to roll down Liz's cheeks as she finally acknowledged the crowd with a wave and a tearful smile. She felt her composure melt as she noticed her father standing next to Becca and applauding. His face was beaming with pride. Hec smiled down at her and clasped his hands together victoriously. She blew him a kiss and clasped her hands together in reply. She knew how hard it had been for him to attend the game and it was a moment of great pride for her.

Finally her eyes met Sheridan's. They looked damp, as if she too was struggling with the emotions of the last game, Sheridan's last game at Chilton College. Liz couldn't dwell on that. She knew it would only bring on a fresh round of tears if she thought about losing Sheridan. The pain was too much to bear. Liz waved again to the cheering crowd then trotted off the floor. She could hear the applause all the way down the hall and into the locker room. She couldn't hold back the flood of emotions. She buried her face in her hands and sobbed. The players filed into the locker room, each one hugging her and offering congratulations to her and the other seniors.

"You were great," Deb said, holding Liz in a bear hug. "I'm so glad you decided to play with us. We will miss you next year."

Liz wiped the trail of tears from her cheeks and drew a deep, cleansing breath.

"Becca has big shoes to fill next year," Deb joked. "A bunch of the players are meeting at the Pizza Barn. We hope you'll come join us."

Liz tried to talk but tears again welled up in her eyes and spilled out.

"Tough leaving, huh?" Deb offered, wrapping an arm around her shoulders.

"Very," Liz replied.

She didn't want to admit her tears were as much relief for Becca's safe return from Sara's malicious attack as they were for the end of her basketball career. The locker room buzz was a blur for Liz. Everyone was laughing and joking about the end of the season and the prospects for next year. For Liz, the excitement and satisfaction over completing her college basketball career was somehow tarnished by the knowledge Sheridan was leaving.

Liz showered and dressed then ceremoniously tossed her sweaty uniform into the bin for the last time. As was the custom with all the seniors, Liz was asked to sign the inside of the uniform closet door. It was a tiny hall of fame for Chilton's Lady Stingers and considered an honor to be invited to stand on the Stinger logo embedded in the tile floor and autograph the weathered oak door. Liz finally said all her good-byes to her teammates and went to meet Becca and her father in the lobby. She hugged them both, tears again threatening to spill out.

"Thank you for coming to my last game, Dad," she whispered, holding him tight. He patted her back awkwardly.

"Grandpa's going to come watch me play next year, aren't you?" Becca beamed at him.

He gave a hesitant nod, swallowing back his fear.

"You play like your mother and I'll be here to watch," he said proudly.

Liz smiled at him, knowing how hard this had been for him.

"I'm taking Grandpa home, Mom," Becca said, locking her arm through his. "He invited me to spend the night and I said sure." Becca smiled at him affectionately.

"You two have a great time. Drive carefully." Liz waved as they headed out the door.

"There she is," squealed a twelve-year-old girl standing in the open door to the gymnasium. She ran up to Liz and pushed her program and a pen in her face. "Can I have your autograph, Miss Elliott?" she asked politely, her face aglow with excitement.

"Sure you can," Liz replied taking the pen and signing her name across the team picture. "What's your name?"

"Melissa," the girl replied brightly. "I play basketball, too. I'm on the sixth-grade team."

"Good for you. What position do you play?" Liz added a comment to Melissa under her signature.

"Point guard sometimes. Sometimes I play center." The girl seemed overjoyed with Liz's interest.

"You keep practicing and maybe someday I'll come watch you play here at Chilton." Liz smiled at her and brushed a stray lock of hair from the girl's eyes.

"Really? Wow, thanks." Melissa read what Liz wrote then ran off to show her parents the autograph. "Thank you," she said, looking back sheepishly.

"You're welcome, Melissa."

Liz stepped into the gymnasium. The bleachers were empty and the only noise came from the janitor unplugging the scoreboard clock from the scorer's table.

"Hi, Miss Elliott," he called, beaming brightly. "Twenty-three points tonight. Not bad. Would you like to try one more shot before you leave?" he asked, rolling a stray ball in her direction.

She set her tote bag on the floor and scooped up the basketball. She bounced it once, the echo reverberating through the rafters. She walked to the free throw line and looked up at the net. She remembered standing here a few short months ago and not being able to hit the rim. Those days were past. She could not only hit the rim, she could almost sink the shot blindfolded. It had been a season of dreams, a season of reliving the most treasured moments in her life and coming to grips with the most tragic times as well. It was also a time of great heartache over Sheridan's change of jobs. She rubbed the ball in her hands like she had done a thousand times. It would be easy to toss it up and hope it would go in one last time. She took a deep breath and let her eyes follow the arc the ball would take. Liz didn't shoot. She set the ball on the free throw line and walked out of the gymnasium. She didn't need to shoot again.

Liz stepped out into the crisp February night. She could feel the first hint of snow in the air. She fought the urge to call Becca to remind her the roads might be slick but she didn't need to call her. Becca was old enough to handle it.

Liz crossed the nearly empty parking lot to her car.

"Sneaking out?" Sheridan called from the doorway.

Liz looked back in surprise.

"Game's over. Time to go home," she replied.

Sheridan pulled on her jacket as she crossed the parking lot.

"Aren't you going to meet the team at the Pizza Barn?" Sheridan asked.

"No. I don't think so. I've lost my festive spirit."

"I'm glad your dad came to see your last game. I know that meant a lot to you," Sheridan said, rolling her collar up around her ears.

"Yes, it did. He said he will come watch Becca play next year, too. She seems to have a strange power over him."

"She's a good kid, Liz. You raised a smart, caring person." Sheridan touched a lock of Liz's hair. "She'll be a coach's dream."

"I guess I should congratulate you on your contract. I'm sorry I wasn't more supportive. You deserve that job at KU. You are a great coach." Liz stiffened her posture, trying to hold back the emotions that threatened to overtake her. She didn't want to discuss Sheridan's leaving but she couldn't help it. She could feel her heart breaking as she stood there staring into Sheridan's eyes. She told herself she would not break down and cry like a baby about it. If Sheridan could walk away from their relationship with a smile on her face, so could she.

"Oh, you mean this," Sheridan said, pulling a letter from her jacket pocket. She offered it to Liz to see.

"I don't want to see it, Sheridan. I really don't."

Sheridan tried to read the letter but the light in the parking lot was too dim.

"I've never had a contract this good before. It surprised even me. Five years with an option for a ten-year extension. Nice increase in salary with a bonus for post-season performance. I could buy a house if we could just win a conference championship," she chuckled. "It's a very satisfying contract."

Liz wanted to scream. With what they had between them, how could Sheridan be so insensitive and cavalier about it? How could she have accepted the job?

"I'm sorry you're leaving," Liz said with restrained emotion.

"You are?" Sheridan asked innocently.

"Yes, I am. You know I am. How can you ask that? I can't believe you signed that contract without talking to me first." Liz placed a hand on Sheridan's cheek. "Don't you know how much I love you?"

Sheridan took Liz in her arms and kissed her deeply. Liz couldn't hold back the tears another moment. She hugged Sheridan tightly as she sobbed.

"Don't cry, sweetheart," Sheridan coed softly, rocking her in her arms.

"You have no idea how much I hate that contract," Liz whispered. "I know I am being selfish. I know you have always wanted a coaching position like that. But I can't help it. I love you. I don't want you to go." Liz buried her face in Sheridan's shoulder and held on tightly.

"I suppose you want to just tear it up and forget it," Sheridan suggested.

"Yes, I do. I would love to do that but you signed a contract, didn't you?"

Sheridan nodded and held up the letter.

"Then it wouldn't do me any good to tear it up. A contract is a contract," Liz added resolutely. She took the letter and opened it. As much as she didn't want to see it, she scanned the letter in the dim light. Something caught her eye and she gasped.

"Something wrong?" Sheridan asked calmly.

"This is a contract from—" Liz started then swallowed back the lump that rose into her throat.

"Yes?" Sheridan said, a small smile pulling across her face.

"It's from Chilton College." Liz's eyes were wide as she stared stunned at the letter then up at Sheridan.

"Oh, didn't I mention that?" Sheridan asked, her eyes capturing Liz's adoringly. "Sweetheart, I could never leave you. I know that now. I'm here for as long as you'll have me. I love coaching at Chilton. I love New England. And most of all, I love you with all my heart. I should have never even considered going anywhere else. I told KU I was turning down their offer. You're stuck with me."

Liz couldn't speak. She threw herself in Sheridan's arms, kissing her wildly.

"So you approve of my new contract?" Sheridan asked coyly.

"Shut up and kiss me, Coach."

Publications from
BELLA BOOKS, INC.
The best in contemporary lesbian fiction

P.O. Box 10543, Tallahassee, FL 32302
Phone: 800-729-4992
www.bellabooks.com

THE KILLING ROOM by Gerri Hill. 392 pp. How can two women forget and go their separate ways?   1-59493-050-3 $12.95

PASSIONATE KISSES by Megan Carter. 240 pp. Will two old friends run from love?
                                                                1-59493-051-1 $12.95

ALWAYS AND FOREVER by Lyn Denison. 224 pp. The girl next door turns Shannon's world upside down.   1-59493-049-X $12.95

BACK TALK by Saxon Bennett. 200 pp. Can a talk show host find love after heartbreak?
                                                                1-59493-028-7 $12.95

THE PERFECT VALENTINE: EROTIC LESBIAN VALENTINE STORIES edited by Barbara Johnson and Therese Szymanski—from Bella After Dark. 328 pp. Stories from the hottest writers around.   1-59493-061-9 $14.95

MURDER AT RANDOM by Claire McNab. 200 pp. The Sixth Denise Cleever Thriller. Denise realizes the fate of thousands is in her hands.   1-59493-047-3 $12.95

THE TIDES OF PASSION by Diana Tremain Braund. 240 pp. Will Susan be able to hold it all together and find the one woman who touches her soul?   1-59493-048-1 $12.95

JUST LIKE THAT by Karin Kallmaker. 240 pp. Disliking each other—and everything they stand for—even before they meet, Toni and Syrah find feelings can change, just like that.
1-59493-025-2 $12.95

WHEN FIRST WE PRACTICE by Therese Szymanski. 200 pp. Brett and Allie are once again caught in the middle of murder and intrigue.   1-59493-045-7 $12.95

REUNION by Jane Frances. 240 pp. Cathy Braithwaite seems to have it all: good looks, money and a thriving accounting practice . . .   1-59493-046-5 $12.95

BELL, BOOK & DYKE: NEW EXPLOITS OF MAGICAL LESBIANS by Kallmaker, Watts, Johnson and Szymanski. 360 pp. Reluctant witches, tempting spells and skyclad beauties—delve into the mysteries of love, lust and power in this quartet of novellas.
                                                                1-59493-023-6 $14.95

ARTIST'S DREAM by Gerri Hill. 320 pp. When Cassie meets Luke Winston, she can no longer deny her attraction to women . . .   1-59493-042-2 $12.95

NO EVIDENCE by Nancy Sanra. 240 pp. Private Investigator Tally McGinnis once again returns to the horror-filled world of a serial killer.   1-59493-043-04 $12.95

WHEN LOVE FINDS A HOME by Megan Carter. 280 pp. What will it take for Anna and Rona to find their way back to each other again?   1-59493-041-4 $12.95

MEMORIES TO DIE FOR by Adrian Gold. 240 pp. Rachel attempts to avoid her attraction to the charms of Anna Sigurdson . . .   1-59493-038-4 $12.95

SILENT HEART by Claire McNab. 280 pp. Exotic lesbian romance.
                                                            1-59493-044-9 $12.95

MIDNIGHT RAIN by Peggy J. Herring. 240 pp. Bridget McBee is determined to find the woman who saved her life.   1-59493-021-X $12.95

THE MISSING PAGE A Brenda Strange Mystery by Patty G. Henderson. 240 pp. Brenda investigates her client's murder . . .   1-59493-004-X $12.95

WHISPERS ON THE WIND by Frankie J. Jones. 240 pp. Dixon thinks she and her best friend, Elizabeth Colter, would make the perfect couple . . .   1-59493-037-6 $12.95

CALL OF THE DARK: EROTIC LESBIAN TALES OF THE SUPERNATURAL edited by Therese Szymanski—from Bella After Dark. 320 pp.   1-59493-040-6 $14.95

A TIME TO CAST AWAY A Helen Black Mystery by Pat Welch. 240 pp. Helen stops by Alice's apartment—only to find the woman dead . . .   1-59493-036-8 $12.95

DESERT OF THE HEART by Jane Rule. 224 pp. The book that launched the most popular lesbian movie of all time is back.   1-1-59493-035-X $12.95

THE NEXT WORLD by Ursula Steck. 240 pp. Anna's friend Mido is threatened and eventually disappears . . .   1-59493-024-4 $12.95

CALL SHOTGUN by Jaime Clevenger. 240 pp. Kelly gets pulled back into the world of private investigation . . .   1-59493-016-3 $12.95

52 PICKUP by Bonnie J. Morris and E.B. Casey. 240 pp. 52 hot, romantic tales—one for every Saturday night of the year.   1-59493-026-0 $12.95

GOLD FEVER by Lyn Denison. 240 pp. Kate's first love, Ashley, returns to their home town, where Kate now lives . . .   1-1-59493-039-2 $12.95

RISKY INVESTMENT by Beth Moore. 240 pp. Lynn's best friend and roommate needs her to pretend Chris is his fiancé. But nothing is ever easy.   1-59493-019-8 $12.95

HUNTER'S WAY by Gerri Hill. 240 pp. Homicide detective Tori Hunter is forced to team up with the hot-tempered Samantha Kennedy.   1-59493-018-X $12.95

CAR POOL by Karin Kallmaker. 240 pp. Soft shoulders, merging traffic and slippery when wet . . . Anthea and Shay find love in the car pool.   1-59493-013-9 $12.95

NO SISTER OF MINE by Jeanne G'Fellers. 240 pp. Telepathic women fight to coexist with a patriarchal society that wishes their eradication.   ISBN 1-59493-017-1 $12.95

ON THE WINGS OF LOVE by Megan Carter. 240 pp. Stacie's reporting career is on the rocks. She has to interview bestselling author Cheryl, or else!   ISBN 1-59493-027-9 $12.95

WICKED GOOD TIME by Diana Tremain Braund. 224 pp. Does Christina need Miki as a protector . . . or want her as a lover?   ISBN 1-59493-031-7 $12.95

THOSE WHO WAIT by Peggy J. Herring. 240 pp. Two brilliant sisters—in love with the same woman!   ISBN 1-59493-032-5 $12.95

ABBY'S PASSION by Jackie Calhoun. 240 pp. Abby's bipolar sister helps turn her world upside down, so she must decide what's most important.   ISBN 1-59493-014-7 $12.95

PICTURE PERFECT by Jane Vollbrecht. 240 pp. Kate is reintroduced to Casey, the daughter of an old friend. Can they withstand Kate's career? ISBN 1-59493-015-5 $12.95

PAPERBACK ROMANCE by Karin Kallmaker. 240 pp. Carolyn falls for tall, dark and . . . female . . . in this classic lesbian romance. ISBN 1-59493-033-3 $12.95

DAWN OF CHANGE by Gerri Hill. 240 pp. Susan ran away to find peace in remote Kings Canyon—then she met Shawn . . . ISBN 1-59493-011-2 $12.95

DOWN THE RABBIT HOLE by Lynne Jamneck. 240 pp. Is a killer holding a grudge against FBI Agent Samantha Skellar? ISBN 1-59493-012-0 $12.95

SEASONS OF THE HEART by Jackie Calhoun. 240 pp. Overwhelmed, Sara saw only one way out—leaving . . . ISBN 1-59493-030-9 $12.95

TURNING THE TABLES by Jessica Thomas. 240 pp. The 2nd Alex Peres Mystery. *From ghosties and ghoulies and long leggity beasties . . .* ISBN 1-59493-009-0 $12.95

FOR EVERY SEASON by Frankie Jones. 240 pp. Andi, who is investigating a 65-year-old murder, meets Janice, a charming district attorney . . . ISBN 1-59493-010-4 $12.95

LOVE ON THE LINE by Laura DeHart Young. 240 pp. Kay leaves a younger woman behind to go on a mission to Alaska . . . will she regret it? ISBN 1-59493-008-2 $12.95

UNDER THE SOUTHERN CROSS by Claire McNab. 200 pp. Lee, an American travel agent, goes down under and meets Australian Alex, and the sparks fly under the Southern Cross. ISBN 1-59493-029-5 $12.95

SUGAR by Karin Kallmaker. 240 pp. Three women want sugar from Sugar, who can't make up her mind. ISBN 1-59493-001-5 $12.95

FALL GUY by Claire McNab. 200 pp. 16th Detective Inspector Carol Ashton Mystery. ISBN 1-59493-000-7 $12.95

ONE SUMMER NIGHT by Gerri Hill. 232 pp. Johanna swore to never fall in love again— but then she met the charming Kelly . . . ISBN 1-59493-007-4 $12.95

TALK OF THE TOWN TOO by Saxon Bennett. 181 pp. Second in the series about wild and fun loving friends. ISBN 1-931513-77-5 $12.95

LOVE SPEAKS HER NAME by Laura DeHart Young. 170 pp. Love and friendship, desire and intrigue, spark this exciting sequel to *Forever and the Night.* ISBN 1-59493-002-3 $12.95

TO HAVE AND TO HOLD by Peggy J. Herring. 184 pp. By finally letting down her defenses, will Dorian be opening herself to a devastating betrayal? ISBN 1-59493-005-8 $12.95

WILD THINGS by Karin Kallmaker. 228 pp. Dutiful daughter Faith has met the perfect man. There's just one problem: she's in love with his sister. ISBN 1-931513-64-3 $12.95

SHARED WINDS by Kenna White. 216 pp. Can Emma rebuild more than just Lanny's marina? ISBN 1-59493-006-6 $12.95

THE UNKNOWN MILE by Jaime Clevenger. 253 pp. Kelly's world is getting more and more complicated every moment. ISBN 1-931513-57-0 $12.95

TREASURED PAST by Linda Hill. 189 pp. A shared passion for antiques leads to love. ISBN 1-59493-003-1 $12.95

SIERRA CITY by Gerri Hill. 284 pp. Chris and Jesse cannot deny their growing attraction . . . ISBN 1-931513-98-8 $12.95

ALL THE WRONG PLACES by Karin Kallmaker. 174 pp. Sex and the single girl—Brandy is looking for love and usually she finds it. Karin Kallmaker's first *After Dark* erotic novel.
ISBN 1-931513-76-7 $12.95

WHEN THE CORPSE LIES A Motor City Thriller by Therese Szymanski. 328 pp. Butch bad-girl Brett Higgins is used to waking up next to beautiful women she hardly knows. Problem is, this one's dead. ISBN 1-931513-74-0 $12.95

GUARDED HEARTS by Hannah Rickard. 240 pp. Someone's reminding Alyssa about her secret past, and then she becomes the suspect in a series of burglaries.
ISBN 1-931513-99-6 $12.95

ONCE MORE WITH FEELING by Peggy J. Herring. 184 pp. Lighthearted, loving, romantic adventure. ISBN 1-931513-60-0 $12.95

TANGLED AND DARK A Brenda Strange Mystery by Patty G. Henderson. 240 pp. When investigating a local death, Brenda finds two possible killers—one diagnosed with Multiple Personality Disorder. ISBN 1-931513-75-9 $12.95

WHITE LACE AND PROMISES by Peggy J. Herring. 240 pp. Maxine and Betina realize sex may not be the most important thing in their lives. ISBN 1-931513-73-2 $12.95

UNFORGETTABLE by Karin Kallmaker. 288 pp. Can Rett find love with the cheerleader who broke her heart so many years ago? ISBN 1-931513-63-5 $12.95

HIGHER GROUND by Saxon Bennett. 280 pp. A delightfully complex reflection of the successful, high society lives of a small group of women. ISBN 1-931513-69-4 $12.95

LAST CALL A Detective Franco Mystery by Baxter Clare. 240 pp. Frank overlooks all else to try to solve a cold case of two murdered children . . . ISBN 1-931513-70-8 $12.95

ONCE UPON A DYKE: NEW EXPLOITS OF FAIRY-TALE LESBIANS by Karin Kallmaker, Julia Watts, Barbara Johnson & Therese Szymanski. 320 pp. You've never read fairy tales like these before! From Bella After Dark. ISBN 1-931513-71-6 $14.95

FINEST KIND OF LOVE by Diana Tremain Braund. 224 pp. Can Molly and Carolyn stop clashing long enough to see beyond their differences? ISBN 1-931513-68-6 $12.95

DREAM LOVER by Lyn Denison. 188 pp. A soft, sensuous, romantic fantasy.
ISBN 1-931513-96-1 $12.95

NEVER SAY NEVER by Linda Hill. 224 pp. A classic love story . . . where rules aren't the only things broken. ISBN 1-931513-67-8 $12.95

PAINTED MOON by Karin Kallmaker. 214 pp. Stranded together in a snowbound cabin, Jackie and Leah's lives will never be the same. ISBN 1-931513-53-8 $12.95

WIZARD OF ISIS by Jean Stewart. 240 pp. Fifth in the exciting Isis series.
ISBN 1-931513-71-4 $12.95

WOMAN IN THE MIRROR by Jackie Calhoun. 216 pp. Josey learns to love again, while her niece is learning to love women for the first time. ISBN 1-931513-78-3 $12.95

SUBSTITUTE FOR LOVE by Karin Kallmaker. 200 pp. When Holly and Reyna meet the combination adds up to pure passion. But what about tomorrow? ISBN 1-931513-62-7 $12.95

GULF BREEZE by Gerri Hill. 288 pp. Could Carly really be the woman Pat has always been searching for? ISBN 1-931513-97-X $12.95

THE TOMSTOWN INCIDENT by Penny Hayes. 184 pp. Caught between two worlds, Eloise must make a decision that will change her life forever. ISBN 1-931513-56-2 $12.95

MAKING UP FOR LOST TIME by Karin Kallmaker. 240 pp. Discover delicious recipes for romance by the undisputed mistress.   ISBN 1-931513-61-9 $12.95

THE WAY LIFE SHOULD BE by Diana Tremain Braund. 173 pp. With which woman will Jennifer find the true meaning of love?   ISBN 1-931513-66-X $12.95

BACK TO BASICS: A BUTCH/FEMME ANTHOLOGY edited by Therese Szymanski— from Bella After Dark. 324 pp.   ISBN 1-931513-35-X $14.95

SURVIVAL OF LOVE by Frankie J. Jones. 236 pp. What will Jody do when she falls in love with her best friend's daughter?   ISBN 1-931513-55-4 $12.95

LESSONS IN MURDER by Claire McNab. 184 pp. 1st Detective Inspector Carol Ashton Mystery.   ISBN 1-931513-65-1 $12.95

DEATH BY DEATH by Claire McNab. 167 pp. 5th Denise Cleever Thriller.
                    ISBN 1-931513-34-1 $12.95

CAUGHT IN THE NET by Jessica Thomas. 188 pp. A wickedly observant story of mystery, danger, and love in Provincetown.   ISBN 1-931513-54-6 $12.95

DREAMS FOUND by Lyn Denison. Australian Riley embarks on a journey to meet her birth mother . . . and gains not just a family, but the love of her life.   ISBN 1-931513-58-9 $12.95

A MOMENT'S INDISCRETION by Peggy J. Herring. 154 pp. Jackie is torn between her better judgment and the overwhelming attraction she feels for Valerie.
                    ISBN 1-931513-59-7 $12.95

IN EVERY PORT by Karin Kallmaker. 224 pp. Jessica has a woman in every port. Will meeting Cat change all that?   ISBN 1-931513-36-8 $12.95

TOUCHWOOD by Karin Kallmaker. 240 pp. Rayann loves Louisa. Louisa loves Rayann. Can the decades between their ages keep them apart?   ISBN 1-931513-37-6 $12.95

WATERMARK by Karin Kallmaker. 248 pp. Teresa wants a future with a woman whose heart has been frozen by loss. Sequel to *Touchwood*.   ISBN 1-931513-38-4 $12.95

EMBRACE IN MOTION by Karin Kallmaker. 240 pp. Has Sarah found lust or love?
                    ISBN 1-931513-39-2 $12.95

ONE DEGREE OF SEPARATION by Karin Kallmaker. 232 pp. Sizzling small town romance between Marian, the town librarian, and the new girl from the big city.
                    ISBN 1-931513-30-9 $12.95

CRY HAVOC A Detective Franco Mystery by Baxter Clare. 240 pp. A dead hustler with a headless rooster in his lap sends Lt. L.A. Franco headfirst against Mother Love.
                    ISBN 1-931513931-7 $12.95

DISTANT THUNDER by Peggy J. Herring. 294 pp. Bankrobbing drifter Cordy awakens strange new feelings in Leo in this romantic tale set in the Old West.
                    ISBN 1-931513-28-7 $12.95

COP OUT by Claire McNab. 216 pp. 4th Detective Inspector Carol Ashton Mystery.
                    ISBN 1-931513-29-5 $12.95

BLOOD LINK by Claire McNab. 159 pp. 15th Detective Inspector Carol Ashton Mystery. Is Carol unwittingly playing into a deadly plan?   ISBN 1-931513-27-9 $12.95

TALK OF THE TOWN by Saxon Bennett. 239 pp. With enough beer, barbecue and B.S., anything is possible!   ISBN 1-931513-18-X $12.95

MAYBE NEXT TIME by Karin Kallmaker. 256 pp. Sabrina has everything she ever wanted—except Jorie.
ISBN 1-931513-26-0 $12.95

WHEN GOOD GIRLS GO BAD: A Motor City Thriller by Therese Szymanski. 230 pp. Brett, Randi and Allie join forces to stop a serial killer.
ISBN 1-931513-11-2 $12.95

A DAY TOO LONG: A Helen Black Mystery by Pat Welch. 328 pp. This time Helen's fate is in her own hands.
ISBN 1-931513-22-8 $12.95

THE RED LINE OF YARMALD by Diana Rivers. 256 pp. The Hadra's only hope lies in a magical red line . . . climactic sequel to *Clouds of War.*
ISBN 1-931513-23-6 $12.95

OUTSIDE THE FLOCK by Jackie Calhoun. 224 pp. Jo embraces her new love and life.
ISBN 1-931513-13-9 $12.95

LEGACY OF LOVE by Marianne K. Martin. 224 pp. Read the whole Sage Bristo story.
ISBN 1-931513-15-5 $12.95

STREET RULES: A Detective Franco Mystery by Baxter Clare. 304 pp. Gritty, fast-paced mystery with compelling Detective L.A. Franco.
ISBN 1-931513-14-7 $12.95

RECOGNITION FACTOR: 4th Denise Cleever Thriller by Claire McNab. 176 pp. Denise Cleever tracks a notorious terrorist to America.
ISBN 1-931513-24-4 $12.95

NORA AND LIZ by Nancy Garden. 296 pp. Lesbian romance by the author of *Annie on My Mind.*
ISBN 1931513-20-1 $12.95

MIDAS TOUCH by Frankie J. Jones. 208 pp. Sandra had everything but love.
ISBN 1-931513-21-X $12.95

BEYOND ALL REASON by Peggy J. Herring. 240 pp. A romance hotter than Texas.
ISBN 1-9513-25-2 $12.95

ACCIDENTAL MURDER: 14th Detective Inspector Carol Ashton Mystery by Claire McNab. 208 pp. Carol Ashton tracks an elusive killer.
ISBN 1-931513-16-3 $12.95

SEEDS OF FIRE: Tunnel of Light Trilogy, Book 2 by Karin Kallmaker writing as Laura Adams. 274 pp. In Autumn's dreams no one is who they seem.
ISBN 1-931513-19-8 $12.95

DRIFTING AT THE BOTTOM OF THE WORLD by Auden Bailey. 288 pp. Beautifully written first novel set in Antarctica.
ISBN 1-931513-17-1 $12.95

CLOUDS OF WAR by Diana Rivers. 288 pp. Women unite to defend Zelindar!
ISBN 1-931513-12-0 $12.95

DEATHS OF JOCASTA: 2nd Micky Knight Mystery by J.M. Redmann. 408 pp. Sexy and intriguing Lambda Literary Award–nominated mystery.
ISBN 1-931513-10-4 $12.95

LOVE IN THE BALANCE by Marianne K. Martin. 256 pp. The classic lesbian love story, back in print!
ISBN 1-931513-08-2 $12.95

THE COMFORT OF STRANGERS by Peggy J. Herring. 272 pp. Lela's work was her passion . . . until now.
ISBN 1-931513-09-0 $12.95

WHEN EVIL CHANGES FACE: A Motor City Thriller by Therese Szymanski. 240 pp. Brett Higgins is back in another heart-pounding thriller.
ISBN 0-9677753-3-7 $11.95

CHICKEN by Paula Martinac. 208 pp. Lynn finds that the only thing harder than being in a lesbian relationship is ending one.
ISBN 1-931513-07-4 $11.95

TAMARACK CREEK by Jackie Calhoun. 208 pp. An intriguing story of love and danger.
ISBN 1-931513-06-6 $11.95

DEATH BY THE RIVERSIDE: 1st Micky Knight Mystery by J.M. Redmann. 320 pp. Finally back in print, the book that launched the Lambda Literary Award–winning Micky Knight mystery series. ISBN 1-931513-05-8 $11.95

EIGHTH DAY: A Cassidy James Mystery by Kate Calloway. 272 pp. In the eighth install-ment of the Cassidy James mystery series, Cassidy goes undercover at a camp for troubled teens. ISBN 1-931513-04-X $11.95

MIRRORS by Marianne K. Martin. 208 pp. Jean Carson and Shayna Bradley fight for a future together. ISBN 1-931513-02-3 $11.95

THE ULTIMATE EXIT STRATEGY: A Virginia Kelly Mystery by Nikki Baker. 240 pp. The long-awaited return of the wickedly observant Virginia Kelly. ISBN 1-931513-03-1 $11.95

FOREVER AND THE NIGHT by Laura DeHart Young. 224 pp. Desire and passion ignite the frozen Arctic in this exciting sequel to the classic romantic adventure *Love on the Line.* ISBN 0-931513-00-7 $11.95

WINGED ISIS by Jean Stewart. 240 pp. The long-awaited sequel to *Warriors of Isis* and the fourth in the exciting Isis series. ISBN 1-931513-01-5 $11.95

ROOM FOR LOVE by Frankie J. Jones. 192 pp. Jo and Beth must overcome the past in order to have a future together. ISBN 0-9677753-9-6 $11.95

THE QUESTION OF SABOTAGE by Bonnie J. Morris. 144 pp. A charming, sexy tale of romance, intrigue, and coming of age. ISBN 0-9677753-8-8 $11.95

SLEIGHT OF HAND by Karin Kallmaker writing as Laura Adams. 256 pp. A journey of passion, heartbreak, and triumph that reunites two women for a final chance at their destiny. ISBN 0-9677753-7-X $11.95

MOVING TARGETS: A Helen Black Mystery by Pat Welch. 240 pp. Helen must decide if getting to the bottom of a mystery is worth hitting bottom. ISBN 0-9677753-6-1 $11.95

CALM BEFORE THE STORM by Peggy J. Herring. 208 pp. Colonel Robicheaux retires from the military and comes out of the closet. ISBN 0-9677753-1-0 $11.95

OFF SEASON by Jackie Calhoun. 208 pp. Pam threatens Jenny and Rita's fledgling rela-tionship. ISBN 0-9677753-0-2 $11.95

BOLD COAST LOVE by Diana Tremain Braund. 208 pp. Jackie Claymont fights for her reputation and the right to love the woman she chooses. ISBN 0-9677753-2-9 $11.95

THE WILD ONE by Lyn Denison. 176 pp. Rachel never expected that Quinn's wild yearn-ings would change her life forever. ISBN 0-9677753-4-5 $11.95

SWEET FIRE by Saxon Bennett. 224 pp. Welcome to Heroy—the town with more lesbians per capita than any other place on the planet! ISBN 0-9677753-5-3 $11.95